Without Words

by

Mae Thorn

Dedication

For those who fight for equal access. I'm rooting for you.

Chapter 1

Rain battered against the glass door, forcing it shut as Cassandra Poole struggled against it. At last, the wind shifted, and she scrambled inside her family's apothecary. Her golden, red hair trailed puddles behind her. She blinked the raindrops from her eyelashes and gave her mother a cheery grin.

"You're late," her mother shook her head, but she couldn't hide her smile.

"I'm sorry, Mama. We visited poor Annie in her sickbed, but her parents didn't want us ill so we went to Mary's. We got carried away with our gowns." She sighed. "It seems wrong to plan a dance when so many are unwell." Her father had said Annie wouldn't last much longer. Now she couldn't say goodbye. She picked at the drenched bouquet of daisies in her basket.

"Perhaps, but you're still young. Everything can't be about fevers and tonics." Her mother gave her a warm smile. "Sometimes your mind needs to be wrapped in ribbons and muslin."

Cassandra nodded, but the day had drenched her spirits. She stashed her floral basket behind the counter.

"You might as well close up before you change. We aren't likely to get customers in this." Her mother slid the backdoor open. "Dinner is on the fire." She left to tend the food.

Cassandra grabbed the mop and soaked up the water dripping from her ruined bonnet. The bonnet ribbons slapped her face. She dashed the garment off to the floor. The splash that followed made her jump in place and then uttered a nervous laugh.

She hummed a solemn tune caught in her thoughts and circled the mop, her skirts shooting rain across the floorboards. Her hum grew to a mournful song. She found herself in the tune, forgetting the rain and the shop sign marked open.

The shop door jingled, stopping her mid-lyric.

"Don't stop on my account." A man's rich accent sent a shiver along her skin. The rolling of his tongue over the syllables made her want to melt into the floor. Eyes like a wild cat's met hers. His gaze shone like bright embers and followed her like a dancing flame.

She shifted in discomfort. "How can I help you, sir?"

A lazy grin settled over his lips. "Any way you'd like."

Her blood raced through her veins. "You can start by stepping around the water. Don't slip." She cocked her head.

His laugh warmed the room. She pushed aside a strand of sodden hair from her eyes. The stranger's hair curled around his head like it had a life of its own and stopped mid-shoulder. His dry hair.

She glanced past him at the relentless rain and back at him. The man didn't carry an umbrella, and not a drop touched his handsome features. She shook the thought away. He must have left his umbrella outside.

He cleared his throat and offered her a shopping list.

As she stretched to retrieve it, her slippered foot slid in the puddle, knocking her to the floor. A shock-like pain shot through her limbs, and a cry escaped her lips.

"Oh, bother."

Without hesitation, the man held out his gloveless hands. After a split-second hesitation, she took them.

A rush like ocean waves stormed behind her ears as though a breath of wind emptied the world of all other sounds. A lance of pain struck through her skull and dimmed her vision. Liquid fire pooled in her ears, leaving behind a throb hammering her ear drum.

She gasped and clutched her head in her hands. Blood trailed between her fingers as she fought to stop the flow. Her chest tightened. She couldn't catch her breath. What had he done?

The stranger spoke, but no sound met her ears. A frown creased his brow, and he grasped her shoulders. At once, her chest loosened, and she gulped down air. Bile rose into her throat. She pushed the stranger aside to purge her stomach. Her sickness was muffled like she was underwater. She hacked onto the floor until nothing but air remained.

Someone rubbed her back, and she jerked away from her mother, who crouched beside her on the floor. The store filled with an emptiness that swallowed all sound. The stranger had left her there.

"Mama." The syllables came out in a whisper. Was that her voice?

Cassandra squinted at her mother's moving lips, and she bit her tongue to hold back the tears. The ocean rush leaked through, but just underneath came her mother's familiar worried tone. She tugged at her ears as she fought with the syllables of her mother's words.

Tears broke through her defenses and washed away the blood on the side of her face, but they did nothing to relieve the cloud that had settled over her ears. She bobbed her head in response to her mother's alarm. Words came through here and there, but the meaning was garbled in her mind. Sound was only so much noise.

She squeezed her eyes shut, holding her ears in her hands. The blood continued past her palms and slid down her arms.

Had she become the next victim of this mysterious illness her father studied? She shook her head, attempting to dislodge the cotton-like stuffiness in her ears. A hand rested across her cheek, and her eyes snapped open. Her mother braced her hands on either side of her face and met her eyes.

In short bursts, the syllables of her name formed on her mother's lips. She blinked, not sure she had heard right. Her mother repeated her name, still muffled but somehow clear as Cassandra focused on her mother's pale blue eyes.

Her mother nodded and tried again. The inflection at the end of her words hinted at a question. Cassandra let out a quick breath and then squinted at her mother to continue.

"…all right?" Her mother's words were caught somewhere between them.

Cassandra's lower lip wobbled, and she bit down on it.

She brought a hand to her ear, but the bleeding had stopped. Her mother pulled her into a tight embrace. She buried her head against her mother's shoulder.

A flicker of movement caught her eye, and she shifted in her mother's grasp. No sound announced her father's approach. His ruddy face studied her. His knobby-limbed apprentice, Roger, stood beside him.

Her mother craned her neck and spoke to her husband, who nodded and pulled Roger from the room. Her throat squeezed tight in panic. Were they afraid they would catch something? If anyone in Coldon could help her, it was her father. She needed his remedies.

"Mama?" Her voice came out an echo of its former self, and it struck her back into silence. Had she spoken, or had she only thought she had?

Her mother hesitated before facing her. Trails of tears marred her warm features.

A sharp pang lodged in her chest. What was wrong with her?

Her father returned with Roger, preventing her mother from answering.

Her mother rushed off toward the kitchen while her father and Roger examined her. They resorted to writing messages on an old chalkboard from when she had learned to read. The chalk made an odd silent scratch against the surface.

She made her clumsy marks. *Is this the illness you warned about?* She avoided speaking. Her distant voice only reminded her of the songs she couldn't sing, and the notes she couldn't hit.

Her father shook his head and took the board from her. *Something else.*

Then what?

He ignored her question, wiping the board clean with his sleeve. *Tell me about this man.* Her father handed her the board.

She settled her hand under his words. *Not much to tell. Never seen him before. Somewhat tall. Dark curly hair and strange eyes.* And a smile and voice that sent a thrill deep in her belly.

He frowned at her, leaning over the chalkboard. *Did he hurt you? Touch you?*

Her cheeks heated at the memory of his hands in hers. *It was an accident.* She wasn't convinced herself. He couldn't have meant her harm with such a thoughtful gesture. Could he?

He sighed, standing from his place. He spoke to Roger, who hurried away and focused his attention on his wares on the shelf behind her. Her mother entered carrying a chipped teacup, steam rising in a trail behind her, and set it beside Cassandra on the counter.

Cassandra eyed the liquid. Her brow wrinkled in a frown. Her mother gestured to the cup with impatience. She wouldn't be refused. Cassandra lifted the tea and sipped the bitter mixture, flinching at the taste.

Her father pulled jars from the shelves, and just in time, Roger returned carrying a box, which burst with all manner of herbs and concoctions. Her father poured an unlabeled jar of liquid into the rest of her tea before leading Roger away under the uncertain weight of his box.

Cassandra sniffed at her tea, her face souring at the smell. Before her mother could intervene, she downed the cup faster than the taste could hit her tongue. A cough forced its way from her throat.

Her mother wrote on the board. *He doesn't want to tell you, but we have seen this before.*

Cassandra's eyes widened.

Your grandma. We thought it died out. Her mother

scrawled the words in her elegant handwriting.

Thought what died out? Will I get better?

Her mother lowered her gaze.

She steadied herself with a sharp intake of breath. Her father could fix this. He was the best apothecary in Yorkshire. By this time tomorrow, she would be bored tending the counter again, gossiping with the same Coldon residents over the latest fashions from London and the newest matches in the neighborhood.

They spent the remainder of the day and the night trying every herb combination her father could concoct. Her stomach ached like a morning star rolled around in it, but her hearing stayed the same. It barely existed.

The next day proved the same.

Cassandra spent her time in bed, hoping she would wake up healed, but she slept little with the quiet tensing of her muscles.

Her father mixed and boiled, studied books and wrote letters. He gave her liquids to drink, massaged balms and clays over her head. He poured oils down her ear canals. The efforts earned her inflamed, pulsing ears.

She tried to keep her smile steady, but a dead weight shifted over her heart with every failure. Nothing could be done.

Chapter 2

Her nightmares carried the sounds that she missed during the day, and she preferred the company of her bed. It was better to hear her own screams than the muffled speech from others. Her eyes red-rimmed, she dragged herself through the day. A gray-lined cloud settled over her as no answers came.

When her mother forced her awake, her daydreams of the past took over her life until a letter arrived from her Aunt Louise, inviting her to the coast. A day's ride by carriage. Her father shrugged at his sister's suggestion. After three months, what more could be done but trust Cassandra's healing to the sea?

Come Monday morning, they bundled Cassandra off into her aunt's carriage. She was stuffed in like so much other baggage next to Aunt Louise's overindulged poodle, Maurice. Her aunt lounged across from her, watching her with slow dramatic blinks. The chalkboard rested on her aunt's lap as though forgotten.

"Really…how…water…" Louise's voice came in and out as Cassandra squinted at her aunt's face. "…good…me." Louise raised a brow in her direction, but Cassandra swallowed her barbed reply and turned to the window as her aunt continued. The words became a muffled anthem to the countryside. Her aunt didn't seem to notice she had stopped trying.

If her father's remedies couldn't heal her, she doubted the sea would do any better. At least now she would have a change of scenery. The chill air promised little enjoyment along the waters, but she fancied her aunt would recommend she immerse herself.

The carriage tossed them along the road, bruising Cassandra's arm as she slammed into the side. Once, she landed on the obese poodle. The poor animal's high-pitched yelp was loud enough that it reached her ears. Head buzzing, she braced herself on the other end of the seat.

Her aunt's ramblings died down as she dozed off. A deep-throated snore emitted from the older woman, and Cassandra blinked at her in surprise. The sound vibrated along Louise's wrinkled throat, up to her lips.

Cassandra shook her head. Why were the unpleasant sounds the most audible?

Dusk settled over the sky like a soaked blanket, drenching the land in drops of frigid rain. They arrived at the inn just in time to be bathed in icy sheets from the ink-black sky. Cassandra's room proved to be even smaller than her room at home, a third of the size of her aunt's. She suspected the room was a closet or servant's room. No matter as long as she was dry.

Nothing could compare to the blissful peace of solitude after a long day of broken communication with embarrassing misunderstandings. Something as simple as passing off a blanket became a series of missteps and failures. The warmth of the coarse wool blanket was close to heaven as she bundled it around her.

She grinned into the covers. The sea was a cherished friend, and she remembered the ocean's roar well enough that the sound greeted her back. In Spray

Cove, it wouldn't matter if she made a fool of herself. A year from now, nobody here would remember, or so she told herself as she shivered for warmth.

The rain stopped sometime during the night. Her aunt stayed abed while Cassandra ventured out of her constricted space. Her back was cramped from the uneven stuffed mattress. A walk would only improve her comfort.

She slumped down the narrow staircase and almost collided with the innkeeper. The worn-faced woman stopped an inch from her face and raised her voice. "Food. Good." The woman rubbed her stomach.

Cassandra narrowed her eyes. Although the woman's words rang clear, the innkeeper must think her hearing made her stupid. Fine. If that was the way the innkeeper wanted it.

"Food. Good," she responded with exaggerated slowness.

The innkeeper nodded and pointed down the stairs. "Eat."

Cassandra flinched as a stream of spittle sprayed onto her face. She pushed herself flat against the wall as the other woman squeezed through, and then rubbed the wet flakes off. Her appetite gone, she bypassed the breakfast table and pushed out the front door.

The town of Spray Cove had never changed in her visits over the years. The same peeled yellow paint decorated the walls of the inn as when she was a child. The bakery across the street sold the same wares by the same thick-mustached man. The fishermen caught the same fish, never complaining of a bad season. The familiarity brought a comfort she didn't know she needed.

She set off up the cobbled street toward the parish church on the hill at the top of the street. The rains had left puddles along the way, which she skipped over, narrowly missing the mud lining her path. Her eyes diverted, she almost didn't see the figure of a familiar gray-clad man vanishing into Morgan's Haberdasher.

Without deliberation, she leapt after him and refused to slow as her booted foot sunk into the murky water, drenching her stocking. By the time she flung open the haberdasher's door, a stitch pained her side. Her gaze raced over the room, but the only occupant proved to be the shop owner who studied her with wide eyes.

"Where is he?" Her words drifted out on a soft exhale. Had she imagined him? Maybe her mind had fled with her hearing.

He said something she couldn't hear, and she stepped closer to him, meeting the man's dark green eyes.

"I need to speak to him."

The man's whole face collapsed into a frown, and he handed her a cloth and pointed to her sodden boot. Her dirty prints followed her across the polished wooden floors. Her gaze snapped back to the man's face. She gave him a sheepish smile as her cheeks warmed.

The man sighed.

She dropped to the floor and soaked up what she could with the cloth. On her knees, she inched along the path of her boot. The rag ran streaks over the last of the boards. She gazed up, expecting to find the shopkeeper standing over her progress, but instead, an elegantly dressed woman stared down at her.

She wore a dark navy ball gown. The silk pooled behind her just beyond the dirty floorboards. Her hair fell in deep brunette curls around her face, and what could only be sapphires decorated her olive-toned throat. Her curious eyes matched the color of her hair.

The woman offered her a gloved hand and gripped her palm, dirt and all. Cassandra made to protest, but the woman had her on her feet before she could get a word out. They didn't stop there. She scrambled along as the woman pulled her past the shopkeeper then through a door at the back of the storefront.

Her new acquaintance didn't pause before pushing them both into a storage closet. The cracked door let in just enough light to reveal dusty linen and cleaning supplies. The woman widened her eyes in a meaningful look then grabbed hold of the fourth hook of a coat rack along the wall. She pushed inward. Nothing happened. The woman did the same to the second hook, and a gust of air swept over Cassandra's face.

The woman led her through the new door behind the coat hooks, shutting the doors behind them. They continued up an iron spiral staircase at a brisk pace. Somehow, her new companion climbed with delicate lightness as though the dress did not hinder her movement, and the train of her dress never once caught under Cassandra's steps.

Her jaw loosened and dropped as the stairs continued upward and upward like they were climbing a high tower. Candles lined the otherwise bare walls. No windows revealed the true nature of their location.

When she thought she couldn't climb anymore, they came to a landing decorated only by a magenta upholstered chair and a side table. Three doors stood on the far side of the room. Cassandra stared wide-eyed as she peered around the small room. From the outside, the haberdashery appeared to be only a single story. How a tower with three rooms sat above the shop seemed impossible.

The woman approached the door on the right and turned the knob. The room beyond the door was like nothing Cassandra had ever seen. Bright-colored silk hangings lined the walls and draped the furniture. Above, the large domed window allowed sunlight to stream in, spilling through the clouds that dotted the sky. Three women sat facing each other around a small table that held a tea tray and a pile of paper.

An ebony-skinned woman dangled an elegant slippered foot over her other leg. She beamed at her and dipped her head topped in coiled midnight hair toward an empty chair to her left. Cassandra hesitated before sitting at the edge of the seat. The woman beside her wrote something on a sheet of paper and handed it to her.

I am Antoinette Westcott. The woman in the fancy dress is Selena. The blonde is Georgiana Hart. Our little mouse is Morwenna Thomas.

Georgiana acknowledged her with a small wave, and her golden-haired beauty seemed to warm her round, smiling face. She studied Cassandra behind long, almost translucent eyelashes, and the woman's dark blue eyes pierced in a predatorial way.

The last woman, Morwenna, sent her a soft smile and cast down her sea-green eyes when Cassandra returned her smile.

Cassandra addressed Selena. "Why am I here?"

Antoinette handed her another paper. *You were*

asking around for someone you shouldn't know. Why?

"He took my hearing."

Selena shook her head and took up the quill. *He didn't take your hearing. You were born this way.*

Cassandra spoke behind grit teeth. "I was not. I could hear perfectly before he touched me."

Selena's brows rose. *He should know better.* She shot a frown in the direction of the door.

"Then, you know him well? Where is he?"

Antoinette pushed a piece of paper in front of her. *Never mind. Have some tea.*

Morwenna poured her tea, adding a bit of honey and cream. It was the exact way Cassandra preferred her tea.

Her brows knit together as she studied the cup as though it would reveal its secrets. Who were these women?

"How do you know so much about me?"

Antoinette tapped the quill over the paper, considering her answer. *Mostly, we know you through him. Through Selena.*

"That doesn't make any sense. How do they know?"

The rest of the women turned to Selena, who stared up at the clouds. Georgiana addressed Antoinette, but only a few words came to Cassandra. "…out…now."

It was Morwenna who answered, taking up the quill. *You are not like regular people. We are like you…but different.*

"I don't understand. I just can't hear."

Morwenna's eyes clouded into a hazy-green. *Yes, we all lose something. A pound of flesh as payment.*

"Payment for what?"

Georgiana reached across the table, placing her hand on Cassandra's.

Cassandra cried out as a high-pitched screech rose in her ears, and she squeezed her eyes shut against the agony.

Georgiana jerked her hand away, and the sound stopped.

She panted. "What was that?"

Morwenna handed her back the paper. *Your ability. May I ask how old you are?*

"What does that matter? I'm six and twenty."

The women exchanged glances.

Usually, we first experience it as a child. I have never heard of it manifesting so late. Have you been living in Cauldron your whole life?

"Cauldron?" Morwenna must have meant Coldon.

No. Not Coldon. The real name of the town is Cauldron. Have you ever traveled outside other than now?

"Well, I've been to Spray Cove a few times but not really anywhere else."

Morwenna smirked. *Scry Cove.*

"That's just ridiculous. Are you trying to tell me you're witches?" She met each of their eyes in turn.

WE are. Morwenna underlined "we" five times.

Cassandra rolled her eyes. "Cauldron. Scry Cove. Next, you will tell me London is called Levitate or some such nonsense."

No. London is not originally a witch town.

"But Coldon—I mean Cauldron is? There are no witches in Cauldron."

Selena wrestled the quill away from Morwenna and bent over the paper. *Yes, there is.* She pointed at

Cassandra, who folded her arms in disbelief.

"Even if I am a witch—and I'm not—one witch doesn't make a witch town."

Selena said something inaudible to Morwenna and then turned to scrawl another note. *Cauldron is an old witch town. Everyone believed the witches either fled or died out.*

Recognition dawned on her. Grandma.

Selena and Morwenna nodded before catching themselves.

Cassandra's jaw dropped. "You aren't reading my thoughts, are you? Please tell me there isn't someone here who can read my mind."

Antoinette burst into laughter and took the quill from Selena. *Not quite. Morwenna's abilities are still weak, and we don't know if they will develop. She's a seer, but so far, she has not lost her "pound of flesh." Selena is a weak empath with unnatural strength. It is her brother you have to watch out for.*

"Her brother? What about you and Georgiana?"

I'm a spellcaster. I practice healing, curses, that sort of thing. Georgiana here is our siren or succubus, if you will. You've already met Niko.

"Will he hurt me?"

Antoinette made a dismissive gesture with her hand. *Unlikely if he hasn't already. I wouldn't cross him, though.*

She bristled at the threat behind her words. "He shouldn't cross me. Being the daughter of an apothecary has some advantages, you know."

Selena gave her a wide grin. *This is why Niko isn't in the room. He sensed you would react this way.*

"He shouldn't be sensing anything about me. If he

doesn't mean any harm, why did he flee after I was hurt? He could have explained everything to me then."

He thought it wiser to leave once he calmed you down. We can't have a scandal. Witches are still hunted.

Cassandra drew in a quick breath. "What did he do to me?"

Selena blinked at her as though struck by the question. Morwenna pushed Selena aside and took up the quill. *You have nothing to fear. He cast his emotions onto you. They've worn off by now. Niko is adept at projecting calm in such situations.*

"I will deal with my own emotions. Thank you. Now, if you don't mind, I've had enough of this madness. If you want to help me, you should restore my hearing. I don't want any part of this witch nonsense." She set her fists on her hips as she glowered at the assembled women.

Morwenna's brow scrunched inward. *We can't.*

"Of course you can. One of you made me like this, and you must be able to fix it."

Once you have lost something in the transition, there is no going back.

Cassandra stared at her, clinging to a stubborn hope that Morwenna was lying. She met Antoinette's gaze, and the woman nodded to her. Selena drew away, and Georgiana gave her a lopsided smile.

She shook her head, unable to believe them. "I can't do this anymore. I need to think." She bolted to her feet. The sudden movement sent her senses into cartwheels, and she steadied her hand against her forehead.

This couldn't be happening. She must be having

some kind of nightmare. Soon she would wake up in her bed at home in Coldon, and Spray Cove would be a distant memory. Scry Cove. Cauldron. She rubbed her eyes to wipe out the words, but she couldn't dispel the ones etched behind her eyelids, the words she dreaded most in the world. *There is no going back.*

No more gossiping at the counter. No more dinner parties. No more calling on friends. No more singing on key. Who would want her now? Few people cared to take the time to write on her chalkboard or explain through notes. These women? Witches? If it hadn't been for Niko, she would be happily tending the shop. This was their fault, and they would only make things worse.

Her throat tightened, strangling her thoughts. It was just as before in the shop, each breath a hissing wheeze. She clutched at her chest, willing herself to breathe and stop panicking. Her head floated as though hung by an invisible thread. Her body swayed. The floor rose to cradle her as she lost the battle with consciousness.

Chapter 3

A heavy knock found her ears and woke her from her sleep. She blinked, seeing the cramped confines of her inn room. Her body was cocooned in the coarse wool blanket.

A dream. It had all been a dream.

Her face brightened. She yawned and rubbed the sleep from her eyes. "All right. I heard you."

Ripping the blanket from her body, she swung her feet down to the floor. Where had her mind come up with such horrible nightmares? Maybe she should have stayed home. She shook her head and hurried to dress for the day.

Suddenly, the door swung open, and Aunt Louise shot into the room, speaking in hurried syllables Cassandra fought to make sense of.

"Come…mustn't…waiting…will…"

Was that a question? She smiled at her aunt, hoping that would suffice. Instead, her aunt thrust her bonnet and gloves at her and pushed her through the door. Aunt Louise beckoned her to follow down the stairs.

Cassandra shrugged and tugged on her gloves. The day must be getting on if her aunt was in such a hurry to leave the inn. Sure enough, the afternoon sun shone in the sky. Cassandra frowned. She never slept in. Maybe this sea cure had something to it. If anything, at least she would return home rested.

As they made their way down the stairs, her aunt continued to prattle on. "No rentals…in the season…" Whatever her aunt attempted to convey, her words lodged a stone in Cassandra's gut.

She tugged at her aunt's sleeve to face her, but the woman pulled her arm back. "Please, Auntie, if you don't face me, I won't understand what you're saying. Do you mean there are no bathing machines for rent? How will I bathe?"

They made it to the street before her aunt faced her. "…served ace…"

Cassandra scrunched up her nose. "What?"

"Served."

"What is served? Are we going to lunch?"

Aunt Louise let out a long breath and closed her eyes for a moment. "Listen." She spoke clearly, holding Cassandra's gaze. "Reserved. Space."

Cassandra gulped down her dread. "You reserved me a space to bathe?"

Her aunt gave her a short nod before setting off again, not bothering to see if Cassandra followed.

She had never heard of such a thing. Where were the bathing machines and dippers? Doubtless, the autumn chill had scared all customers away and the services with them. Her hearing couldn't wait for a warmer season. Besides, summer hadn't been all that long ago. The water still might be warm enough.

It wasn't.

The frigid sea shot a jolt through her like falling feet first off a tree. The shock froze the scream in her throat, and her teeth chattered the instant she was in the water. At least, she wouldn't have to worry about being seen. Her aunt had indeed reserved a private place for her to bathe on private land.

Aunt Louise shivered on the shore and watched her wade out into the water. The older woman held up a hand and gestured that she would return. She held Cassandra's clothes under her arm as she retreated to the town.

The cold must have been too much for her. Cowardly old woman.

Cassandra cast a scowl after her and braced herself as the water reached her chest. She turned her back on her traitorous relation and resigned herself to her sea cure. Clothed in nothing but her undergarments, the water bit into every scratch she never knew she had. Her feet were dead weights along the seafloor, having lost sensation.

Bracing herself, she took in a great gulp of air and ducked her head under the water. Hair slapped against her face as she emerged. She pushed the hair out of her eyes, and a figure appeared where her aunt had stood.

She squinted at the figure. A man. His face was in shadow. Her eyes scanned the beach, unable to locate her aunt. At first, she thought the man was the stranger from her family's shop. The man on the beach had cropped hair and a bulky form, nothing like what she remembered. Whoever this man was, he wanted to speak with her. Now of all times.

Her limbs were numb. Knowing her aunt, she wouldn't return for some time. She cursed her aunt for her unconventional bathing methods. The man needed to leave and soon before she froze. She didn't fancy the idea of revealing her body in scanty wet undergarments.

"Go away. Can't you see I'm trying to bathe?" Her throat closed up as though frozen shut.

The man shifted from foot to foot and called back to her, but she couldn't make out the words.

"I can't hear you. I'm not decent. You're very rude."

He shook his head and then gave a sudden start when he gazed to the side. Someone walked toward the man but stopped in his tracks as he noticed Cassandra in the water. He hesitated before facing the first man. They talked, and the first man backed away, holding his palms in front of him.

She wrapped her arms around herself, the shivering a violent quake abducting her body. Saltwater stung her eyes, hindering her view of the beach.

The first man hurried in the direction of the town.

The second man stopped at the edge of the water, his shoes likely victims of his choice. On closer inspection, the man's familiar curls rustled behind him in the chill breeze. His immaculate clothes were out of place on the wild coastline. The stranger had found her.

He pulled off his coat and settled it just out of the water and beckoned to her before turning his back. Out of options, she kicked back against the seafloor. The faster she could cover up, the better. The water resisted her heavy limbs.

She clenched her teeth as the time weighed on her to escape the water before he looked.

At last, she grasped the coat and huddled into it. The warmth settled over her like a patch of sun heating her shoulders. His scent lingered on the fabric, a warm exotic spice that reminded her of summer nights. A wild, intoxicating aroma she wanted to curl up in.

With slow precision, the man faced her. His golden eyes assessed her condition. Her skin heated under his gaze, but she shivered despite it.

He pulled his hand out of his glove and offered it to her.

Her heart hiccupped. She narrowed her eyes at his hand. He must be joking.

Instead of waiting for her answer, he grasped her wrist. The crash of ocean waves grew to a roar. She jerked at her arm, but he held fast, and a dull heat crept along her skin as though she had drunk a glass of wine.

All at once, he released her, and she stumbled back. The coat slid off one shoulder, but the resulting breeze only whispered over her skin. She no longer shivered. A crisp air resided in the edge of the wind, but her body refused to react.

Cassandra caught him focused on her bare skin and adjusted the coat again. He swallowed, his gaze flying to hers.

She sent him her best glare. "What did you do to me?"

He cocked his head in thought and bent down to write in the wet sand. *I convinced your body to be warm.*

She lowered her brows. "I would rather you didn't manipulate me."

He shrugged. *I will try to remember that.*

"Who are you?"

He peered up at her, an eyebrow raised in a question of his own. He smoothed over the sand. *Niko, did you injure your head when you fell?*

"Fell? I didn't fall—" The dream. Only it wasn't a dream. She took an involuntary step back. "How did I get back to the inn?"

The side of his lips tugged upwards. *I carried you.*

Her gaze fell on his arms, and her imagination found the flexed muscles beneath. She pictured herself hoisted like a child in those arms, her face resting next to his on his shoulder. The exotic scent of him clouding her senses. She shook the image away.

His smile widened as he watched her.

Shame burned over her cheeks. "Are you reading my mind?"

A sigh fell from his lips, and he shook his head. *It doesn't work that way.*

"However, it does work. Please stop invading my mind. And another thing, why didn't your sister carry me if she has abnormal strength?"

He rolled his eyes. *How would it look for a woman to carry you?*

"All right, then how did you get past my aunt without her knowing? Or without anyone knowing for that matter? Did you do something to their minds?" She didn't want to believe it had all been real. Witches. Abilities. Him. She had enough trouble without these complications.

His jaw clenched. He took his time, brushing the writing out of the sand as though wiping out his anger. *I walked in the front door. Nothing to it. No abilities were necessary.*

She dismissed his explanation with a wave of her hand, unsure whether or not to believe him. A strange man carried her to her bed. She couldn't think of anything more compromising at the moment. Not to mention, he was *the* strange man. This excruciatingly attractive man with a lazy smile and wild hair and eyes.

His empathic nature only complicated matters further.

"What are you doing here, anyway?"

Niko stood, wiping the sand off his hands. He pointed in the direction the other man had retreated. "He's trouble." The sound of his voice still resonated from their first meeting, so much that she could swear she heard it now.

"You came to chase him away?" She swallowed back her disappointment that he hadn't sought her out. Then, she internally kicked herself for her foolishness.

He nodded and gestured toward the town.

She followed his movement. A distant figure approached their location. This time, she was sure it was Aunt Louise. With one swift motion, she shrugged the coat off and handed it back to Niko. A slight chill spread over her still-damp body, but the cold was better than her aunt finding her alone with a man. With any luck, her aunt's failing vision would serve Cassandra well.

Niko's eyes widened at the sight of her. His gaze darted away, and he shook his head as he offered the coat back to her.

"Please. Take it and go. If my aunt sees me half-naked with a man, she will tell my parents. I can't fail them again."

His gaze swept to her face for a brief glimpse. He gave a short nod and trotted off in the other direction.

Sure enough, her aunt hadn't spotted Niko, or if she had, she didn't seem concerned. Cassandra dressed while her aunt huddled into herself. The day had grown old while Niko distracted her. Her stomach's angry rumble reminded her she needed food. To her relief, her aunt led her back to the inn where a meal awaited them.

The mutton stew sent the chill from her body, and she soaked up every drop with fresh-baked bread. Her aunt ate with slow sips as if she were unsure of what she ate. Cassandra drew her brows together in confusion.

"Is something wrong, Auntie?"

Louise met her gaze, her eyes unfocused. A tear slid down her aunt's cheek. She rubbed it away and stared at her damp hand in confusion. In all of Cassandra's life, she had never seen her aunt cry and didn't believe she was capable. By Louise's face stone face, she must have had similar notions.

"Auntie, should I help you to bed?"

The older woman nodded her head, a single drop of her chin. Cassandra moved around the table to offer her arm to her aunt, but instead of accepting help, Louise's hand flew to her chest. Her mouth dropped open, a silent gasp.

Cassandra hesitated, staring at her aunt's darkening face. Louise clawed at her with her free hand, pressing her niece into action.

"Help." She screamed the word until her throat hurt. "Send a doctor."

Cassandra continued to scream until the innkeeper rushed into the room, her face pale. The innkeeper said something to Cassandra, shaking her shoulders in her hands. When she didn't respond, the innkeeper pushed past her to Louise, who was now sprawled on the floor.

Cassandra moved with mechanical bursts of speed, racing around the inn until she found the stable hand who she directed to fetch a doctor.

The inn cook came across Cassandra and saw her

frenzied state. The cook tried to get answers, but Cassandra could only shake her head. She led the cook to her aunt.

Her aunt's features were tinged in purple. Her hands formed claws against her chest. The cook rushed off at the sight of them and came back with a bottle of brandy. None of them could get Louise to drink or hold the bottle.

A thin foam bubbled at the corner of her aunt's mouth, and Cassandra leaned in to wipe it away. The sharp whistle of breath from Louise's lips reached her ears. She searched her mind for a cause for these symptoms. The heart seemed the best possibility, but she had none of the treatments her father used. If he were here, he would know what to do.

At last, the stable hand returned with the doctor. A disheveled man in his thirties examined her aunt with worn hazel eyes. He faced Cassandra. "...long?"

"It just happened while we were eating." She hoped she had answered his question.

He spoke to the other occupants in the room, his lips out of her view. Cook turned a shade of green she hadn't seen on any human, and the innkeeper covered her mouth.

When she heard no more voices, she tried to get a word in.

"I can't hear you. What's happening to her?"

The doctor's gaze read her face as though seeing her for the first time. He pointed to the bowls of stew and back to her aunt.

"You're mistaken. I ate the stew, and I'm all right. I'm better than all right." She stammered over her words for fear they might prove wrong. A tight-fisted grip squeezed her stomach.

He held up a hand for her to wait then shuffled over to her aunt. Once her aunt was in her bed, and the others had left, the doctor beckoned her out into the hallway. She focused on his kind expression as he spoke.

"She must…sensitive..damaged…" He handed her a bottle, the instructions marked on the label. She didn't recognize the liquid, but everyone had their own remedies.

"Why am I not sick?"

"I don't know." At least he was honest. The country doctor in Coldon was known for making up ailments and giving obscure diagnoses. Spray Cove appeared to be a different case entirely.

She sighed. "Will she get better? My father is the apothecary in Coldon, should I send for him?"

He paused, his gaze settling on the door. "…unlikely. Nobody…village quack."

Her heart stilled. "What? Do you think she'll die? My father's a brilliant healer. He might be able to help." It wasn't the first time her father had been insulted to her face, but she believed this doctor meant well by it. Too many apothecaries made a mess of the profession by pedaling ridiculous cures that caused more harm than good.

He nodded.

So the bottle was to make her aunt comfortable. Her knuckles whitened around the glass. She fought to keep herself from crying in front of him, taking hard swallows to push down the tears. He seemed to sense this and pulled a handkerchief from his pocket.

At once, she dropped the handkerchief and then

bent forward to catch it. Her head slammed against the doctor's. A rippling wave of pain shot through her forehead and whooshed out through her ears. She cupped her hands over her ears, frowning at the doctor.

His brows shot up. His stare was wide and unblinking.

"You too?" She dropped her hands. "I don't suppose you have a special talent for healing you haven't shared?"

His lips quirked up despite the situation. "No."

She rubbed at her forehead. "Oh well, I assume you all know each other. Would you tell Antoinette about my aunt? It couldn't hurt to have her opinion."

"Indeed." He gave her a short bow. "I'm …Gabriel…"

"Gabriel what?"

He caught her gaze and raised his voice. "Scott."

"Dr. Gabriel Scott?"

He bobbed his head.

"Dr. Scott, do me a favor?" She swirled the liquid in the bottle. "Tell Niko I appreciate his help, but I don't need it. Better yet, tell him to stay away from me. I crowd my mind enough not to need him in it."

Dr. Scott burst into laughter at her words and pivoted on his heel. His laughter echoed down the hall and back to her in a low hum.

Chapter 4

Once again alone, Cassandra wrote a detailed explanation of her aunt's condition to her father. She emphasized the need to make haste with his response. Spray Cove must have an apothecary that she could consult for remedies and supplies with her father's advice. If only his answer would make it in time.

Antoinette presented another possibility. Although the woman had shown her some proof of their words, Cassandra was skeptical the witches could be of any use. If they couldn't help restore her hearing, preventing death was probably out of the realm of possibility. Yet, she would try anything with the remotest chance of success.

She spoon-fed her semi-conscious aunt the medicine from the bottle, a bitter smelling inky fluid. Her aunt's skin continued to darken until her fingers and lips held a purple hue. Although Cassandra massaged the affected areas, nothing brought back Louise's usual pale pink features. No fever flushed her skin, but instead, it remained cool to the touch. The only progress Cassandra made involved Louise swallowing the broth she fed her, but her aunt never spoke a word.

Night washed over Spray Cove. A fire in the grate provided her aunt's room with just enough light to know Louise's fate was out of her power. Nothing more could be done.

A deep ache settled on Cassandra's nerves. She slumped into the chair beside the bed and broke down into heavy sobs.

A breeze brushed over her, and she opened her eyes to the dying fire. When she lifted her head, her neck protested the movement. She must have fallen asleep in the chair.

The cause of the breeze gathered around the bed, staring down at her aunt.

Antoinette, Selena, and Niko stood with identical expressions of concentration, ignoring her presence. Cassandra rose to her feet, tripping on the chair she had vacated. Did these people always come and go as they pleased?

A flush bloomed over her cheeks. Well, she had asked for help, and she was grateful they overlooked her rude behavior. Regardless of her message, Niko had turned out to assist.

Niko's brow twitched, but he avoided her gaze. He set his palm over her aunt's forehead and closed his eyes. Selena followed him, grasping her aunt's hand.

Antoinette cocked her head in thought and approached Cassandra.

Cassandra folded her arms around her middle. "Can you help her?"

Antoinette drew in a deep breath, holding it briefly before expelling it in a great puff of air. She shook her head.

"Can't help her or won't help her?"

Selena handed Antoinette the long-forgotten chalkboard and chalk from her aunt's table.

Antoinette frowned at the offering but took it up.

Can't. Don't know what ails her. Can't fix the unknown.

"Surely, this is just some heart condition or other."

Antoinette scrunched her brows together. *No. There is an underlying cause. Her heart is the result. Something she ate.*

"Why help us then?"

We don't abandon our own. Antoinette set the chalkboard down and met her eyes. The sadness in her gaze mirrored her own and drained Cassandra into an exhausted husk.

She faced the certain death of her aunt. Even though she had never really related to Louise, her aunt had always been there for her. Now, Cassandra would need to be there for her. It seemed Antoinette and the others would not make her do it alone.

Antoinette took a place beside the bed, exchanging a glance with Niko. He nodded to her once and moved around the bed to Cassandra. She dropped her gaze, her focus glued on the floorboards.

He stepped into her line of sight, and she stared at his shoes. Even the leather was immaculate. His intoxicating spicy scent hovered between them. When she refused to acknowledge him, he raised her chin with a gloved hand. His eyes darkened to dying embers as he searched hers.

Her first impulse was to pull away, but she didn't have the strength. All of her fight and tears were used overnight. The emptiness of the last few weeks opened into a violent chasm, and nothing remained but pain, physical and demanding pain.

Niko dropped his hand, and the rest of his body seemed to mimic the action. He peered back at Aunt

Louise, who now slept with even breaths.

"Niko." His name was on her lips before she could stop herself.

His wide-eyed surprise at her address forced a giggle past her throat. A near-hysterical laugh that died almost before it began. She didn't think it was possible to surprise him. He raised a brow in question.

"I feel as though I might lose my mind." As much as she hated his manipulations, the pain was worse. She had to stay strong for her aunt until her father could be reached, but she had to function to do that.

He smirked.

She wouldn't blame him if he refused her. Hadn't she spent most of their acquaintance warning him off? "I'm sorry. Perhaps I was wrong."

He held out a hand to her. She took it without hesitation. Before she knew it, he swept her into the hallway.

She shut the door behind her and rested her back on the wall next to it. Her heart stomped heavy thuds inside her chest.

She shifted under his gaze.

Niko waited until he had her attention before he spoke, "Are you sure?" He appeared to take great care with his words.

"Just this once. I have to get through the day."

Instead of removing his gloves as she expected, he leaned into her, taking her lips with his.

A gasp caught in her throat as the crash of waves settled in her ears. The pain dulled, and a fever lit between them, becoming two parts pleasure and one part pain. His kiss was bold, caressing, an unexpected dare that left her stunned.

The fog inside her thinned.

His lips caressed hers until she responded in kind. She pressed into him, letting his closeness consume her. Raw need rose inside her and demanded more.

He stilled and stepped back from her. Her breath came out in bursts. She ached for him to reel her back in, but his focus fell on the door beside her. The knob turned just as she followed his gaze.

Selena favored her brother with a scowl. Niko lifted his hands in surrender and set off down the hall toward the stairs. His sister watched Cassandra, her brows drawn together with worry. Selena beckoned her back into her aunt's room, where she took up the chalkboard.

What has my brother done this time?

Cassandra slouched under Selena's questioning stare. "I asked him to help me get through this."

Selena snorted. *As a distraction?*

A flush crawled over her ears. "That isn't what I meant."

The chalkboard fell from Selena's hands, hitting the floor with a clank that made Cassandra jump. Selena stared down her nose at her before sweeping up her gown and exiting the room.

Antoinette shook her head at the door, then handed a bottle of brown liquid to Cassandra, who puzzled over the contents. She fetched the chalkboard off the floor, and Antoinette leaned over to write across its surface.

Two drops at bedtime. No more.

"This will help her sleep?"

For you. Don't ask Niko for favors. He will make them his own.

Cassandra rubbed at her temples. "All right. What

do I do about my aunt?"

Give her Dr. Scott's medicine every time she wakes. Just a few drops will do. He gets it from me.

"How long does she have?" As much as she dreaded the answer, she had to know.

Days. Maybe weeks, if you're unlucky.

She read the message across the board again and once more. "Will it be that difficult for her?"

No. The medicine will keep her comfortable. Hard for you. I will come tomorrow. Antoinette placed the chalkboard on the table and opened her arms to Cassandra, who hesitated.

Antoinette rolled her eyes and embraced her.

No pain or sounds invaded Cassandra's ears, but their skin never touched. The gesture sucked her in. She couldn't remember the last time someone hugged her, really hugged her, and let her take comfort in their arms. Antoinette gave her a final squeeze and released her.

"Take care." Antoinette mouthed the words. Her lips curled into a warm smile that reached her eyes.

Cassandra sighed but nodded her agreement.

Satisfied, Antoinette waved as she closed the door behind her.

Touch. She had to touch someone to sense their abilities. Everyone she had touched seemed to sound different. Niko had understood this when he chose to kiss her as though he knew the sensation would carry his mark. Her cheeks blazed anew.

And what a kiss.

The press of his lips lingered over her like a vibration that tickled the air above her skin. She raised her hand to her lips. Niko shouldn't have done that, and she should never have let him. The opportunity to stop him had been wide open, and yet, she returned his kiss. Wanted more.

He had broken it off. Now, he was back in his tower, laughing at her expense.

She raised and dropped her shoulders. She must be blind as well as deaf. Niko couldn't possibly want her. Cassandra was a used, broken, and aged apothecary's daughter. Ashley, her ex-fiancé, had shown her that much when he abandoned her for better prospects. She had no reason to believe that Niko would be any different. He would use her up then throw her away when he was done with her, just as Ashley had.

Cassandra lifted the bottle Antoinette gave her up to the bright firelight. The dark brown liquid sloshed against the glass. Most likely opium, but she couldn't be sure. Her father didn't usually carry it. He detested its addictive nature and had seen too many lives ruined from it.

What did she have to lose? She tugged the stopper from the bottle and dripped what she hoped was two drops onto her tongue. Her mouth screwed up at the bitter taste. She poured herself a glass of port from her aunt's things to wash it away.

She jumped when she was nudged awake, and daylight streamed into her eyes. She shielded her vision. The innkeeper stood over her, and a frown etched on her brow. Cassandra glanced over to her aunt, who still slept with even breaths.

She sighed with relief before addressing the intruder. "What is it?"

"A caller." The innkeeper drew out the word, making it difficult for Cassandra to process what the woman was saying.

"Send them in then."

The innkeeper shook her head and pointed toward the door before edging out into the hall. With an annoyed huff, Cassandra followed her into the dining room.

A familiar wide-shouldered man hunched over the table, nibbling a piece of toast.

The innkeeper gestured to the chair across from him and set a plate in front of her loaded with eggs covered in something creamy. Little triangles of toast sat on the edges. Her stomach rumbled at the offering. She hadn't eaten since the stew.

Instead of inhaling her food as she wished, she returned the man's stare. His cropped brown hair tugged at the back of her mind. "Do I know you?"

He shook his head and said something in a low voice.

"What? I can't hear well."

He met her eyes and swallowed another bite of food. "Eat first."

"Really, I'm not hungry. What did you want to speak to me about?" Her stomach gurgled then, giving her away.

The man widened his eyes at the sound of her traitorous organ.

She twisted up her lips and scooped up some of the eggs. The sauce proved to be made with cream, some kind of sharp cheese, pepper, and something else she couldn't quite identify. The taste lingered over her tongue. Before she realized it, she had finished her plate. She soaked up the last of the sauce with the toast. A moan escaped her lips.

The man gave her a satisfied smile. "Good?"

Cassandra leaned back in her chair. She was stuffed, and yet, she wanted more. The hunger was like an itch that refused to leave. "Wonderful. What did you want? I need to get back to my aunt. She's very ill."

"Direct…" He gave her a wry smile. "…sent…my…speak…"

She focused on him, waiting to make sense of his words. "You were sent?"

He nodded. "For you."

She frowned. "Why would anyone send for me? I must be here to care for my aunt. I can't just leave."

"Agreed…this…aunt."

Cassandra furrowed her brow. "I can't hear much of anything you are saying. Don't you have something you can write on? Or maybe we can just agree to do this another time?"

He rose to his feet. Suddenly, Cassandra remembered where she had seen him. On the beach. He had stood there staring at her while she took the sea cure. Niko said he was trouble, but what did he know? They both seemed like questionable men.

She stayed seated with her nails embedded in the chair as he fetched paper and writing instruments. Should she run back to her room? She would be alone there, though, and more vulnerable. At least, here she would be more likely to be heard if she called for help.

Once he returned to his seat, he dipped the quill in ink and wrote. *My employer sent me to escort you to speak with him.* He tipped the message toward her.

"Again, I can't leave here."

It is in regard to your aunt. We think we know what may be the cause. Come with me, and he can explain.

She tightened her jaw. "Who are you? How do you know what's happening to my aunt?"

I am Mr. Abraham Sutton. Spray Cove is a small town with small town tendencies. Will you accompany me?

"Why should I trust you?" She knew already she would go with him. If there were any chance these men could help her aunt, she would take it.

Mr. Sutton seemed to sense this, as well. He gave her an encouraging smile. *We are not the ones you should fear. There are prying eyes and ears everywhere. I am sure you know what I mean.*

Her face paled. "Let me see your hand."

His smile widened, and he extended his arm over the table.

She hesitated a moment, eyeing the innkeeper's turned back, then inched her hand over the table to grasp his gloveless palm. No rush of pain, no unusual sounds. She released him and grabbed it with her other hand. Nothing. Mr. Sutton was normal. He wouldn't have an unfair advantage over her, other than being twice her size.

Mr. Sutton allowed her to linger a moment longer before he returned his hand to the quill. *Are you satisfied?*

The lack of questioning on his part raised the hairs on her neck, but she had no choice. If only someone were here to accompany her. Someone she trusted. That list dwindled every day. She would have to face this alone. She hoped her aunt would hold out until she returned.

"All right. I'll come with you. Let me go to my room and fetch my shawl and chalkboard. Will we be walking?"

His eyes lit up at her acceptance. *I brought a carriage. Bring your board if you so choose. My lord has plenty of paper and ink.*

Cassandra took her time finding her warmest shawl then asked the innkeeper to watch after her aunt. She left behind the chalkboard and opted to bring a knife from the kitchen, which she put in her reticule. If anything happened, Cassandra wasn't sure what to do with it, but it eased the frantic beating of her heart. She considered for a moment using the liquid Antoinette gave her. Her head needed to be clear. Besides, who knew what was actually in the bottle? Perhaps this man would have her answers. She dropped the bottle in the reticule next to the knife and made her way back to Mr. Sutton.

Stepping into the carriage suffocated her like closing her coffin lid. Her breaths came out short and weak. The jostling of their ride pricked at her skin. Nothing seemed right anymore. Her world had been turned upside down, and she crawled by the tip of her fingernails to bring it back upright. More than anything, she wished she had stayed home, but home didn't hold any answers to her hearing. The man at the end of their drive might.

Chapter 5

When they reached their destination, it was
midday. The sun shone behind the grand bulk of Lyme
House before them, casting the front in shadow. As a
child, she had often wanted to explore the old-fashioned
three-story structure, but the residents of Spray Cove
warned her parents not to ask for a tour.

The fountain in the courtyard had long since been
out of use, collecting water and insects. Yet, the stone
walkway was maintained. The hedges along the
property were pruned to perfection. The result was a
stern, no-nonsense property. Not exactly a welcoming
home.

Cassandra followed Mr. Sutton to the door, where
a long-faced butler greeted them. He sniffed at the
appearance of Cassandra and ushered her in.

Mr. Sutton turned on his heel with a promise to
return within one hour or one minute, but he walked off
before he could clarify. She stared after him a moment
before hurrying to catch up with the butler. He waited
for her with a frown in the doorway of a massive
library.

The library, like the rest of the front of the house,
was all marble and polished wood. Books lined the
walls on neat shelves, and no dust peeked out beside
books. A fireplace took up most of one wall, flanked by
green damask chairs. On the far side of the room, a

monstrous desk sat, and behind it was the rigid form of an older gentleman.

He gestured to the chair in front of the desk, and she perched on its edge. Steepling his fingers in thought, he studied her. His brows rose, and he pointed to the sheet of paper before him. She nodded, and he bent over it to write.

I apologize for my rude manners. I thought it better that we meet in private at my estate. Allow me to introduce myself. I am Edward Moore, Baron of Lyme. I am told you are Cassandra Poole of Coldon, is that correct?

He waited for her nod and started again on another sheet of paper.

Mr. Sutton is my assistant. He runs errands for me from time to time. You see, I am not often in town.

Lord Lyme pushed away from his desk and revealed he was confined to a wheeled chair. His legs were covered in a plaid blanket. Once he was satisfied with her assessment of him, he rolled forward to another sheet of paper.

You see, I am like you. I lost something once. Unlike you, I did not gain anything. You can check me if you wish. My associate discovered your gift through our contacts in Coldon.

She frowned at his offered hand but took it all the same. Nothing. He had written the truth.

He gave her a grim smile. *This injury of mine was not an accident. I hear you met the man responsible for my condition. Nikolas. I believe he goes by Niko.*

Her mouth fell open, and her stomach twisted. "Niko did this to you? He didn't seem violent to me." If anything, he was gentle.

I am sorry I have to tell you this. He is not to be trusted, and those women he spends his time with should also be avoided.

"But they were helping me. My aunt can rest." She shook as she spoke.

That may well be. Did they ask you for anything in return? That lot does nothing for free.

She stilled.

He took her silence as answer enough. *They will. The price will be more than you are willing to pay.*

Her gaze scanned the paper, hoping it would provide guidance. "What should I do? Can you help my aunt?"

Only God can help your aunt.

"Then, how does this concern her?"

His writing became frantic, almost illegible. *You misunderstand me. I do not know how to heal your aunt. I do know who is responsible for killing her.*

She grew pale. "I thought she had some strange illness. Do you mean someone is killing her? That can't be right. Nobody would hurt Louise." She scrunched up her forehead.

She was not the target; you were.

Her hand trembled as she read the message over and over again. "That's insane. Why would anyone want to kill me?"

He poured himself a glass of whiskey and offered her one. She drained the glass, and he refilled hers again before sipping his now.

Indeed. That is the question. Why would your new witch friends want to kill you?

"It was them? I—I don't understand."

Perhaps we can help each other. Lyme House can

protect you against those trying to harm you and your aunt. While you are here, we will deal with them. You will both be safe in the end. Witch hunters still track witches though most of the outside world is unaware.

"That would put me in your debt. There's nothing I can do for you in return." She chewed her lip.

He gave her a small smile. *Good. You are learning. There is something you can do for me. I need to know the identity of the witches in my association. All you have to do is shake some hands. Do this, and I will grant you sanctuary.*

Use her powers to find witches? She took a long gulp of her whiskey to wash the idea away.

"No. I've met these people. I'm not convinced they're a threat to me."

His knuckles whitened as he gripped the quill. *I thought you would say as much. If you help me, I am offering to send you to a special hospital in Florence for your condition. They have had great success in the past, but you must relocate here immediately.*

Her gaze fixed on the amber liquid of her drink, and the color reminded her of Niko's strange eyes. She would be betraying him. If what this man said was true, then Niko needed to be stopped. If not, she would have to live with the consequences.

"What will happen to the witches I identify?"

That depends on a lot of factors. If they mean harm, they will be dealt with. Witches are an affront to God and are the Church's domain. I will seek guidance there.

The guilt gnawed at her stomach, begging her to refuse. The witches in Spray Cove were good to her, and even now, Niko made her pulse flutter. Yet, she could be healed. She would never be able to afford the trip to Florence, and even if she could, she didn't know where this hospital was or how much it would cost her.

Cassandra shut her eyes as though she could escape her decision. "You have a deal."

He had already written his reply to her acceptance and pushed the paper over to her. *Mr. Snoot will show you to your room. Mr. Sutton will arrange for your aunt and your things to be collected. My doctor will tend to her, and I assure you she will be in the best of care. I would advise you to stay on the property where we can be of most help to you.*

Lord Lyme rocked his chair back to pull at the rope behind him. At once, the butler, Mr. Snoot, waited for her to follow him. Stunned into silence, Cassandra left the library without another word. What more could be said? She had already sold her soul.

The walk to her room seemed like miles. She was asleep on her feet, exhausted by the long night and unsettling day. Some hours remained before nightfall, but they would have to do without her tonight. Tomorrow would be a new day.

The marble floors went on through each hallway, above and below stairs. Her room was located on the second floor and down a set of corridors. The lighting was darker here, as though the glow from the candles could not penetrate the space. She wanted to cry out to see if she heard her voice call back to her. No doubt, Mr. Snoot would frown on the behavior.

At last, they came to her room. He unlocked the door without ceremony and waited for her to enter and shut the door. The sour-faced man didn't even bother to show her the room. After a moment of hesitation, she locked the door.

Lord Lyme had given her a modest guest room that was still larger than her space at home. The room was decorated in an unremarkable maroon. The bed was twice the size of her own, taking up the far wall beside a curtained window. A small fireplace, dressing table, writing desk, and chest took up the rest of the space.

Already the room was stocked with extra blankets and freshwater as though she were a guest in an inn. Lord Lyme had expected her to accept. His assumptions made her want to change her mind.

As much as the bed called to her, she needed to take care of her correspondence first. The letter to her father was a quick message of her relocation to Lyme House without further explanation which eluded her at present. The other letter was a warning to Niko to stay away and warn other witches to do likewise. She enclosed the two letters in a third letter to the innkeeper with instructions to forward them. She handed off the letters to a maid who came to build up the fire. Having finished her only task, she crawled into bed, only bothering to kick off her shoes before closing her eyes.

The same maid, Alisa, who had lit the fire, woke her for her aunt's arrival. Cassandra rolled from the bed and righted her clothes. The maid led the way to Louise's room, saying nothing as the darkened hall seemed to require. Her aunt's room was larger than hers, but the air had a musty quality to it.

The patient still slept soundly as if she had failed to notice the transfer to Lyme House. Cassandra halted in the doorway as the doctor and nurse busied themselves to make Louise comfortable while another maid fetched supplies.

Her aunt's pallid complexion and whistled breaths chilled her. Cassandra wrapped her arms around herself. The woman who was a constant in her life had withered into a corpse-like replica of herself.

As promised, Louise was well taken care of. The nurse shooed her off, and a weight lifted from Cassandra's shoulders followed by a nauseous wave of guilt. As her niece, she should have the responsibility of Louise's care.

Unsure what to do with herself, she wandered until she found her way to the library and front door. A slim gray tomcat greeted her at the other side of the door, and he rushed past her up the stairs before she could catch him.

A faint smile tugged at her lips as the feline's tail waved in his flight.

She startled when Mr. Snoot found her in the otherwise silent house. He guided her to the dining room where a light supper was served. She squinted at the bright light of the numerous candles about the table. Lord Lyme already occupied the end of a heavy mahogany table. At Lord Lyme's right, Mr. Sutton rose at her entrance and invited her to sit to Lord Lyme's left with a sweep of his hand.

When Mr. Sutton returned to his seat, the two men seemed to take up their earlier conversation. She pecked at her plate with little interest. The food seemed to agree with the men, but to her, it resembled eating hair ribbons. After taking a bite of her chicken, her eyes caught on Lord Lyme watching her.

He smiled, a mere curve of his lips. "The food wouldn't suit you." He spoke in a loud, clear voice after repeating himself three times. "You will like dessert."

His patience with her hearing warmed her. She burst into a wide grin. Nobody took the time to really talk to her. The paper and chalkboard always seemed like second-hand information without the tiny movements and emphasis involved in speech.

Dessert arrived just then to compliment his words. Baked apple pudding was placed in front of her. The aroma of warm apples and sugar made her mouth water. Appetite restored, she dug into her dish.

She closed her eyes. The chewy flesh of the apple on her tongue forced a moan from her throat. The fruit seemed drowned in flavor. Cinnamon, sugar, and cloves coated her lips in a loving kiss. Nothing existed except for this moment.

Before she knew it, she finished the last crumbs as though she was desperate for just one more taste. It wasn't enough.

Lord Lyme nodded to her in approval as he finished his own. "A fine treat."

"Mmm. When do I start?" The rest from earlier had worn off, and her eyes fluttered half-open.

Mr. Sutton beamed at her. He pulled ink, paper, and quill from the side table. *Tomorrow. We would like to check the household staff first. At the end of the week, Lord Lyme is giving a party. You will attend to perform your duties. Do you have any questions?*

She rubbed at her eyes. "Will there be more of that dessert?"

Lord Lyme gave her a pleased smile.

Mr. Sutton scribbled on the paper. *Yes, and so much more. Lord Lyme's cook has remarkable talent.*

Her face fell. "What will I wear to the party? I haven't any suitable gowns for such an occasion."

Cassandra had never possessed a gown worthy of such an event, but they didn't need to know that.

Mr. Sutton nodded. *Leave that to me. Leave everything to me. For now, relax. You are free to use the library or walk the gardens. If you need anything, simply summon a servant. Visit with your aunt if you choose but try to keep well-rested. What you will be doing requires a great deal of energy. We would like you prepared.*

She gave him a lazy smile and yawned.

Lord Lyme leaned over the table toward her. "Go to bed."

"Mmm."

Cassandra giggled as she rose to her unsteady feet and held to the walls as she went back to her room. The events of the past couple of days had caught up to her. She would do as they said and rest.

On her way to her room, she stopped to check on her aunt. The nurse sat at her bedside, knitting, and raised a finger to her lips as Cassandra peered in. Louise slept on. A weight lifted from Cassandra's chest. Now Louise would get the care she needed.

Her room wasn't far. She managed to stumble back without running into anything. When she entered and locked the door behind her, she noticed the gray cat lounging across her bed. He watched her with the cool, unconcerned gaze of felines.

She blinked. "What are you doing in my room? Don't you have mice to catch?"

The cat blinked at her, unphased.

"Fine. Just don't bring me any presents in the night."

He proceeded to lift his leg and bathe himself.

Cassandra snorted. She started to undo her buttons but stopped. Her gaze fell on the cat, still bathing. Turning her back on the creature, she threw on one of her nightgowns that had arrived from the inn.

Stretching under the blankets, she reached out to scratch behind the cat's ears. "If you're going to sleep with me, I should at least give you a name." She thought for a moment. "How about Mikel? I once had a cat named Mikel."

The cat narrowed its eyes as if he understood her.

"Hmm. How about Lucky?"

He darted his gaze away, no longer acknowledging her.

"Pounce? Smokey? Milo?"

She poked the cat in his side, and he gazed back at her through slit eyes. "All right. I know. Mist. It's perfect for you since you seemed to materialize from air."

He curled his body next to her belly, lowering his head to his paws.

"Mist it is then. Well, Mist, we have a big day tomorrow. Lord Lyme is putting me to work already. I don't know what I would do without his help. Louise can't possibly travel back home."

Mist yawned, his breath revealing his fish dinner.

Cassandra's lips screwed up. "Disgusting creature, stop that. You'll make me yawn." She finished her sentence doing just that.

She ran her fingernails along the cat's fur and was rewarded with an answering rumble from his throat. Looking back, she couldn't recall being this relaxed. Her body rested like jelly among the pillows and blankets. Mist offered her the companionship she hadn't realized she needed.

Perhaps, she wasn't so alone after all.

Chapter 6

Mist had vanished when Cassandra woke the next morning. Cat or no cat, at least she was rested.

She pulled back the curtains of the window to reveal the garden below bathed in sunlight. More of the same hedges from the front of the house occupied the grounds, but she couldn't make out much more than that.

The memory of the dessert from last night was still fresh in her mind, and she hurried to dress in hopes that breakfast would be equally pleasant. Her simple, pale blue gown seemed underdressed for such a grand house. To make up for her lack, she paid particular attention to her golden-red hair, placing the curls just so.

She peeked her head into her aunt's room, and the nurse was quick to send her away. Cassandra caught a glimpse of Louise, unchanged from her last visit. Why wouldn't they let her see her aunt? Louise didn't seem contagious. She would have to sneak in later.

Shoulders slumped, she shuffled to the empty breakfast room. The servants hovered over her, the last of the breakfasters, cutting her time short. Her meal of buttered rolls and strong tea failed to meet her expectations.

This morning, she would explore the garden until she was needed. The weather was fair, but a threatening mass of clouds in the distance promised the possibility of rain. As she approached, the hedges turned out to be a well-tended maze. An iron gate marked the entrance near the back door to the house.

Directionless, she made a series of right turns until everything appeared the same. She backtracked only to become further lost, having missed a turn somewhere. The maze offered a challenge to Cassandra, and she defied every dead end with renewed enthusiasm. The sun was well overhead before she decided she needed to find her way out, choosing to mark the paths as she went. She came across a statue of Artemis and a stone bench in the center of the maze.

Her feet throbbed, pleading to rest. She gave in to the urge and took up the bench to study the statue. The goddess wore a swath of clothing with a bow slung over her shoulder, a stag rested at her side. Her lips had a slight gap like she was in awe of the sky above.

A gloved hand went over her mouth, and her right arm was seized.

Her stomach leaped in her throat. She struggled against her assailant and bit into the leather over her mouth. The grip on her only tightened until she stopped her futile protests.

A gloved finger went to her lips to indicate her silence.

Her breath caught. She nodded against the hand in understanding.

The hand on her arm moved to her shoulder, and her attacker spun her around. Niko kept a firm hold of her mouth and arm as he assessed her reaction with his bright eyes.

Cassandra jerked against him in a last desperate

attempt to free herself. Her efforts yielded nothing. Her heart thumped a mad race in her chest. She was at his mercy.

Niko cocked his head and listened, his eyes fixed on the sky. Then, he gave a short nod and met her gaze once more. He pursed his lips in a shushing gesture. His hand dropped from her mouth. He pulled her back into the maze.

She stumbled on the gravel path as he brought her into an alcove she hadn't seen before. Once inside, he replaced the hand on her mouth. The space in the maze wall provided little movement, and Cassandra pressed up against Niko's chest as he listened.

Her heart thudded against him, and her breath was reduced to a broken rhythm. This man. His spicy scent. That kiss.

Then she heard the voices. A low murmur at first, growing louder as they approached their location.

She glanced around in quick, panicked movements.

Niko watched her, a warning in his eyes. She surrendered and laid her head on his chest, having no notion of what he was capable of.

He pressed her further into the shadow of the alcove just as the voices descended on them. He stilled against her, waiting for them to pass.

Mr. Sutton and another man in shabby clothes walked past without stopping. She couldn't make out most of their words, but she heard her name more than once. They must have been searching for her, but she kept her peace.

A smile tugged at his mouth. With a start, she grew aware of her arm pressing against his groin. She raised her arm between them, placing her hand on his chest.

This was a mistake.

Her heart skipped when her hand met the hard plane of his chest, and her first thoughts involved peeling the fabric off of him. He stood around her like a shield that wrapped her in warmth. Although they were in danger of discovery, his presence made her weightless. Their skin never touched, but she wanted him. She needed space before she lost all reason.

At last, Niko seemed to conclude the men were far enough away, and he dragged her out of the alcove. He lowered his hand from her mouth but kept his hand on her arm to prevent her from bolting.

Their lost closeness left her naked.

"Didn't I tell you to stay away from Lyme House?" Her voice came out short, and she barely managed speech from her stunned state.

His grin revealed a devilish dimple on his chin.

She wasn't sure if she wanted to slap or kiss him. Maybe both. Her gaze dropped. "What do you want with me?"

He tilted up her face with a gloved finger. "Cassandra."

Her name on his lips sent a shiver down her spine. It was the most erotic thing she had ever heard. She cleared her throat. "Why don't you just kill me now? You've wasted enough time. Lord Lyme told me everything."

Niko let out a sigh and shook his head. "…want to."

Her stomach jumped into her throat. "Then, why don't you?"

He pinched his brows together. "Don't want to." He repeated his words, speaking in a clear voice.

"Then why hurt my aunt? Why look for me here? I don't understand." She didn't understand the stirring in her belly either.

His hand dropped from her arm, and he ran his fingers through his curly mane. She could run now, run like death was on her heels, but then, she would never have her answers. If he wanted her dead, she would be already. She didn't want to believe Lord Lyme, but his was the only story she knew.

Without warning, Niko set off back the way they came. Taken off guard, Cassandra stared after him a moment before following him. He dropped down on the stone bench and put his head in his hands. Against her better judgment, she sat next to him and waited for his response.

He straightened beside her, his expression thoughtful. Removing his glove from his hand, he extended his palm to her.

Her face turned sour as though he had offered her a live eel to eat. He pressed on, nodding toward his extended hand. She tugged at her glove with deliberate slowness, and he rolled his eyes at her dramatics. In a hot-headed act of defiance, she grasped his hand. The roaring ocean filled her ears, making her flinch.

Beyond the pain, a slow trickle of sadness filtered through to her. The golden hue dulled in Niko's eyes, and she found the hurt behind them. Threatening tears stung her eyes. She braced herself against them.

"Did you hurt my aunt?"

The sadness deepened to hopelessness. Was he giving up?

"If you didn't hurt my aunt, why would Lord Lyme say you did?" She clenched her teeth on a new rush of pain, followed by fury. No, not just fury, betrayal.

"Lord Lyme was on your side once?"

Niko sighed and nodded.

Guilt crept along her skin to their clasped hands, and Niko's eyes widened.

"I'm sorry. I don't know what to believe anymore. I can't undo this."

He raised his brows.

"He wants me to test them. His staff. His friends. Everyone. I'm afraid of what he might do to them."

At first, she thought the dead weight in her stomach was her own dread, but the set of Niko's jaw told her it was his.

"Niko." A wave of pleasure made her pause, a curious sensation in herself. "He promised to help me to help my aunt."

A tight jab to her stomach, this time. Hard enough that Cassandra considered pulling her hand back.

"You, Antoinette, and Selena couldn't help me, and as much as I appreciate your efforts, he said he could. I can't just turn away from the possibility. I have to see this through."

He frowned, and she didn't need their connection to tell her he was disappointed. He must have sensed her stubborn resolve when he pulled at his hand. She tightened her grip, drawing his gaze to hers.

Her stare stayed firm. "Prove to me what you've been telling me is true, and I'll find a way out of this. I don't want anyone to get hurt, regardless of what you must think of me." She didn't believe her own words. Healing her hearing was everything to her, and now, Niko would know it too.

Red, hot anger rushed through their hands. She

flinched back at the same time he jerked his hand away. He had sensed the lie from her lips. Of course, Niko excelled at reading emotions.

He shot from the bench and faced her. His eyes burned like lit kindling under lowered brows. He stuffed his hand in his glove and then suddenly paled. Pivoting on his heel, he scanned the area behind him.

The low murmur of voices had returned. His eyes darkened in their weary lines, and he set off toward the alcove.

Pulling her glove onto her hand, she steadied her face into a calm mask. Mr. Sutton came across her just as Niko disappeared.

"…young lady…off to?…assistance."

"I don't understand a word you're saying, Mr. Sutton, but I'm so glad to see you. I'm afraid I'm lost in this maze. Would you lead me back to the house?" The lie flowed from her lips like honey. As much as she questioned Niko's motives, she still didn't wish him harm.

He chuckled low under his breath, almost too low for Cassandra's ears. He held out his arm in response, and she took it. Patting her hand, he strolled off down the path where Niko hid.

She held her breath as they came to the alcove. Mr. Sutton stopped in his tracks. The sudden tightness in her chest was like a giant fist suffocating her.

"Miss Poole." He spoke as though he measured the sound of his voice. "…seen anyone…?"

Her shoulders relaxed as she realized he hadn't noticed Niko. She stepped forward to move Mr. Sutton's gaze away from the alcove.

"Who?" She tilted her head.

The man studied her face and then nodded. She had always been a good liar, which made Niko's ability that much more unnerving.

She caught a glimpse of Niko over Mr. Sutton's shoulder. He winked and blew a kiss at her. A smile tugged at the corner of her lips, but she coughed to hide it. Even when he was angry with her and evading discovery, he tried to make her laugh. Maybe he was insane, but his wide grin made her stomach turn cartwheels. The man was dangerous in more ways than one. What was the matter with her?

She cleared her throat. "If you would lead on, Mr. Sutton. I'm especially famished. This maze has been…well, it has been rather interesting."

Mr. Sutton nodded, lowering his eyes as though he were ashamed of himself.

Cassandra stuck her tongue out at Niko, and he covered his mouth to hold in a laugh.

As Mr. Sutton showed her the way, she took special care to note the route for future reference. She wouldn't be caught unaware in the maze again. Even though she believed Niko meant her no harm, she couldn't be sure of anything else. Too many questions swirled around her mind.

Experiencing Niko's emotions first hand had been a whirlwind, an intimate connection she hadn't shared with anyone else. The wave of pain she associated with his touch was bittersweet. She suspected he gained more from the exchange than she did.

Could he fake his emotional reactions? Lie through the bond? It seemed likely. He certainly had more experience with the practice than she did. On the other hand, she couldn't imagine a reason for his falsehood.

At any moment in their short acquaintance, he could kill her as he proved today when he snuck up on her and withstood her struggling.

She sensed there was something more to his abilities, something dangerous she hadn't experienced. What Lord Lyme said about Niko injuring him had a ring of truth to it that she needed to explore, but she had no idea when she would see Niko again.

She wasn't sure she *should* see him again.

Her life didn't need any further complications, and getting involved with Niko was the last thing she wanted. Heartbreak was something she was all too familiar with, and she wasn't going to let it happen again. As tempting as the handsome devil seemed, she had to guard against the inevitability of rejection. Nobody wanted a broken spinster to burden them. She was a dried husk of her former self.

For now, she would look after herself and her aunt by fulfilling her promise to Lord Lyme. With his help, she could mend the pieces of herself and reclaim her life. She had warned Niko, and hopefully, he would spread the word with haste. It would have to be enough. Her future depended on her service to Lord Lyme, and nothing Niko did could stop her.

Chapter 7

Cassandra was ushered into Lord Lyme's library, where the man himself rested behind his desk. She sat on one of the green damask chairs to await the first of dozens of staff members.

She sipped at her tea, wishing it were something stronger, and nodded to Mr. Sutton to get started. She sent a silent prayer to Niko that he had warned people away.

Mr. Snoot entered and placed himself before Lord Lyme, not acknowledging her presence. Lord Lyme frowned at his butler and said something Cassandra didn't catch. The butler spun in place, looking down at her with a sneer. At Mr. Sutton's urging, Mr. Snoot removed his glove and offered his hand to Cassandra.

With a long sigh, she took the offered hand. As she expected, nothing happened. She had just started, and already the task wore on her.

When the butler left, she addressed Lord Lyme. "Can't we line them up in the hall?"

Mr. Sutton shook his head and jotted off a note to her. *No, Miss Poole. Who would run the house? There are too many servants. We cannot spare the time before the party. Besides, if we find a witch, it would be in our best interest to keep it a secret from the rest of the staff. So far, aside from Mr. Snoot, most of the staff members only see this as an introduction to Lord Lyme's niece.*

She caught Lord Lyme's gaze. He gave her a reassuring smile. She attempted to smile back and gave a slight twitch of her lips, but he took that as permission to continue.

The next servant was the housekeeper, who she hadn't met. She didn't gather much from Lord Lyme's introduction, but he must have explained her hearing. When the housekeeper turned to shake her hand, she spoke in a high-pitched voice that most women reserved for infants.

Cassandra couldn't make out a word of the demeaning speech. Why did people insist she was simple as well as deaf? "That is quite enough. You must speak to me in a normal voice and remember to face me at all times."

The woman nodded sagely as though she had already been doing just that. Cassandra wanted to shake her. She almost wished the housekeeper was a witch. At least, she wouldn't have to experience this forever.

Cassandra decided early on not to bother learning names. Lord Lyme would have to write them down for her, and she wanted to get this done sooner rather than later. Besides, if she could help it, she would be in Florence before she would need them.

The next three servants were as uneventful and disrespectful as the housekeeper. She was reminded of the way people treated her Aunt Louise like she was not an adult with a head on her shoulders. She was ready to run screaming from the library.

"Lord Lyme, is this really how your servants would treat your niece? If so, you don't need them to be witches to dismiss them. We can save time now."

Lord Lyme chuckled and took up his quill. *I do*

apologize for their behavior. If I let go of every employee who stared at my wheelchair, there would be nobody left in Yorkshire to tend my home. Chin up, this will not last forever. Remember Florence.

Indeed, Florence was the only thing keeping her in her chair. Well, that and the delicious tea in her cup. The cream sweetened the strong pot in such a way that she relished each sip like it was her last.

A footman entered the room next and delighted her with his contagious smile and easy manner. His green eyes shone when he took her hand. A bolt crashed through her, forcing her to the ground and out of his grasp. Her ears rang from the encounter. The footman stared wide-eyed between the occupants of the room, backing up as he did so.

Mr. Sutton stopped him in his tracks, holding the man firmly in place.

The footman's expression fell all at once. "Why?" The word pierced clean through the ringing.

A deadweight set in her stomach, and she dropped her gaze, unable to respond.

"Why?" His voice came again, full of hopelessness and anger.

She shuffled her feet. He deserved an answer, didn't he? "I need to get back what I've lost." She shook her head. "I can't go home without it. Lord Lyme promised to help me."

The footman spat to the side.

Mr. Sutton slapped him across the back of the head, and the footman slumped in his grip.

Cassandra's mouth dropped open. "Please don't. I deserve as much. What are you going to do with him?" The weight in her stomach grew to include her shoulders.

Lord Lyme watched the footman with a grim frown and picked up his quill. *That remains to be seen. This man has served with me for more than a decade. Such deception cannot be overlooked. Once he reveals his abilities and intentions, we will make a decision. You may go rest. This discovery has been exhausting for you, as using your new sense will be. You have exceeded my expectations. I will send for you when your services are further required.*

She opened her mouth to protest and shut it once more. A hazy, floating sensation blanketed her. Her eyes settled on the footman, going in and out of focus.

The man slouched into himself, but the look he returned to her was full of pity. He pitied her. She expected anger and hatred, both she could handle. Pity was the scrapings at the bottom of the barrel. It was the uttered words of regret soon forgotten.

She couldn't swallow over the lump that had lodged in her throat.

She nodded to nobody in particular as she placed one foot in front of the other toward the library door. Her steps were blind, half asleep, and half numb. The tears came when she shut her door behind her, but she dried them with an angry jerk of her hand.

Once she gained her room, she locked the door, but at the back of her mind, she realized what little purpose it served. Someone had a key to it.

For the first time, she fetched the knife from her reticule and placed it beside her pillow. Lord Lyme needed her, but if word spread, she wouldn't trust her safety to the servants. Too many factors rested on her usefulness to others. If she was dead, she couldn't harm anyone else.

The anxiety was no match for the unnatural sleepiness consuming her. Her eyes fell shut as she nodded into her pillow. Her last thought was of Niko and the slim hope of warning the rest of the witches in her path.

Sunlight shone along the edge of the curtained window, waking her. The knife still rested in her hand. She started as she saw the time. Twelve hours had passed. Too early for breakfast but too late to go back to sleep. A visit to check on her aunt was long overdue, and she dressed herself to make the trip down the hall.

The nurse sat dutifully at Louise's bedside and nodded to Cassandra when she entered. Her aunt lay just as before, motionless and at peace.

Cassandra frowned down at her. "Has she woken at all?"

The nurse shook her head in response and went back to the book in her hands.

Louise's forehead was cool under her hand. Her heart beat a steady rhythm. In all appearances, her aunt should wake up at any moment. It was another lie to herself. Yet, she took up the other chair next to the bed and held her aunt's hand.

By now, she should have received a letter from her father, but at this point, she no longer believed anything could be done. He had seen this illness weeks ago, and when she left home, he was no closer to an idea than he had been then. He hadn't discovered it had something to do with food or drink. It was unlikely he had solved the rest of the mystery in her short absence. If by some slim chance he had, it was already too late for Louise.

Cassandra took in a deep breath and resigned to

spend what time she had left with her aunt. Already, she had missed a day with her and hated herself for her selfishness. Lord Lyme would have to wait. She wouldn't have a second chance at this.

How many times had her aunt been there when she was ill? She had complained of Cassandra as a child, but beyond her sour mood was the hint of a smile in her eyes. Louise was a hard woman, and she had thought hard women lived forever.

She stared at the space just above Louise, unaware of anything but the woman in the bed. At times, her chin dropped to her chest, and she lost time. Her aunt's condition never wavered as though she were an adult-sized doll with the barest hint of movement.

It was Mr. Sutton who came to find her. He looked over the patient with a critical eye and handed her a pre-written request to return to her duties.

She handed him back the note. "Perhaps another time. The servants have been with Lord Lyme for years, and I don't think there is any hurry. It will have to wait until my aunt passes. I can't leave her now."

Mr. Sutton glared at her through lowered brows but said nothing as he left her to her aunt. Cassandra continued her vigil over Louise. She couldn't ignore the building hollowness in her stomach, urging her to run downstairs and earn her hearing back. A part of her wanted to see things through, while another wanted to buy the rest of the household time. Lord Lyme wouldn't take this as a failure of her duties, would he? He couldn't fault her for wanting to be there for her aunt in her last moments.

Hours passed before she would have her answer. The door to her aunt's room opened, and Mr. Sutton walked in. He held the door open as Lord Lyme wheeled himself in. The effort to bring Lord Lyme upstairs must have been some undertaking.

Lord Lyme wheeled his chair up to the bed to get a better look at the dying woman. After several moments of silence, he squinted at Mr. Sutton in a silent command. Mr. Sutton nodded and peered out into the hall.

Muffled voices came from the hallway, followed by a maid carrying a tea tray laden with the tea Cassandra was so fond of and little sandwich triangles. Her stomach grumbled at the sight of food. The maid set the meager meal next to Cassandra and departed once more into the hall, where she fetched the quill, ink, and paper for Lord Lyme.

Cassandra poured two cups of tea, offering Lord Lyme one of them. By then, Lord Lyme was busy with his quill, and he waved the cup away. He gestured between the cup of tea and her aunt.

I admire how much you care for your dear aunt. I thought I would come and see the woman for myself and bring you some refreshments. Take as much time as you need with her. Of course, there is no hurry. I presume you will be at the party?

Cassandra gave him a quick nod, not daring to refuse. She sipped her tea to drown the voice screaming to get out of there, but the party couldn't take any more than a few hours.

I will have another cot brought up to help you rest. I insist you take all of your meals as well. You can't be there for your aunt if you waste away.

She forced a small smile. Or there to perform her duties.

Don't worry yourself. I know what you must be going through. My dear wife perished as I watched at her bedside. I am forever grateful to have been there for her in those final moments. If only my children had been there.

Cassandra raised her brow, meeting his gaze. "I'm sorry, my lord. I had no idea you had lost your wife or had children. Are they away?"

His lips turned down, but she couldn't tell if he was sad, disappointed, or angry. *Thank you, my dear. I am afraid I lost my children too. That was long ago, though. Now, you are here, and I won't allow you to miss this time with your aunt. Let us know if there is anything else we can do to make you comfortable.*

"Yes, my lord."

He nodded to Mr. Sutton, who helped Lord Lyme out of the room.

She poured herself another cup of tea and offered the pot to the nurse to give to her aunt. The tea provided some rest from the draining day. It was just what she needed to restore her efforts over her aunt.

Lord Lyme's actions backed up his promises, but if he was sincere, it meant Niko wasn't. She wanted to believe Niko was the considerate and understanding man who turned her to jelly with his breathtaking looks and unexpected humor.

True to his word, Lord Lyme sent up a cot for her. She stared at it with longing for some moments before she gave in. Her eyes were heavy, and a short nap could only do her good. The nurse would wake her if there were any changes with her aunt. Cassandra surrendered to the now-familiar exhaustion.

A violent shiver shook her from sleep.

The nurse was absent from her aunt's bedside. Indeed, the woman was no longer in the room.

Cassandra pulled her blanket around her as she got to her feet, and summoned a maid to help her restart the fire. She stumbled about the room, and she was able to light a candle for her aunt's bedside table.

"There now, Auntie. We'll have the fire going in no time." Cassandra fumbled around for her aunt's hand. It was ice cold.

"The fire must have been out for some time. Where is that nurse? We need to get you warm, or you'll catch your death." A laugh caught in her throat at the last part. Her hand trembled when she found her aunt's face.

No breath eased from Louise's wrinkled lips.

"You can't die now." She must have been mistaken. Her aunt had slept peacefully just hours before. She placed her ear against the woman's chest. Of course, she couldn't hear anything. Not when she needed her hearing the most. Louise's chest remained still underneath her head.

"You can't leave me alone. Not here. Not in Spray Cove." She choked on her words as she tried to contain her tears.

Cassandra knew the inevitable truth. She was warned her aunt would not last much longer, but nothing could prepare her for the raw fact of it. She stared through tear-hazed eyes at Louise's frozen face, willing her aunt to take a breath, to moan in her sleep, to twitch an eyelash. To do anything that would erase the truth.

A hand rested on Cassandra's shoulder. She didn't move, didn't speak to whoever had entered the room.

For a moment, she thought it was Niko, and she wanted to lean into him for comfort. No, that was a dream. Niko wasn't who she thought he was.

Mr. Sutton moved to crouch in front of her. "She's gone." Cassandra heard no voice from his lips as he mouthed the words.

"Where is the nurse? We need to warm Louise. Would you rebuild the fire?"

Mr. Sutton sighed and took her hand in his.

The gesture broke the sobs from her throat, and she held her mouth with her other hand. "How could I sleep through it? I should have felt something."

He squeezed her hand in response, seeming to know no words would comfort her.

"I did this. She was in Spray Cove to help me heal." She jerked her hand back from Mr. Sutton and straightened. "I need to tell my father. We'll have to take her back to Coldon."

Mr. Sutton rose from his crouch and pointed toward the window.

She guessed what he was trying to convey. "Yes, I know it is late, but my father will want to know as soon as possible."

He grasped her shoulder again, this time with a firm grip. Before she could protest, he guided her out of the room. She grew numb when she sat on her bed, unaware of the glowing fire already lit and the click of the lock on her door.

Chapter 8

On the day of the party, Cassandra frowned down at the white dress and matching slippers Lord Lyme had provided her for the occasion. On short notice, there was no chance of dyeing the dress black, nor did she have the time or the money to order something appropriate. She had used the rest of her funds to pay the innkeeper in Spray Cove, and she had used the rest of her tears, sending off her aunt's corpse along with a letter to her father explaining her promise to Lord Lyme.

She had pleaded with Mr. Sutton for an appropriate mourning period, but in the end, her promise must be kept. Already, she had postponed her service. No more excuses, however dire, would be accepted. She dragged herself through the job, her mind a haze with thoughts of Louise.

Wasting no time, Mr. Sutton stood by as she tested the rest of the staff that morning. To her relief, she revealed no other witches and could only speculate if her delay saved anyone.

Lord Lyme provided a maid to assist her, expressing the importance of looking her best for the guests. She was to attract interest, which translated to her as smiling despite her aunt and laughing when she would rather be left alone. The guests were important associates of Lord Lyme's gathered from London, the first group of many such occasions she was to attend.

The maid pinned her hair up with neat curls falling against the white dress, emphasizing the red in her hair. A string of pearls borrowed from Lord Lyme completed the look.

Mr. Sutton advised her to come late after all the guests had arrived and were well distracted by the wine punch. She suspected they intended to watch the exits. This employ was a mistake. No news came of the footman she had identified. The thought of asking turned her stomach in knots.

Nor had she heard what happened to the nurse the night of her aunt's death. It was as though the woman simply vanished from the estate without a word from anyone. Her hearing kept her trapped in her uninformed bubble no matter how many questions she asked Niko or how much Lord Lyme chose to include her.

She was a tool, and the only thing saving her was her agreement to be cured. She hoped it would be enough. How many witches would she have to reveal to earn her place? How much would she lose before she gained herself?

Once she decided she had waited long enough, she entered the ballroom and made straight for the refreshments. Mr. Sutton would come looking for her soon. She needed the extra fortitude that only wine would provide. She took a place along the wall beside the terrace door, ready to bolt at a moment's notice.

The guests were unfamiliar to her, and each sip of her wine separated her emotionally from them. If she could think of them as less than people, then revealing their private lives wouldn't seem so horrible. Right?

As she contemplated the tired, gaudy costumes

before her, a gloved hand brushed her shoulder. Suppressing a yelp, Cassandra gazed behind her to the curtain bordering the terrace door window. Niko stood a step away, but it wasn't the Niko she knew. The man had outfitted himself as a dandy. His pale blonde wig matched his pants and waistcoat to perfection. His sky-blue overcoat was made to hide his true form, but to Cassandra, the outfit only made her more aware of his alluring closeness.

She snapped her gaze back to the ballroom, hoping nobody had noticed her drawn attention. Her senses honed in on his closeness, and her heart drowned out the rest of her hearing. She admired his daring, but what was he thinking coming here?

He tugged her unoccupied hand back toward the terrace, and the soft brush of his lips sent a crashing jolt up her arm.

She brushed him away. "Go away." She barely made out her whisper.

Just as his hand left, Mr. Sutton approached her, leading an all too familiar figure. She blinked at the man in his ensign uniform in disbelief. She downed the rest of her glass.

Mr. Ashley Barrett, her ex-fiancé, made a neat bow as though they had parted on nothing but happy circumstances. Her hands clenched and unclenched as she fought to restrain herself.

To her surprise and annoyance, Mr. Sutton had fetched the chalkboard. He now wrote something for her. *I am told you are already acquainted with Ensign Barrett? He is stationed in Spray Cove. Lord Lyme has business with him, but we had not realized you were old friends.*

Friends? True, they had been dear friends from early childhood up until he abandoned her just before their wedding day to run off with the baker's daughter, Bertha. The memory of the cold note he had left for her sent a boiling roar through her. They weren't suited. More like, the baker's daughter was willing to abandon her family and run away with him.

Mr. Barrett appeared a decade older than she had last seen him only a few short years ago, his hair now a splash of white. His round face was lined with worry, most likely from his rumored excessive gambling debt. She noted he favored one of his legs, perhaps a new injury? How desperate was the Prince Regent for soldiers that he would enlist ill-equipped men?

He grinned at her, no doubt expecting some kind of welcome. It wasn't as though he had ripped apart her heart.

She returned his grin with a glare. "I assume Bertha is here as well?"

Mr. Sutton returned to the board. *Mrs. Barrett is resting back in Spray Cove. Unfortunately, she fell ill yesterday.*

Cassandra held back a smile. Maybe she was some kind of monster to be amused by the other woman's misfortune. "Indeed? How awful." She could be civil, but she would not express condolences.

Her eyes widened when Mr. Sutton handed Mr. Barrett the board and excused himself. Could tonight get any worse? With that thought, Niko joined her with a teasing grin, giving her a fresh glass of wine.

Niko introduced himself to Mr. Barrett with a false name that sounded much like Mr. Michael Hunt. He gave Mr. Barrett an elaborate bow and a suggestive smile, making Cassandra cough to cover the laugh forced from her belly.

Mr. Barrett introduced himself and, from what Cassandra could gather, he proceeded to tell Niko his relationship to Cassandra while Niko inched closer to him. Mr. Barrett cleared his throat and stepped back, not taking the hint, Niko closed the distance between them.

Cassandra fought with the laughter bubbling in her throat and sipped her wine to cover up the rest of the damage.

At last, Mr. Barrett faced her. "Cassandra…talk…so long."

Hopefully, this meant he would leave, but unfortunately, she had misheard him, and his voice wove into the other noises around them. Niko came to her rescue, tugging the chalkboard away from Mr. Barrett.

He says he wants to renew your friendship. Niko gave her an exaggerated frown.

Cassandra shook her head. She wasn't about to open up Pandora's box.

Niko addressed Mr. Barrett to translate her gesture. His voice came out loud, even to Cassandra. "She said she doesn't want to talk to you."

Mr. Barrett shifted from foot to foot, choosing to ignore Niko as he spoke again. This time, she didn't catch any of the words, and instead of asking for clarification, she gave Niko a pained look.

I don't like him either. Were you supposed to marry this roach?

She glowered at Niko, and he sighed.

Mr. Barrett continued to speak over this exchange,

his face turning a comical shade of red. It was only a matter of time before the man threw one of his regular tantrums.

Niko must have sensed Mr. Barrett's growing frustration when he brought his full attention to the other man. He grasped Mr. Barrett's shoulders in his hands and pulled him into an embrace. Cassandra's eyes nearly jumped from her face when Niko caressed the other man's back like an old lover.

Mr. Barrett attempted to step away but couldn't untangle himself from the overly affectionate gesture. His face transformed from red to purple. At last, when the surrounding area had grown quiet, and Cassandra considered intervening, Niko released him. Mr. Barrett wasted no time as he rushed away, not stopping to make his excuses.

Niko waggled his eyebrows at her. *How did you ever let him get away?*

Her wine traveled to her nose as she choked on it. She took the board from his grasp, hoping it would afford her more privacy. *Aren't you afraid of being recognized? Lyme will have your head if he catches you in his house.*

Niko smirked. *I fear nothing.*

She spoke over her wine glass. "Liar."

I am sure Mr. Barrett is a witch. Only a truly powerful witch would resist my attention.

She snorted. *He is no more witch than Mr. Sutton or Lord Lyme. Not in the way you mean, anyway. Besides, I can resist you, and I am not powerful.*

Niko beamed. *I will take that as a challenge.*

His golden eyes held a dare as he pivoted on his heel and left her to stare after him. A moment passed before she realized he wasn't just ending their conversation but evading Mr. Sutton's return. She smoothed away the writing on the board before the other man could see it.

Mr. Sutton frowned after the form of Niko departing. He appeared to want to say something, but instead, he beckoned her to follow him, offering his arm.

She avoided his gaze and settled on his offered arm without hesitation, allowing him to lead her to Lord Lyme's wheeled chair on the other side of the room. She mourned her empty wine glass, wishing she had stopped to get more. She would need it for what Lord Lyme required of her tonight.

Cassandra was introduced to the throng of people surrounding Lord Lyme. Wearing gloves, she had to be creative about testing each of them. A brush of an arm here and there was not as effective as the handshake from before. Mr. Sutton remedied the problem by starting up the dancing.

Music, aside from singing, had never been a problem for her hearing. The songs beat through her as did the steps to the dances, and she freed herself to the music the way one celebrates the removal of a cast after a long injury. Each note was a blessing to her ears.

As much as she enjoyed dancing, she was subjected to dance after dance with whoever Mr. Sutton threw her way. At least, some of the men were eliminated when she passed by them in the course of the dance, but it became apparent that her innocent touches would not serve her long. Already, some of the men were drawing conclusions about her loose ways. They argued with Mr. Sutton for more dances with her.

One man went as far as to ask to walk with her about the garden, but Lord Lyme intervened. The chilly outdoors was no place for a young lady.

Near midnight, Cassandra longed to rest her throbbing feet, but Mr. Sutton refused to let her sit out a single dance for fear they would miss someone. The current song ended, and she tripped over her feet only to be caught by a man on the edge of the dance floor.

A familiar wave washed over her, increasing her lightheadedness. She didn't need to look up to see Niko held her. The crashing jolt of his presence in her ears revealed concern until he removed his skin from hers.

Before she could protest, he pulled her onto the dance floor. Her eyes snapped to his when the music erupted into a waltz, the first one that evening and, she suspected, not one of the scheduled dances. He raised a brow, daring her to comment.

She fell into step with him. "You're insane. They're watching me. What if they recognize you?"

A grin split across his face.

Her eyes snapped wide when she realized he must have removed his gloves sometime earlier in the evening. She stared at their clasped hands, the thin leather of her glove the only thing keeping her from sensing him, drowning in him.

"Niko, you know I have to touch you. For appearances, of course."

The tilt of his grin told her he didn't believe her excuse any more than she did.

She swallowed. "Just do whatever it is you do to make this less painful." Less overwhelming. Less intimate. Less him.

He gave her a solemn nod, keeping his gaze locked

on hers.

She adjusted her arm to touch his when Niko raised the hand at her back to stroke his thumb along her cheek.

She missed her step, and he adjusted to hide the clumsy movement. The split-second ocean roar from his gesture jolted in her ears to deep in her belly, resting there as her cheeks burned under his golden gaze.

She gasped. "That was uncalled for."

He frowned and said something she couldn't grasp over the music.

She shook her head. "It's impossible for me to understand you in here." When the dance ended, Niko gave her up to another partner, but first, ran his hand over her arm.

Remorse. Was he sorry to stop the dance, or was he sorry for insulting her? Both she hoped. The man was impossible. He had no boundaries and refused to keep to hers. The worst part was that with his abilities, he knew her boundaries were just words. The wall she had built around her heart thinned when Niko crashed into it. It wouldn't do. Once this job was done, she would be away from the madness bred in Spray Cove's citizens.

Her new dance partner was a round man with a polite air and bright hazel eyes. Given his size, his grace was unusual. He attempted to engage her in conversation, but with the music and her traveling thoughts, she didn't catch a word.

She made a sour face and willed him to be quiet, pushing all her frustration and disappointment into keeping the man from uttering another word.

His mouth fell shut, mid-sentence.

She blinked at his wide-eyed stare. How curious.

She willed him to speak again, but the man only paled.

Nausea climbed up her throat, and her gaze jumped about the room. She let out a long breath. For once, nobody seemed to be watching. She turned her gaze back to the poor man.

With the sudden jerk of his head, he coughed, jarring them both out of step. He shook his head, regaining his senses as he took back up the dance. Perhaps the man was ill? At least, the color had returned to his face.

The song emitted its final notes when she remembered herself and brushed her arm against her partner's. A gong erupted in her ears, echoing off the sides of her head. The touch had been brief, but the pain lived on, gnawing at her ears with oversized hammers. Her skull would be smashed under pressure.

Not since her first encounter with Niko had she been so consumed. She found herself curled on the floor, her head cradled in her hands. Mr. Sutton stood over her, his fingers to his lips as though he tried to silence her.

Her mouth shut on the scream she hadn't heard. Like the beginning with Niko, everything had fallen silent. Her fingers moved to test her ears for blood, but thankfully, they came back clean. She breathed out a long breath and leaned onto her arm. Mr. Sutton helped her to her feet just in time to see her last dance partner being escorted from the room by two broad-shouldered footmen.

Cassandra caught sight of Niko among the onlookers. His lips pinched together. She tried to meet his gaze, to send some message of apology without words. He either didn't see or ignored her when he reached into his coat, but someone behind him pulled him into the crowd, and he disappeared.

Her stomach twisted and left her lightheaded. Again, she had given up another witch, or had she given up something more?

Chapter 9

Although she wanted nothing more than to leave, her hearing worse, and her limbs limp, Mr. Sutton insisted she continue. At least, he let her sit out the rest of the dances but took possession of her gloves. Of course, it was Lord Lyme's house. He set the rules here. Without her gloves, it was easier to come into contact with the guests, and the process became smooth.

Except now, she was dead on her feet, carrying the iron weight of dread through the paces. Any one of the people she met could send her writhing on the floor. She didn't know what to make of her last dance partner and wished she had tried harder to catch the man's name.

Perhaps Lord Lyme would let her travel to town. There she would find the answers from the witches above Morgan's Haberdasher. He had advised her to stay in the house, but what could be the harm in visiting the haberdashery shop for some much-needed supplies?

Her mind refused to focus on the task at hand. Mr. Sutton cast her annoyed frowns as the evening wore on. The guests were pleasant enough, and none of them mentioned what had happened. She knew they spoke of it when they were sure she couldn't hear. She stopped short of laughing in their faces about how careful they were. She couldn't hear them most of the time when they spoke directly to her face. It was a fine joke.

She found herself searching the crowd for Niko, knowing he had left after she revealed another witch. An icy touch claimed her chest. Was he as disgusted with her as she was of herself?

After what seemed like years to Cassandra, the party concluded without any further discoveries. The last of the guests had left in their carriages, having escaped their interrogation unknowingly. She shook the thought from her head. As dishonest as Lord Lyme was to his associates, it wasn't her place to worry over them.

With leaden steps, she made her way to the stairs. Mr. Sutton caught up to her and placed his hand on her shoulder, getting her attention.

He swept his hand toward him. "Come."

She sighed, and her body protested the movement. Hadn't she done enough for one night? She trailed him in silence, rubbing her temples as she went. A week of sleep would do her good. No, a month. From the way Lord Lyme had pressed her tonight, she doubted she would get another day. She must have been paying for her time with her aunt.

Lord Lyme sat composed behind his desk as though he hadn't been playing host for hours. One would think he was a healthy man of twenty instead of an injured man twice her age. He handed her a note as she approached his desk.

His usually neat handwriting was strained. *Miss Poole, You have done well tonight. The man you identified was Mr. Bartholomew Shaw, a long-time business associate. My people were able to uncover some disturbing information about him tonight.*

She paused in her reading. Had they questioned him? They couldn't have found the time, but the man had already given up his secrets. She frowned to herself, better not to ask. She took up her place again.

Mr. Shaw's unusual charisma and sway are not simply positive character traits. Looking back, I question many of my decisions when investing in his business affairs. He has cost me a good deal of money in the past, and I wonder at my never noticing his greedy motives. Your help has been vital in uncovering this nefarious business.

A flaming blush crept up her cheeks. Cassandra loosened her shoulders and regarded him with a small smile. Working for Lord Lyme had always been for herself, to gain her hearing back. She hadn't believed they would uncover anything harmful. Perhaps she hadn't given the threat of witches enough weight. Lord Lyme was a baron in the middle of Yorkshire. She couldn't imagine the harm Mr. Shaw's influence would do in London or, more specifically, Westminster.

"What of the footman?"

Lord Lyme frowned and spoke, perhaps not deeming the subject important enough for paper. "He's been dismissed."

She scrunched up her nose but said nothing. Who was she to judge what Lord Lyme decided was best for his employees? After the discovery of Mr. Shaw, she couldn't deny there was a danger working with witches. She had witnessed it herself with Niko. She shook her head. Why had she let the man with golden eyes into her trust? Or was he really harmless to her?

Lord Lyme hunched over another note to her and passed it off to Mr. Sutton to hand to her. *I have decided to take Ensign Barrett into my employ here at Lyme House to help with your task here. Mr. Sutton already does the work of a dozen men and could use another set of hands. Since Ensign Barrett is an old friend of yours, I thought you would be more comfortable working with him. He will be present for the dinner party I have arranged for tomorrow. The dinner will proceed like the party tonight. You will make contact with all of the guests. Don't waste any time with a guest after you have ruled them out.*

The paper in her fingers shook as she scrambled to keep it secure.

She attempted a smile, but her lips shook as it faltered. How could she refuse Mr. Barrett's help without displeasing Lord Lyme? She sensed she was on shaky ground with him after Louise. What had they talked about while she tested the guests? If Mr. Barrett didn't already know about her ability, he would soon, and it would become yet another reason for him to be disgusted with her.

Cassandra inched to leave, but Mr. Sutton stopped her with a raised hand. Lord Lyme leaned back over his desk. *I took the liberty of writing to your parents when we sent your dear aunt to them, reassuring them of your well-being. I gave them an advance payment for detaining you from your work in the shop. They responded and agreed that you are needed here and said for you to take the time you needed to fulfill our arrangement. Rest assured, everything at your home in Coldon is as it should be. Your aunt has been laid to rest in the family plot, waiting for your visit when you are restored to your true self.*

Her shoulders tensed as she read the note. Her parents hadn't responded to her own letter. She wanted the comfort of her father's neat script or the loving advice of her mother. Why had they answered Lord Lyme and not her? Perhaps they hadn't been able to respond with the grief of her aunt's death. Tears stung in her eyes, and she took in a sharp inhale, willing them away. She would write to them again.

A knot tightened in her chest. She needed to be home to mourn with her parents. All at once, she reverted to the child she had been, lacking her mother's arms around her, soothing her to sleep. Her eyes were wide awake now, the anxiety weighing over the long day, reminding her how alone she was here at Lyme House.

Lord Lyme must have read her expression when he gave her a warm grin. "Your parents… proud…good work you're doing here. Don't…witches in Spray Cove to poison your thoughts. Steady the course." Gaining familiarity with her hearing quirks, Lord Lyme conveyed his words well enough for her to get the message after his second attempt.

She chewed her lower lip. Had he known Niko had been there tonight? No, Mr. Sutton or Lord Lyme would have made it clear if they had known. They had warned her away from the witch, and she doubted they would allow her to endanger herself. After all, they needed her to remove the rest of the witches in their path. They must have noted when she spent too much time with the unknown dandy, the only time during the party that had been too short.

At last, Cassandra returned the man's smile and excused herself from the room. This time, they didn't stop her. Yet, as late as it was, she couldn't shake the ache resting along her bones, screaming to be released. Her feet led the way, traveling unknown corridors without any direction.

All at once, she wanted to scream, to cry. How could she spend time with Mr. Barrett, pretending like he hadn't abandoned her? Their reunion was long overdue, and she knew they would eventually cross paths, but why did it have to come at the worst of times? Already she had enough to occupy her tired brain.

An echo of her shattered heart weighed on her chest. She knew this reunion would hurt, knew it would evoke happy memories she wanted to erase along with the bad. What bothered her the most was the compassion overwhelming her and nagging at her conscious. He had been injured, most likely in battle. No longer was she the one to soothe his pain or calm his worry. Their countless hours together sharing smiles and secret kisses meant nothing to him. She no longer had any bearing on his well-being. It was as though she had never existed in his world.

The upset blinded her as she plunged into the labyrinth-like halls. She stumbled and almost trampled Mist as he brushed across her path.

"There you are, you little demon. I thought you'd forgotten all about me." Cassandra regarded the cat as he planted himself in her path. "Come along if you must, but I would rather not fall on my face just now."

Mist cocked his head but didn't move.

She sighed and stepped to the side of the cat. Mist had other ideas, as he rose from his seat, and rubbed up against her advancing leg. She pushed him with a gentle nudge, but the feline took her movement as encouragement then butt his head against her.

"All right." Cassandra bent to scoop the cat up, but

Mist dodged her hands, venturing just out of her reach ahead of her. Her scowl did nothing to scare the beast away. "What is it you want?

A faint meow issued from the cat's throat, a short hum of recognition. Mist whisked his tail behind him as he advanced a few paces and craned his head back to watch her. His amber eyes slit at her.

"I must be losing my mind." Cassandra shook her head. "All right, I will follow you, but if you lead me to a den of mice or a pit of snakes, I will throttle you."

Mist squinted his eyes at her before giving another swish of his tail and sashaying down the hall. She followed him a short distance away, avoiding his abrupt stops to check on her progress. Her aimless wandering hadn't been much different, and she reasoned if someone came across her, she could claim she was lost. It wasn't a lie.

At last, Mist stopped in front of a wooden panel along the wall. Only, it wasn't a panel, but a door, only noticeable after Mist traced his nose along a crease in the wall. She studied the outline of the door, searching for a handle or keyhole. Nothing was visible under the low light of the hall.

The cat sat back on his paws and blinked up at her. She couldn't help but think the beast criticized her.

She snorted. "This is ridiculous. I'm going back to my room."

As she moved to leave, a meow stopped her. A command if she ever heard one.

Mist rose from his place on the floor and stretched to paw at the wall. He gave a yowl back at her.

She knelt beside the cat, running her fingers over the smooth surface beside him. Her index finger caught on a whorl in the wood and she pressed it experimentally. A click sounded through her fingers, inaudible to her ears. The wall cracked forward, allowing a gush of chill air into the hallway.

Cassandra clicked her tongue. "Clever boy." She scratched Mist's head before widening the entrance.

A shiver raced along her spine. She stood beneath a cloudless night sky, a sliver of moon cast faint shadows along the ground. They had long gone past the edge of the house, and this must be an atrium somewhere near the center of Lyme House. A pool of water reflected the moon back to her, but she could see little else.

Mist bolted into the dark as though chasing some unknown apparition.

Cassandra groaned. "Here, kitty, kitty. Come back here."

Surely, if the cat couldn't let himself into the atrium, he would have no way out. She cast her gaze among the shapes, hoping one would materialize into the cat. Her teeth chattered as she rubbed her arms to warm them. A streak of movement snapped her gaze to the left.

The tone of her voice heightened. "Kitty, I'll find you some nice tasty fish." She blew out a breath. "If you come back here now, I won't skin you. Although I could use some nice new slippers." Her voice trailed into a laugh. Who was she kidding? The cat was probably having the time of his life.

For a moment, she shivered in place, catching glimpses of Mist among the silhouettes of what appeared to be a garden. At last, he pranced toward her, a still form dangled from his mouth. Cassandra crouched down to get a better look. Her lips screwed up when she identified the toad.

With a tentative hand, she tugged the creature out of the cat's mouth. "This thing will kill you, stupid beast."

Mist surrendered his catch without any fuss, wandering back into the hall with a puffed-out chest. She set the toad aside and rushed back to shut the cat in before he got other ideas. The door snapped into place as though it had never existed. She would have to return during the day. She made note of the location of the door and left in the general direction of her room. Mist was nowhere in sight, not that she believed the cat would guide her back to her room.

It was a half-hour later when she reached her room. The fire was lit but low in the grate. She must have wandered for hours. Her mind had run circles around her troubles, leaving a well-worn path she didn't care to continue. What she longed for was something to forget. Seeing Mr. Barrett had been the last push needed to send her into a freefall, she could not escape.

Cassandra dug the forgotten bottle of liquid out of her reticule. It was what she had. She knew what she wanted—Niko's comfort. With her aunt, he had shown himself to be a tolerant and caring man. His presence was like a drug, as addictive and pleasurable as the brown substance sloshing around the bottle.

Antoinette said two drops, but that was then. That was before she had lost her aunt. Before Mr. Barrett arrived. The last time she saw Antoinette, her life had been a sunny day at the beach. She hadn't given up any witches then, and her ability had been just a side effect of her hearing loss, easily ignored, and never to be used.

She placed four drops of liquid on her tongue then hesitated a moment before a fifth drop.

Let me forget.

Chapter 10

Toads surrounded her.

They crowded her in bed, their throats expanding and contracting in a chaotic chorus of movement. Their pebbly skin was a wash of brown, blending and bending into the maroon bedspread. No sound came from their throats as though they were ghosts.

Mist stretched his way over the toads, paying them no attention as he climbed above her. He sat on her chest, his head tilted as he studied her face.

Her gaze lingered on the toads, her heart beating in time with their movements. If she stared at them hard enough, they might vanish from her will alone. Mist pawed at her, his amber eyes demanding her attention. At last, she met his gaze.

If a cat could look concerned, Mist showed as much worry as a mother hen. He pawed at her again until she reached out to pet him.

The toads continued their frantic beat around her. With a start, she reached back to find one in her hair, tugging at its length. The knobby skin of another brushed at her legs under the covers. She kicked back the blankets, scrambling to her feet.

They were everywhere.

Her head grew burdensome, as though trapped in a whirlwind, both light and heavy all at once. Her stomach splashed around in her middle as she fought back against nausea. She couldn't step without coming across another toad. Where had they come from? Had Mist brought all of them in here? Why did he act as though they weren't there?

Just like that, the throats quit expanding. All movement stopped as if the world was frozen in place. No, not frozen. Dead. The toads were dead.

The maddening orchestra of throats had stopped, but this was worse. The toads showed an accelerated rate of decay. The smell filled her nostrils all at once, forcing a gag from her throat. All reasoning escaped her. She doubled over on the floor, giving up the sparse contents of her stomach, heaving out the last of her strength.

When she dared steal a glance at the room, the toads were gone. Not a bone remained.

Mist peered down at her from his perch on the bed.

"What did I do?" She steadied her shaking body against the bed before throwing herself next to the cat on the bedspread. Her body curled around Mist, hoping for any outside comfort. Of course, the cat hadn't seen the toads. They had never been there. At least, nobody was around to see the heat burn her cheeks. Nobody but Mist, anyway.

Antoinette said two drops.

She shivered inwardly and wrestled the blanket out from under her weight. Mist seemed to take her action as an invitation and burrowed his way under the covers, nestling beside her stomach. The cat soothed he. It wasn't long before she found her rest. A dead sleep devoid of dreams.

****

Cassandra slumped on a bench along the terrace in

the forgiving autumn sun. If someone hadn't had the foresight to send a maid with more of that delicious tea, she would still be abed, unknown, and unfazed by the world. It was just after two in the afternoon. She had hoped the sun would shock her back into consciousness.

She sipped another cup of tea, though the contents also failed to rouse her. The house was a blur of activity she could not comprehend. Toads lingered in her mind like a nagging unfinished chore at the edge of her thoughts. She itched to go back to the atrium if only to reassure herself that it wasn't a dream. She sensed the atrium was a forbidden place for her. Lord Lyme had never hinted of any such area, but the artfully concealed door told her enough. The knowledge only increased her desire to return.

Why conceal an atrium? Perhaps it was a secret place for Lord Lyme to escape to. She doubted the man had any trouble making people disappear when he needed, but what other uses could a secret atrium have to a man in a wheeled chair? The more she thought about it, the more ridiculous the idea appeared. She should march back there and throw open the door for all to see.

As she considered doing just that, an unwelcome visitor approached.

Mr. Barrett strode toward her, bearing her chalkboard in hand. Some infernal idiot had found it for him, but he was the last person she wanted to talk to. She would have to get a hold of the board so she could hide it away. Sitting in silence was far more preferable than enduring this man's company.

He gave her a face-splitting smile as he bowed and

then settled down next to her on the bench. His steady hand moved over the chalkboard.

She scowled back at him. What fantasy world was this man living in?

He handed her the chalkboard. *I wanted to talk to you before dinner. Our meeting at the party came as a surprise, and our conversation was cut short.*

Not short enough. What could they possibly have to discuss? She gave him a reluctant nod. Better to get this over.

I wanted to tell you last night you looked as beautiful as ever. I am glad Spray Cove agrees with you.

Her cheeks heated, and she handed the board back to him, her gaze averted. Words were lost to her.

He shoved the board in front of her. *You do. I am afraid you have outgrown your old friend.*

Her gaze flicked to his, and she gritted her teeth. "You know that isn't what happened. You left me. I had nothing to do with it."

He nodded. Forgetting about her hearing, he spoke. "I can't help…"

"I don't hear half of what you say. You can't help what? Can't help abandoning me? Can't help betraying our friendship? Can't help letting all of our friends and family down? Ashley, what is it you think you can't help?"

His face turned a deep purple. "I can't help what I feel." His words slammed into her ears.

An inferno rose inside her, blazing over her skin like so much kindling.

"What is it you feel?" She knew the answer, didn't want to hear it, but she needed to.

His head turned away as though he wanted to flee. Run. It was what he was good at, avoiding his problems and never caring who he hurt. She had spent months defending him to her friends, to their families. He had been her closest friend, the love of her life. He had thrown it all away for a pretty skirt and a mountain of debt.

A shadow of his voice came from his turned-away lips. A croak of words she couldn't hope ever to decipher. She had known him most of her life, and he couldn't even bring himself to face her. Coward.

"You're going to have to face me if you expect me to understand you. I need to see your lips." How was she going to work with him?

The pain in his eyes when he turned back to her was enough to make her reconsider her whole outlook. He had hurt himself more than he could ever hurt her and didn't need her to make it any worse.

Her voice dropped. "What is it?"

He appeared near tears. "I'm sorry. You're right, but I can't help what I feel." His voice had become quiet, difficult to hear.

She gestured to the board for him to continue.

I don't love you.

She stared down at the words, blinking. Of course, he didn't love her. Love wasn't something that just came out of the air. It was something you worked at, something you gained from mutual fondness and respect shared with another person. After he fled, she realized his heart had never been in the wedding or their relationship. Other people didn't factor into Ashley Barrett's world.

As much as she reasoned his written words away,

the crushing weight in her chest told her she still loved him. It wasn't the same deep longing of their youth, but a love of the memory of what she thought they once had, who he had once been.

His hand shook against the board. *I am truly sorry. If you want, I will withdraw from Lyme House.*

She bit her lip, fighting back the words to tell him to run away again. He needed this job. The set of his shoulders and the cast of his eyes told her he dreaded her answer. After all this time, she still wanted to lash out, to hurt him the way he had hurt her. Taking this away from him would serve no purpose. It wouldn't change the past or erase the pain he had caused.

Her conscience left her no choice. Losing this job would destroy him.

"Stay." She patted his leg, and his lips turned up a fraction. The sadness lingered in his eyes. She knew then he would have destroyed her in the end. He would never raise a hand to her. No, that wasn't his way. Her need to take care of him would wear her down until nothing was left of her.

All at once, the tightness in her chest released. He had no more power over her, and she was free for another chance at love.

"Stay." It wasn't like he could make her situation much worse.

He cleared his throat and nodded. *Thank you. Maybe you can fill me in about what happened to you. I heard about your hearing. Lord Lyme told me what you can do. Is it true?*

"Unfortunately, yes."

A maid appeared with a fresh pot of tea and a plate of dainty sandwiches. Her stomach grumbled at the sight of them. She glanced toward Mr. Barrett, who nodded to the tray for her to eat. Once the maid left, Mr. Barrett held up the board for her to read as she poured more tea.

Forgive me for being so bold. I thought you could use some food.

She gave him a tentative smile and shoved a sandwich in her mouth. Smoked salmon with a creamy spread. To die for. "You remembered."

His lopsided grin was answer enough. She offered the plate to him, but he shook his head. This was the Ashley she remembered.

He rubbed away the writing on the board and took up the chalk again as she devoured another sandwich. *How did you get this ability?*

She swallowed the bite of deliciousness, wondering at the abilities of the Lyme House cook. "I came into contact with a witch in Coldon, but I didn't know what it was until I came to Spray Cove. The witches here explained it to me."

He raised his brows. *Did the witch do this to you?*

Her mind shifted to Niko's feral gaze and wild hair, and the image gave her a wide, playful grin.

A laugh bubbled up into her throat. She had drawn the same conclusion. "No, he's quite harmless." For a moment, she believed her own words. "My abilities woke when I sensed his. Niko wouldn't hurt me." At least, she was sure of that.

His gaze searched her face. *Are you sure? These witches are dangerous. Mr. Shaw proved this.*

So, Mr. Barrett had already started working with Lord Lyme. A quick hire. The sandwiches in her stomach gave an uneasy churn. She pushed the plate away.

"I'm sure. Niko has proven to be a gentleman." At least, in a sense. "Besides, he has had every opportunity to manipulate me with his ability, and you can see I'm well." A curl of doubt threaded over her skin. Had he manipulated her? She knew he had used his empathic talents to help her, but had she missed something else? She shook the thought away. It didn't matter now.

He blinked at her. *Neeco? Was that who you were talking to last night? I thought he said his name was Mike Hunt.*

Her hand clutched her side as she doubled over with laughter. Leave it to Mr. Barrett to not catch the joke. No amount of this delicious tea could get her to explain it to him. Her face colored at the thought. She took the board from him.

Niko.

He rolled his eyes and took back the board. *I don't care how you spell it. You are getting yourself into trouble. Does Lord Lyme know?*

She snorted. "Of course not. I was told to stay away from him, but he keeps showing up at the most inconvenient times."

His hand rubbed out the chalk as he shook his head. *They told you that for good reason. I cannot believe you have not turned him over to them. Your job is to turn over the witches, not consort with them. Next time, if you do not turn him over, I will.*

Her face paled at his declaration. "Ashley, please, that won't be necessary. I'm sure he's grown tired of Lyme House. He saw what happened to Mr. Shaw, and he would be a fool to return." If she could only convince Niko of that. The man had no sense of self-preservation, and she had no reason to believe he had learned anything since she last saw him. He had shown no intent to harm anyone there, and she wasn't about to turn him in for being a minor nuisance.

Or that was what she told herself. Even now, her breath hitched at the memory of his kiss and his piercing golden eyes. Her face regained a fury of color as she noticed Mr. Barrett watching her.

Are you in some kind of trouble? We should tell Lord Lyme.

She shook her head with such violence that he set the chalkboard down. "I can take care of myself. Lord Lyme can't know. He had some kind of feud with Niko, and he wouldn't understand."

He let out a long breath and held out a palm for her to continue.

"Ashley, the witches in Spray Cove know what I'm going through. It would be like turning myself in. They can't do us any harm here. Please, try to understand." She thought of the bottle of medicine Antoinette had given her. "They didn't have to help me when I asked, but they did anyway knowing I could at any time identify them and others like them. I'm in their debt."

She had repaid them by turning on them.

She grew numb. Her tea was cold, but she swallowed the last of it, anyway. She wished she was back in her room consumed by the peaceful sleep of Antoinette's cure. Was it too early to take a nap? Her fingers worked at her temples. So much and so little of the day had already passed.

Mr. Barrett pressed a hand to her shoulder and pushed the board to her. *I am sorry. Put it out of your mind. We will get you back to your old self and forget we ever heard of witches. Are we friends again?*

Her lips dropped into a thin line. "If we're going to be working together, then I suppose so." For a moment, she was back in Coldon with him, and they had their whole lives together in front of them. "How is Bertha?"

His face fell at the mention of his wife, and he ran a hand through his hair. He stared down at the board a moment. *She returned to Coldon.*

She frowned. "Is she sick? Maybe you should go to her."

He shook his head. *Thank you for your concern. No, she is well.*

When he didn't continue, she willed him to meet her eyes, but he kept his gaze on the board. "Ashley, is everything all right?"

His hand reached over to hers. He gave her fingers a gentle squeeze and released them to take up the chalk. *No, but it will be. She returned to her family.* With no further explanation, he wiped the half confession away. Bertha had left him.

She waited for the thrill of justice to swell in her breast or even the pleasure and awe at the harmony of the universe. It didn't come. She couldn't feel joy over another person's heartache, even if it was his.

"I'm sorry." The lie flowed from her lips. No celebration would ring out over his misery, and yet, she had no sympathy for him.

He nodded then rose to his feet.

An uneasy weariness crept along her brow, and the anger of before made way for pity. When her task for Lord Lyme was finished, she would leave him with a heavy mind, but she wouldn't look back. Never again.

Chapter 11

Mr. Sutton solved her skin contact problem and had a pair of gloves altered to allow tiny slits on three fingers of each glove. The gloves matched the tone of her skin, making the slits on her fingertips almost invisible. Along with the gloves, she was given another white dress.

If they had taken such care on short notice to outfit her and alter a pair of gloves, why couldn't they allow her to wear mourning clothes? Taking more time off would have been out of the question, but outfitting her in the proper attire wouldn't have been too inconvenient.

She took a long breath as she entered the drawing room. She had avoided every dinner party since losing her hearing, aside from an awkward event hosted by her mother. Dinner conversation would prove interesting tonight. At least she wasn't expected to actually carry on conversations with the guests.

Mr. Barrett approached her with a grim-faced man in well-kept but ill-fitting attire. The man escorted a golden-haired, grinning woman in a light lavender dress. Her smile was infectious. Cassandra found herself beaming from ear to ear.

"Miss Poole…introduce Mr. Nathan Powell and Mrs.….Powell."

She curtseyed to Mrs. Powell and gave her hand to

Mr. Powell. Her fingers graced his, but with no effect. Her gaze drew back to the other woman. "Mrs. Powell, is it? I do apologize but my hearing has failed me of late."

The other woman's eyes shone. "Please, call me Katrina." Her voice came out clear as she leaned toward Cassandra. A faint hint of flowers rose from her skin.

Mr. Barrett cleared his throat. "Mr. Powell...the...ove."

She blinked at Mr. Barrett and turned toward Katrina. "What did he say? I often find him impossible to understand."

Katrina giggled. "Aren't all men impossible to understand?" Her chocolate-colored eyes crinkled when she smiled. "Mr. Barrett said that my husband is the vicar in Spray Cove."

A corner of Cassandra's lips twitched up. "Mr. Barrett has a husband?"

Katrina fell silent, and all at once, her face crumbled into laughter. She covered her mouth. Mr. Powell's grim visage brightened, and a hint of a smile crossed his lips. All eyes went to Mr. Barrett, who had turned a familiar shade of puce.

Katrina wiped away a tear from her eye. "I like you, Miss Poole. I do hope you plan to stay in Spray Cove for a while."

"We'll see." Cassandra pressed her lips together. She wouldn't stay there a minute longer than she had to.

The drawing room was filled with at least a dozen people she would have to meet with each of them in various states of ease. She needed introductions, and she would be damned if Mr. Barrett did the job.

Cassandra let out a sad sigh. "Mrs. Powell, I'm afraid I don't know anyone here except the host."

"Katrina, please. Of course, as the vicar's wife…to know everyone in Spray Cove. I…to introduce you, my dear." Katrina laid a gloved hand on Cassandra's arm and guided her to the nearest group.

Cassandra glanced back at a solemn-faced Mr. Barrett and a bright-faced Mr. Powell. Her ex-fiancé's presence sent her teeth on edge. Worse, he insisted on looking away when speaking to her and spoke under his breath when he forgot she couldn't hear. His hand had a way of covering his mouth, a rude gesture that she couldn't decide if it was deliberate or not.

She managed to touch everyone in the first group without incident. Mr. Sutton watched her progress from the other side of the room. He appeared to anticipate her finding someone, but he gave her no hint at whoever that may be.

Cassandra examined the eyes of each guest as though Niko would appear among them though the dinner party was too small to conceal him. As careless as he seemed, she knew he had better sense than that. The crowded drawing room was empty without him. This dinner lacked a humorous someone she didn't have to pretend with.

Her thoughts of Niko cast a sour cloud over the introductions, and her smile faltered after she tested each individual. He didn't approve of what she did, none of the Spray Cove witches would. How could they? She betrayed them with each brush of her fingers.

Cassandra's steps wavered as she reached out to a portly man in a fine waistcoat that reminded her of

Niko. The man steadied her to her feet as she brushed a hand along his exposed wrist. Now was not the time to become scatterbrained by pretty buttons. At the back of her mind, Niko's golden eyes bobbed with laughter.

Her face flushed.

The butler entered to announce dinner before they reached the final three people. Mr. Sutton's sharp gaze told her he had noticed it. He gave her a short nod. They would have to find time later.

She was separated from Katrina at dinner and seated next to two gentlemen. Having tested both of them, she gazed off in their company. The man on her left, a neighboring landowner with a lisp, spoke to the other woman next to him after receiving a dull reception from Cassandra. Her dinner partner to her right, another landowner with a high voice and silver wing-tipped hair, didn't seem to notice as he prattled on about his prized hunting dogs and the hunt he had planned.

Mr. Godfrey Carter's passion for the sport was such that Cassandra almost enjoyed listening to what she could hear. She had never been hunting, of course, but the way the man's face animated when he spoke was enough to turn anyone into a fan.

She sipped her lemonade, having been deprived of anything stronger by Mr. Sutton. A fact one of the footmen had discreetly informed her when she asked for wine in the drawing room. They wanted her fully aware as she performed her job. Lemonade didn't help to brace her for Mr. Carter's conversation. At least, they could have given her more of her favored tea.

Cassandra agreed to attend Mr. Carter's hunting party, though she doubted she would be around for it.

The man wouldn't take anything less than acceptance and by the close of dinner, she would agree to anything short of marriage if the man would stop talking.

When the men joined the women in the drawing room, Mr. Barrett approached her and brought the three sportsmen she had missed during her earlier rounds. He must be making up for her leaving him behind.

Katrina stepped in before Mr. Barrett could perform his duty. The auburn-haired man was addressed as Mr. Tallmadge. He took her hand with a haughty smile, and a shiver raced down her spine at his unwanted touch, but not any magic ability.

The dusky-faced man, Mr. Jones, was more reserved beside his friends. As before, the breath caught in her throat and escaped her after she touched his bare hand without event. Of course, she couldn't tell on sight who the witches were. If she could, then this whole process would be complete.

A giddy relief engulfed her. She met the chestnut-haired man, Mr. Harris, with a genuine smile. He avoided her touch with a swift bow and a step back, throwing Cassandra off balance. She teetered forward with the grace of a drunken horse, falling between Mr. Harris and Katrina. Her hands grasped out as she fell, clasping onto them.

All at once, a crackling storm erupted behind her ears. A melodic bell sang behind it. The sounds waged a battle in her head, like Thor crashing down on the heads of giants. Her hand flinched back from Mr. Harris, and the storm cut short. The bell continued its song in a faint imitation of a church bell. The pain in her ears was a soft pinch in the background.

Cassandra stared into the horror-stricken face of

Katrina, her hand still grasping the woman's arm. She jerked her hand away, but not soon enough. Mr. Sutton had reached their group. Hadn't she ruled Katrina out earlier in the evening? Somehow, she must have missed her, or Katrina had avoided it.

"I'm so sorry." Cassandra mouthed the words to Katrina, and her lips shook as she spoke.

Katrina shook her head and swallowed. Her golden head leaned toward Cassandra as she spoke in that voice, not unlike the bell. "Niko warned me. I should never have come."

From the solemn cast of Mr. Harris's eyes, he must have had similar thoughts. The pair had both avoided her touch throughout the night. If it weren't for her determination to do her cursed job, they would have gotten away.

Three footmen appeared to help Mr. Sutton escort the two guests out.

Cassandra willed Katrina to meet her gaze, but the woman kept her head turned away. Mr. Harris had grown pale, his peach waistcoat now too bright against his skin.

A shout erupted from the center of the room. Mr. Powell inserted himself between Mr. Sutton and Katrina. "What…this?" The vicar's voice rose and fell where Cassandra's hearing couldn't follow.

Mr. Sutton answered him in a low inaudible voice.

A crimson flush crawled up Mr. Powell's neck and into his cheeks. He rounded on Cassandra, and this time she didn't miss his words or his steel eyes. "You did this. Traitor." He spit the accusation into her face.

His anger dropped away as he turned to his wife. "My angel…"

Cassandra averted her gaze; this moment between the couple was for them alone. She continued to look away as Mr. Powell shouted at Mr. Sutton and the footmen. When Mr. Barrett guided her out of the drawing room, she didn't protest or look back. Her head hung limp as though the life had drained out.

The bright star Cassandra met that night was now in Lord Lyme's control. The power she observed from the other woman was faint, a small trickle of power next to what she had experienced from Mr. Shaw. The energy that radiated off Mr. Harris had almost overridden Katrina's, but he was no match for Mr. Shaw or Niko.

Her throat clenched tight on the emotions she refused to acknowledge. This was the job. She couldn't afford to have sympathy or love for these people. Her abilities had seemed impersonal when she agreed to help Lord Lyme. What she could do was like a foggy dream, a surreal consciousness not fully formed.

When the haze cleared from her thoughts, her gaze darted around the room they now inhabited. Mr. Barrett had taken her to the library. For once, Lord Lyme was not behind the desk. Ashley seated her in a chair near the desk and took up the one next to hers. He slid back into the chair, watching her as they sat in silence.

Lord Lyme entered the room, and a footman pushed him behind his desk.

Cassandra narrowed her eyes at him but waited for the footman to leave before she threw verbal daggers at him. "Katrina is harmless. Why don't you let her be?"

Lord Lyme let out a long sigh and turned his gaze to Mr. Barrett, who leaned toward Cassandra.

"You…that."

She shook her head.

"Give me the bloody chalkboard." Mr. Barrett reached over Lord Lyme's desk.

A stab of hurt pierced her chest. Her hearing was erratic, and she found herself catching things she shouldn't hear. People believed they could talk about her while she was present without fear of her overhearing them. If only he would give her a chance to understand what he said. Katrina had spoken with such clarity, but then again maybe that was part of Katrina's ability. She banished away the thought.

He shoved the chalkboard toward her. *You do not know if they are dangerous. It is up to Mr. Sutton to find out.*

She scrubbed away the words with her gloved palm and tossed the board onto the desk.

Lord Lyme closed his eyes against her anger.

Mr. Barrett fetched the board from the desk and wrote with whitened knuckles. The chalk broke under his hand, but he continued to scribble with the stub. He held the board out to her, but she pushed it back at him without looking at it. His anger scrunched his face into the ugliest expression, forcing a laugh from deep in her chest.

She took the board with a smirk.

Why do you have to act so bloody childish? You were hired to do this job, and you will do it. Lord Lyme did not have to offer you anything for your help. He could have taken it. Be grateful for this opportunity. You will not get another chance.

A chill slithered up her spine. Lord Lyme would force her to work for him whether she liked it or not. She was a tool for him to be wielded as he saw fit. She knew he wouldn't harm her. He needed her to find witches for him. He couldn't bring his guests to her if she were tied up, kicking and screaming. The whole countryside would know.

Lord Lyme handed her the paper he had finished writing on. *My dear, you are performing your job superbly. Do not let your kind heart cloud your judgment. Mrs. Powell may be just as dangerous as Mr. Shaw. She is not to be trusted. I fear their numbers are far greater than I ever anticipated. We need to work faster. Already word of our purpose is spreading among them. We will be holding a house party with a ball and hunting party. You will attend all events and cease all contact with Niko.*

She stared above the letter, no longer reading it. Had he found out about Niko at the party or in the maze? Her gaze snapped to Mr. Barrett, who gave her a smug smile. "Does our friendship mean nothing to you?"

Lord Lyme's eyes blazed as he took back the letter and underlined the last sentence three times.

Mr. Sutton arrived beside them, and Mr. Barrett got to his feet. All eyes went to Cassandra. She shot to her feet and strode for the door. Mr. Barrett caught up to her as she strode away and stopped her in her path.

"Let go of me. I need to walk."

He jerked her toward the stairs, not bothering with an explanation. She knew from experience that she didn't have the strength to fight him. The memory of her childhood friendship slammed into her chest with a leaden weight.

"I don't know how you can live with yourself. You aren't the person I thought you were." Who did she really know anymore? She didn't even recognize herself.

He chuckled to himself then pushed her to mount the stairs. She tripped, slamming her hands and knees against the stairs.

Alisa rushed down the stairs to help her up, casting a glare toward Mr. Barrett. The maid braced Cassandra against herself and helped her up the remaining steps.

She murmured her thanks to the maid in dismissal, but Alisa refused to leave her, walking the rest of the way to Cassandra's room. Mr. Barrett trailed close behind them. Her back hummed in warning at his proximity. The man had become a monster possessing the body of the man she once loved. She could no longer predict what he would and wouldn't do.

Alisa jerked the door shut inside her room before Mr. Barrett had the chance to advance, but Cassandra had no doubt he would stand there until she was alone and lock her away like some valuable heirloom.

The maid never spoke as she made up the fire and inspected Cassandra's scraped palms. The wounds to her body were minor. The burn of betrayal raced through her like so much tinder. She had let him in. Again.

At last, finding no more excuses to linger, Alisa let herself out with promises of tea to help her sleep. Cassandra nodded her thanks, but already she moved toward the bottle of brown liquid. Rest would not be a problem tonight.

Chapter 12

Retching echoed off the walls, waking her from a deep sleep. She slumped over the side of the bed and coughed out the retching sounds. A groan followed the last dry heave. Her stomach now empty, she rolled over.

A shape moved near the window. No doubt it would be Mist moving in to take advantage of the mess on the ground.

"Please don't eat my vomit."

The snort came from across the room, and she sat bolt upright in bed. The low fire in the grate cast around the contours of a man standing near the foot of her bed.

She grasped the blankets closer as if they would ward off any harm he meant her.

The man stepped closer, and Cassandra jerked to the side, withdrawing the knife from under the other pillow. She swept the weapon forward only to find Niko at the end of her blade. He raised his hands in surrender.

Her heart hammered in her chest. "What are you doing in my room? Have you lost all sense?"

He raised his brows as he indicated the blade still pointed at his chest.

She rolled her eyes. "I'm not lowering it. You're in my room. Explain yourself."

He made a sound, half sigh and half grunt, then

turned away from her. He stalked about the room until he halted near the fireplace. A spark brightened the room and dimmed. The candle in his hands illuminated his face as he returned.

Of course, the chalkboard was still in the library. She would never make out his words without the extra light. She softened her grip on the knife but didn't lower it. Who did he think he was?

He stopped just out of her reach and considered her. No doubt, she looked like she had just escaped from a bog. Her fingers itched to draw the blanket over her head. Of course, his clothes were as impeccable as ever. She wondered if he had been born in a finely tailored waistcoat.

"How did you get in?" Her gaze scanned him. The servants would have noticed him. It was impossible not to. Maybe that was just her.

He waved a hand toward the window.

"Are you trying to tell me you can fly?"

A laugh burst from his lips. The candlelight danced under his breath. He shook his head and took a step closer. "A tree." Her ears almost didn't catch the words.

"You climbed a tree in that?" She indicated his clothes with an upturned palm.

He looked down at himself, and a frown creased his brow. He spoke, but she couldn't grasp what he said. Trying again, his voice still escaped her. Ignoring the blade, he took another step toward her. "I didn't have anything else."

Her laugh was part embarrassment and relief. So much effort went into such a small, unimportant message. A wide grin split her features as she shook her head. She tossed the knife to the floor.

He returned her smile, his eyes brightening behind the candle flame. "Who did you expect?" One of his brows rose.

The relief at hearing him the first time made her nearly miss his meaning. Her cheeks heated. "The cat who thinks he owns Lyme House. I call him Mist."

"Mist doesn't eat vomit." His hand pulled a flask from his coat, and he offered it to her to wash down any lingering taste, no doubt.

She sniffed the unidentified liquid inside. Maybe brandy? The drink burned as it went down, and she flinched against the onslaught. "That is vile." Already the acidic vomit was seared from her mouth.

She took another long gulp and handed the flask back to him. Her mind was still hazy from sleep as the meaning of his words became clear.

"What do you mean, Mist doesn't eat vomit? Do you know him? What's his name?"

Setting the candle down on her bedside, he eyed the edge of the bed like he expected her to offer him a seat. It was bad enough he was in her room in the middle of the night. He didn't need to sit on her bed.

"Mist. He has always been Mist."

Her eyes squinted at his face. She must have misheard him. "That's impossible. How can he be named Mist? It was the name I chose for him."

Niko tilted his head, looking much like the feline in question. "No."

"Are you intentionally being difficult?"

The smile playing on his lips told her everything. She wanted to shake him, to push him back out the window where he came. Even more, she desired to take his lips with hers and push him onto the bed. What was in that flask?

She knew he had read her emotions, but he gave no hint of it. Her gaze turned away to avoid any further thoughts concerning his body. "What did you want?"

He waited for her attention and then spoke. "You need to stop."

Her back stiffened. He would ask her to stop working for Lord Lyme even though he admitted he had no solution to her problem. As much as she sympathized with the witches she turned in, she couldn't give up this chance. Katrina and Mr. Harris had known about her beforehand. Still, they attended the dinner. Of course, she regretted revealing them, but how was she to know they were witches?

Mr. Shaw manipulated and used people for his own gain. He was one witch nobody would miss. It was those with abilities such as his that drove Lord Lyme to hire her. The limits of witchcraft were a dangerous unknown. Any one of them could put regular people in harm's way. If someone like Mr. Shaw used his powers to take control of the Prince Regent, nobody could stop them.

"You know I can't do that."

He raised his hand to touch her, but she pushed back into the bed.

He focused his gaze on hers. Neither of them looked away as a moment passed in silence. A laugh bubbled up from her throat from nowhere. Her hand slammed over her mouth as she attempted to stifle her giggles. Despite her best efforts, the laughter continued. She rolled onto her side on the bed and clutched her sore gut.

The laughter receded, and she gasped for breath.

The corner of Niko's mouth twisted up.

She spoke between gasps. "You did that to me." Her breathing slowed. "You don't even need to touch me, do you?" Her skin itched like she was dirty. She wanted to wash his invasion off of her skin. At any moment, he could be playing with her emotions, and she wouldn't know it.

"Touch helps."

Her fists clenched around the blankets. "Are you the only one who doesn't require touch?"

He studied her a moment before responding. "No."

Her attention snapped back to him. "Am I the only one that requires touch?"

His feet shifted under his weight. "For the most part."

"What do you mean? I suppose some abilities would need proximity, but I don't understand why I can't sense witches further away." She huffed out a breath of air. "This whole business is unpleasant."

Dawning fear rose in her breast, a restless discomfort she couldn't shake. Lord Lyme was right. They were in more danger than she realized. Mr. Shaw may have done far worse than gain money or power. What if he had taken it upon himself to charm women into bed? Or convinced someone to harm another?

Niko reached his palm out to her.

Her brows pinched together as she considered what he offered. He had demonstrated he didn't need to touch her. He offered her a way to read him on equal footing. Trust went both ways.

She closed her eyes and took his hand.

The wave crashed into her with full force, jolting her back. Her ears hummed against the onslaught, and her skin sparked from a pool of anger. She nearly pulled back her hand at the sensation, but she ventured on, digging deeper. Her eyes snapped wide open, scanning the room for an exit, a place to hide.

How could he stand so calm under such fear?

Flecked bits of anger shone in his eyes. She concentrated on them, soothing them away with a balm of peace. His lashes lowered as though he had consumed a particularly fine wine, and his shoulders softened ever so slightly.

"Bloody hell." He mouthed the words.

Comfort mirrored back to her, accompanied by surprise. The connection resembled the click of a lock in place, and she had acted on instinct without reservation or thought. The same way she had silenced Mr. Shaw.

He regarded her with a wary cast to his eyes but didn't release her hand.

A hollow sensation filled her chest. "I don't know. I wanted to help you." She wrapped her other arm around her middle. "Nothing makes sense anymore."

He blew out a breath. A strand of hair fell into his face. She suppressed the urge to push it back, tame the wild curl away from his dimpled chin, and those lips that beckoned her. The space between them seemed a mile wide.

He released her hand and pushed his hair back behind his ear. Sometimes she wondered if he had lied about not being psychic. He cleared his throat then looked away.

The loss of their connection and its accompanying hum left her empty. How strange to miss the pain, the crashing waves of his ability. She berated herself for her foolishness. It was clear he had no real interest in her. In any case, it would never work out. She would be gone before they were even started.

"You've wasted a trip. I can't go back on my word. Who would find witches like Mr. Shaw? In any case, Lord Lyme promised to help me. Warn your friends if you have to, but leave me out of it. By the by, you will be rid of me."

The scowl he turned on her dashed away the rest of her thoughts. He scanned the room, looking for something. The chalkboard or writing supplies she guessed. She had used the last of her paper to write to her parents again.

He must have more than a few words to say to her. She knew it was challenging to speak to her, near impossible at times. It only reinforced her resolve to see her job done.

He paced the room, his gaze distant. His rough, deliberate walk seemed foreign to his usual good humor and easy charm. At last, he appeared to reach a decision then headed to the window.

Her emptiness deepened. "Niko, wait." She swung her legs off the bed and stood.

He froze in place without turning.

"It isn't that I don't care." She approached his turned back but stopped short of touching him. "It's that I can't afford to care. I want to help you and keep innocent witches from Lord Lyme. I just…I don't know how."

He appeared to consider her words a moment and then faced her. The hurt in his eyes required no empathic connection. His eyes widened as he took in her appearance in the light.

She crossed her arms over her chest in a feeble effort to cover herself as she remembered she only wore a thin night rail.

His crooked smile said her efforts were too late.

Her chin dropped in an attempt to hide her blush. The hair on her neck rose as she sensed his gaze linger over her, the shock of it rendered her motionless. She chanced a glance up at him, their difference in height more evident than ever. She would have to stretch to meet his parted lips.

She wanted to look away, but he caught her chin in his hand, and she stilled with his touch. The familiar crash of waves overcame her, but the jolt of pain softened almost at once.

His expression was unreadable as he seemed to search her, his gaze trained on her face as he got his fill. Her emotions, and who knew what else, were rendered bare to him. The moment was only a few seconds, but to Cassandra, an eternity passed between them.

She tired of his silent interrogation and pushed back with her mind. The hum deepened in her ears. She suspected she caught him off guard. Indeed, an awe-like sensation met her probe, similar to gazing at the late-night stars. She wanted to drown in the depths of his mind.

His eyes darkened to the golden-brown of whiskey.

He leaned down to take her lips, a short brush of his mouth before a feral spark ignited inside her. Encouraged, he pressed into her. The spark turned to ripples of heat from deep in her chest. Her hands grasped behind his neck and the crash in her ears sent her deeper into his embrace. His arms encircled her, and she opened her mind to him.

In one swift motion, he pulled away, stepping out of her reach. His brows drew together as his gaze searched the room, coming to the place on her bedside. She tried to block him, but he pushed past her with little effort and scooped up the half-empty bottle on her bedside.

He held the bottle up to the light and waved it in front of her.

She rubbed the back of her neck. "It has been helping me."

His finger tapped the place on the bottle where the liquid sat.

She sighed. "What do you want me to say? I can't sleep at night. Two drops isn't enough. I would drink the whole bloody bottle just for some peace."

He inhaled and closed his eyes. She raised her chin, waiting for the coming storm.

It never came.

When he opened his eyes, she thought she saw disappointment. The look hit her deep in her gut. It was worse than anger. Disappointment was bordered with pity and halted short of contempt. She was too familiar with contempt, the emotion she shared with Mr. Barrett.

He gripped the bottle then made for the window. Instead of climbing out, he raised the bottle above his head and flung it hard into the distance.

She stared after it like the iron door to her cage had been slammed.

Niko placed a hand on the sleeve of her night rail and urged her to bed. She jerked her shoulder away, never touching him.

He spoke, facing away from her. It took her a moment to realize he said her name.

Her gaze left the window to find him. "Who are you to make decisions for me? My father is an apothecary. I think I know what I'm doing."

He raised a brow, probably sensing her lie. She hated that about him.

"Fine. I have no idea what I'm doing. I'm probably my father's worst student. I don't care. It doesn't matter anymore. I've lost so much." A tear escaped her eye, and she brushed it away with a hurried gesture.

His face softened, seeing her inner war. "Are you done?"

"What do you mean?" She spoke through clenched teeth. His words dashed all tears away. She must have misheard him.

He put his hands on her shoulders. She allowed him to guide her to the mirror. The first thing she noticed was the sheen over her pale blue eyes and the bruise-like circles under them. She frowned at her reflection and saw the horror in the mirror parallel her movements.

"Yes, I look horrible. What's your point?"

He rolled his eyes and pushed her reddish-blonde hair behind her ears. The brief brush of his fingers sent a sizzle through her ears. She met his eyes in the mirror. He nodded at their reflections.

She peered over her shoulder at him, but he gestured again at the mirror. A long breath seeped from her lips, and she returned her gaze to her own. The empty person before her was nothing like the woman she had known. The exhaustion and heartache etched over her face as though each tear had left their impression. Nobody deserved this.

He addressed her in the mirror, his mouth near her

ear but visible in the glass. "Are you done?"

She studied his solemn face and swallowed back the tears. No more. She gave him a short nod.

A small grin curved his lips. "Good. Stop feeling sorry for yourself. All of us have lost something." His success in communicating such a speech was in no way small. If only, she could always understand every word.

Her throat tightened against her reply. She had never thought to ask what he had lost, what any of them had lost. Her hearing weighed her down to the point where it was her only concern. Nothing else mattered.

The faint tick in his smile was all that hinted at his sadness. Of course, he had guessed at what she was thinking.

"My mother."

Her hand flew to her mouth. "I'm sorry." She spun to face him.

He attempted to widen his grin but failed.

"Niko, I had no idea. You must think I'm a fool." She couldn't imagine losing one of her parents to gain power. When her hearing went, her parents were the first to help her. "What about your father? Did he support you?"

The grin on his face vanished. He looked away and mumbled something.

"What?" A pang of hurt slapped her chest. After such success, he would resort to the same tendencies as everyone else?

He placed a hand on his heart.

A laugh burst from her throat at the gesture. "Are you trying to apologize? You better be."

The smile that split over his face was genuine. He

gave her an elaborate bow.

Her eyes crinkled. "Much better."

He held his hand out to her. She took it without hesitation and met the onslaught with an iron will. He brought her hand to his lips. Her lashes lowered under a leaden weight, and she remembered nothing of the trip to the bed where she rested well for the first time in days.

Chapter 13

Cassandra awoke to Alisa bustling about her room. She must have made some noise since Alisa immediately faced her. The maid held up a hand and brought over the chalkboard that was fetched from the library while she slept.

Alisa scrawled her message in a neat loopy hand. *Good morning, or should I say good afternoon, Miss Poole. Before you ask, all of the servants can read and write thanks to Lord Lyme. He made it a condition of employment with him. I have come to make sure you are comfortable. Lord Lyme advised us to let you sleep since you have no duties until the house party. Mr. Barrett wanted to see you, but I turned him away. Would you like me to get you some food? Maybe some tea?*

Cassandra gave a contented sigh and stretched up in bed. "Some food and tea would be lovely. How long was I asleep?"

Alisa cocked her head as though thinking. *Two nights, two mornings, and almost two afternoons.*

"That long?" She rolled her feet to the ground.

The maid waved her back to bed and made a staying gesture with her hand.

"What am I? A dog?" Cassandra's misplaced anger caused Alisa to scrunch up her nose. "I'm sorry. I've just lost so much time."

Alisa snorted and turned her back to grab something off of the dressing table. She handed the folded letter to Cassandra and bent to write another note. *This letter was left for you. I did not read it, nor has anyone else been in your room. Do be careful. If Lord Lyme finds out you are being visited in your room, it will be a disaster. Not to mention who is visiting you.*

Cassandra frowned at the maid. "I thought you said you didn't read the letter."

I did not have to. I have worked in this household since I could scarcely scrub a pot. My parents both served the family before me. I would recognize that script anywhere. Remember my warning. I will see about your tea.

When she looked up again, the maid was already gone. Jealousy gnawed at the back of her mind. The slim, smiling maid with smooth blonde hair and bright green eyes knew Niko's handwriting on sight. Alisa wasn't just beautiful, she was intelligent with a backbone of granite. Niko must have been a frequent visitor for Alisa to come to know him so well.

A thought nagged at the edge of her mind that she couldn't grasp. She would dig it up later. For now, she unfolded the letter. Niko's handwriting was careful, unlike the cramped script he displayed on the chalkboard. It was all flourish and curves, almost feminine. Indeed, it would be easily recognized. She had the urge to strangle him. He put her in danger, leaving her this letter.

Dearest Miss Poole.

Really? Working with Lord Lyme did not make her dear.

I calculate you will wake to this letter sometime in

the afternoon. I returned last night to be sure you slept soundly and to leave you this letter. Yes, I helped you sleep again. You need the rest after drugging yourself senseless.

Since you have repeatedly refused to stop your actions, I must warn you about the danger you put yourself in. Lord Lyme hates witches with no exceptions. It is unlikely that he grants you any favors. It is not too late to leave. I can arrange for your safe journey.

Be careful.

Witches must stick together. Already there are too many against us. I don't approve of your choices, but it is a difficult time we must all go through.

The illness that took your aunt has been witnessed throughout Scry Cove, and we can't find a particular food source affected. The nurse and doctor who cared for your aunt have also died from it. The innkeeper was ill, but she recovered. Nobody knows why you were not taken ill, but you may still.

I do not want to go into further detail. I have already put you in danger by visiting you and leaving this. We will talk again soon. N

Her face fell. The correspondence was cold and unlike the man who kept finding excuses to unnerve her senses with kisses. At least, he didn't try to persuade her again. The mysterious illness spreading was news but not surprising. She had witnessed similar outbreaks alongside her father, and they always died out over time.

It had already occurred to her that Lord Lyme might go back on his word. She had to take the chance, she wanted her life back. Helping her parents at the shop had been her life, and without it, she was nothing. One by one, her friends had forgotten her. She was broken. Everything would be restored the way it should be, and she would be normal again. Acceptance as a witch was pointless if she wouldn't be one soon.

Cassandra wanted to believe Lord Lyme, but what Niko said held weight. She was tugged in two directions. She needed answers before she was ripped apart.

She refolded the letter and leaned toward the low burning fire, allowing the flames to dance over the paper. It crumbled in her hand. She dropped it just before it burned her fingers. Her gaze narrowed toward the flickering flame as she tried to identify the source of a shuffling noise. Fear like an iron fist gripped her chest, but it was only Alisa returning with her tea.

The maid brought her the creamy tea and a bowl of some kind of stew. It was mutton or beef. She couldn't tell through the heavy spices. She sat at a tray near the fire and beckoned for Alisa to remain with her.

"You said you've worked at Lyme House for some time. How did you come to know Niko?" She kept her voice calm, hoping the maid wouldn't sense her nervousness.

Alisa watched her a moment. Finding the chalkboard, she pulled the remaining chair next to Cassandra.

You must not say these things out loud. It is good we have this board already. Lord Lyme has positioned footmen outside of your door.

Cassandra's eyes snapped wide, and she leaned in to take the board from Alisa. *Am I a prisoner?*

Alisa twisted her lips to the side and took up the

chalk. *As good as. I think the dinner party made Lord Lyme afraid. He does not like being questioned. I believe Mr. Barrett suggested it to ease his fears.*

"That's ridiculous—"

Alisa raised a palm to stop her mid-sentence and indicated the board.

They couldn't be afraid of me. I can't do anything to them. She handed the board back.

But they are. People talk around Lyme House. Something worried Mr. Sutton enough to want himself and Lord Lyme away from you. Mr. Barrett was already there as their shield. All I know is Mr. Shaw screeched like a banshee when they questioned him. Mr. Sutton came out pale. His hands shook so much he dropped his hat.

Mr. Shaw, afraid of her? Of course, she had silenced the man as she had comforted Niko, using their own abilities on them, but she had no idea how to use that as a weapon. She required touch to manipulate witches, or at least, she thought she did. Had she been touching Mr. Shaw when she silenced him?

At the time, she hadn't realized what she had done. After her last encounter with Niko, her power over Mr. Shaw became clear. Perhaps Niko was right. Lord Lyme probably would not help her.

A chill brushed over her skin. She glanced at the window to reassure herself that it was closed. Alisa caught the action and checked. The maid shrugged back at her from the closed window and went to prod the fire back to life.

Cassandra wrote as Alisa worked. *How do you know Niko?* She wasn't sure she wanted to know the answer, but she had to know.

The maid looked over her shoulder at the message. Cassandra handed her the board, and she wrote as she walked back to her seat. *Everyone here knows Niko.*

She rubbed out Alisa's writing. *That is not an answer.*

I do not know if I should tell you, but it is by no means a secret. Alisa frowned at her own words and started again. *Did you know Lord Lyme was married?*

Cassandra nodded in reply, and Alisa continued. *They had two children. Twins. A boy and a girl, Nikolas and Selena.*

An involuntary sound escaped her throat, something between a gasp and a cough. She tugged the board away from Alisa then scribbled over it. *Lord Lyme hates his children? What did they do that is so unforgivable?*

Alisa regarded her with patience and accepted the board. *He blames them for the death of his wife, Giovanna. I do not know why.*

Cassandra peered around the room. *What about his injury? Did Niko and Selena do that?*

The maid tilted her blonde head to the side and shrugged. The gesture was all the answer Cassandra would get from her. Alisa wiped off the chalkboard then rushed to the door.

The room had been silent, and Cassandra still hadn't heard the knock at the door. Maybe her hearing had gotten worse. However, she did hear the murmured voice from the other side of the door though she couldn't tell what they said.

Alisa closed the door behind her and picked up the board to scrawl a hurried message. *Mr. Barrett wants to see you. He refuses to leave. I bought you enough time to compose yourself. He thinks you need to dress.*

Cassandra made a sour face. When they had been together, Mr. Barrett would tease her about his desire to see her without proper clothes or any clothes. Now, he was kept away by the idea. Niko didn't seem to mind seeing her in just her night rail. Her neck and chest flushed at the memory of him staring at her barely clothed body.

Alisa handed her one of the new hated white gowns Lord Lyme had provided for her, but Cassandra took her time removing each article of clothing. Hang Mr. Barrett. If he wanted to see her, he would have to wait. And wait, he did.

An hour passed before Mr. Barrett knocked again. This time, Cassandra heard the hurried thump and the fury behind it. Alisa stood braiding her hair into an elaborate crown. She had caught onto Cassandra's reluctance and pursued the goal with a crooked smile. Her hair only needed a few more pins. Alisa had already stalled as long as she could.

Cassandra let out a long breath then got to her feet. Shouldn't Mr. Barrett be off chasing his wife? Or better yet, shouldn't he be fighting Napoleon? Either Lord Lyme had offered him a ridiculous sum, or he loathed her. Or both.

She followed Alisa out the door. Mr. Barrett beckoned to her with an impatient wave to accompany him. The footmen trailed behind her, but Alisa had other duties to attend to and separated from the group.

Her glare pierced the men surrounding her. How ridiculous for her to need an escort. She had tested all of these men, and she couldn't do anything to people who weren't witches. What did they think she would do?

Run. They thought she would run. She had enough incentive to stay under Lord Lyme's control. Why question her loyalty now?

As expected, they entered the library. Lord Lyme sat in his usual place, soaking in the shadows. However, Mr. Sutton was absent.

She remained standing before his desk and folded her arms. "My lord, you need more sun. Perhaps we can move this meeting into the garden? It seems warm enough." It looked like it could rain at any moment, but she didn't care. The house suffocated her.

Lord Lyme frowned as he peered up from his work. He shook his head and bent back to the book he wrote in.

Mr. Barrett tugged at her sleeve and gestured to a chair. She stiffened and pulled back from him. He threw up his hands in resignation then took the chair opposite the one he offered her. His gaze focused on his hands as he chewed at what was left of his nails.

Long moments passed. She shifted from foot to foot, and her feet ached in their slippers. If she took the chair now, she would show Mr. Barrett he could command her. It was childish, but she couldn't spare the man any more power. It appeared Lord Lyme had the same notion concerning her.

Lord Lyme cleared his throat. The sound boomed in the emptiness of the library. Probably for her benefit.

Mr. Barrett accepted the note offered to him from the side of Lord Lyme's work. She scowled at the paper. It had rested on the man's desk this whole time. Mr. Barrett pursed his lips and passed the note to her. If this was the way they planned to communicate with her, she might as well have stayed in bed.

She held the paper with a dirty sensation, wanting nothing more than to throw the thing in the fire. Lord Lyme's note skipped all formalities.

You have been advised to perform your duties and warned against contact with other witches.

She stopped and reread the line. It made no sense. She had done everything asked of her. Well, almost everything. They couldn't possibly know about Niko climbing into her room. She continued.

I have assigned footmen to guard you. It is for your own safety.

She snorted.

Mr. Sutton and Mr. Barrett assured me that you will be safe as long as you remain in your room. The footmen or Mr. Barrett will escort you when the house party begins.

Her gaze jumped from the page to Lord Lyme, who watched her read. "I'm not a child. I don't need a guard. Give me a pistol or some other weapon to defend myself. There is little reason to think anyone wishes me harm." Of course, they didn't know about her knife.

Lord Lyme raised a hand to the paper, urging her to read on.

The illness has spread to my home. I have every reason to believe Niko has caused the death of some of my most loyal servants. He and his band of miscreants have gone too far. You will be safe once you leave for treatment. For now, special care will be made for your food and drink. Your late meal has already been arranged.

The end of the message was a dismissal. The man hadn't bothered to talk to her in days, and he had given her a letter she needn't respond to in person.

She couldn't speak from the rage coursing through her veins. The letter dropped from her hand as Mr. Barrett escorted her from the room.

When they entered the hall, she turned on him with a fist raised. "You're just going to go along with all this? I'm a prisoner here now."

A shadow fell over his face, but the lighting never changed. He bared his teeth at her and clasped her shoulder with a heavy grip. He wheeled her about on her feet without much effort but remained silent. She no longer had the patience to speak with him anyway. What purpose would it serve?

She thought for sure he would lead her to the dining room or the terrace for her meal, but instead, he brought her to her room. They didn't even want her out of her room for meals. She wondered again why they would bring her out of the room for a simple note.

When she opened her door, she saw her answer.

The room was disheveled. The covers of her bed were upturned, her few valuables had been disturbed, and even her discarded night rail was searched. Alisa stood over the mess, brow furrowed. Her usual calm was tinged with anger.

At least Niko's letter was nothing more than ash.

Alisa set into motion to right the turmoil. Cassandra joined her, moving to tidy the bed. Sleep was her main goal now. She wasn't going to allow Lord Lyme's dogs to deprive her of it.

A tightness grasped her chest. They had been through her things, and not a secret remained. The invasion resembled them reading her thoughts and witnessing her darkest moments. The room wasn't much. She had added little to it. Yet, the small space had become her source of safety. Not quite a home, but a refuge away from her work and Mr. Barrett. The violation left a queasiness in her stomach.

She bit her tongue to recall back the emotions climbing up her chest. It wasn't like she was without protection.

Her hand stopped mid-work. She rushed around the bed and moved a hand under the pillow. Nothing.

Her heartbeat was like a stampede in her chest.

She pushed the pillow to the side and searched the bed. The tousled sheets failed to produce the knife. The pressure in her head deepened while blood rushed to her ears.

She frantically tossed around the blankets and pillows. She checked behind the bed then on the floor, once in shadow and a second time with the light of a candle. Alisa joined the search after her choked explanation, but it was no use.

The knife was gone. With it went her last defense.

Chapter 14

After consuming far too much creamy tea and biscuits in an attempt to comfort herself, she sprawled over the bed in hopes sleep would take her. Tightness threaded over her muscles and roped along her neck as though it would trap her in consciousness.

She stared at the ceiling, counting the not-so-hidden water spots. In her darker moments, she considered jumping from the window or attempting the tree Niko somehow used to ascend to her room. The only possibility of her escape relied on her growing another hand-width to make the nearest branch. It was a shame witches couldn't fly. At least, this one didn't.

Time passed without meaning. Alisa came and went with her meals, which Cassandra ate with little enthusiasm. She drained the tea in gulps, always eager for more. Alisa watched her with equal parts amusement and sadness, her smile not quite reaching her downcast eyes.

At last, the sun dipped behind the horizon. She cursed Niko for throwing out her bottle of liquid sleep.

Cassandra stroked Mist as he purred next to her. "He could have at least left me with something." She tossed a pillow at the wall. "I give you leave to bite him when he shows his ridiculously attractive face. Better yet—claw out his eyes."

Mist squinted at her in contentment as though

smiling at her musings.

"Maybe he will think twice before leaving me a prisoner. The two of us, though, we'll run away, and I will feed you nothing but fresh-caught fish on a gilded platter. Would you like that?"

The deep rumble from Mist's throat was answer enough.

She scratched the area behind his ears and sighed. "Maybe Alisa will sneak me in something. Maybe a book or laudanum. If it weren't for the tea, they might as well end my misery and be done with it."

Mist kneaded the skin on her forearm, and little pinpricks indented her skin just before they bled.

"Ouch. I love you dearly, but you need to put those somewhere else." She moved his paws onto her night rail-covered shoulder. "Well, you have a weapon to attack him with. Station yourself by the window. It will give you the element of surprise. Shred his clothes, but keep the hair intact. I rather like the hair."

She could swear Mist grinned and craned his neck to peer toward the window.

"Bloody hell. Is he here?"

Echoed laughter answered from the shadows of the window.

"Mist, you little traitor. Why didn't you tell me he was here?" She frowned down at the beast. "How long have you been hiding there?"

Niko advanced on the bed and dropped down beside her in full view of the candlelight at her bedside. He spoke, but the words came out meaningless like syllables on the wind. He tried again, and still, she made him repeat himself.

She shook her head, her face blooming pink. "I do

have the chalkboard now if you so choose. Or would you rather listen to me ramble on to this traitorous feline?"

His eyes scanned her face. He reached out his gloved hand to her and squeezed her fingers. The board rested next to the candle, ready for use in case Alisa returned. He seemed to hesitate before taking it up.

I have been here long enough to know you intend to send my childhood friend to attack me.

A rush of warmth swam up her neck. He had heard everything, and Mist had known all along. The cat's laughter filled face had new meaning now. Well, she hadn't told Mist about what she thought of Niko's piercing golden eyes or his hard limber body. He could sense emotions, but she assured herself her private thoughts remained her own.

She closed her eyes a moment to regain her composure. "What are you doing here, Master Nikolas?" She emphasized the formality. "Your father has guards on my door. Someone is probably watching the window."

The scratch of chalk prompted her eyes to open. Niko wrote with a heavy hand, and his frown would scare small children. *That man is not my father. He may have provided the seed, but he was never my father.*

He angled the board for her to read, and she sat up to his level. He wiped out the message when she finished.

She swallowed then lowered her voice. "Still, they must know you've been here. It's not safe for you to visit."

He finished his scribbling and showed her the board. *Worry about yourself. He is too much of a coward to come after me. Besides, I am his only male heir, and as much as he hates me, he would rather his blood kept the title.*

"How do you know this?"

He spread his fingers to indicate his body. He was still alive.

"But why risk it? You can't know for sure he doesn't mean you harm." She scooted closer to him to lower her voice further. "He needs me too much to hurt me now."

Niko shook his head.

"Fine. Get me out of here then. You said you could. Please tell me it doesn't involve sheets and the window."

He bent down to the board. *It did, but things have changed. No, not the guards. They might have proved inconvenient, though. We need you here now. We have to find out what is causing the deaths in Scry Cove.*

He wiped out the board again and continued. *The only connection between the victims is Lyme House and you.*

She raised a hand to her neck. "You can't mean I had something to do with it. I know less than you do."

No, you misunderstand me, but it cannot be a coincidence. Our contacts in the house have fled, or the old man took them somewhere. You are our only link. We need you to be our man.

Humor sparked the golden hue in his eyes.

"Your man?" She smirked and slapped his hand with the back of hers. "I don't see how you can joke about this. I mean…" She leaned into a breath's distance of him. "You want me to spy?"

His gaze fell to her lips, but instead of closing the

hairbreadth between them, he leaned into the chalkboard.

The rejection crushed her chest, and she looked away to hide her clenched jaw. Not that it did any good with him.

Find a way to investigate the house. I will return for updates.

She glared at the board. "That isn't very specific. What am I looking for?"

He shrugged. *Anything out of the ordinary.*

"Niko, this whole house is out of the ordinary. The cat knows his own name and somehow tells others. Witches inhabit Spray Cove." She stared down her nose at him. "Witches. How am I to judge what's ordinary? I think you have the wrong girl."

A dry smile creased a slight curve to his lips. *You are a witch.*

She dismissed his comment with a wave of her hand. His face grew solemn.

That reminds me, you should not be taking laudanum. Antoinette was a fool to give the bottle to you. Witches often struggle with addiction. Not all witches, but some. Now that we know which group you belong to stay clear of it. Addiction is forever.

She handed him back the board, and he rubbed away the chalk. "I've only been using it for a few days. I can't possibly be addicted. Besides, I can't seem to rest well without it except when you help me."

He set the board onto his lap and tapped the chalk against the surface. His focus remained on her face. At last, he set to write.

Addiction does not always take time. As much as I want to help you, I cannot.

Her shoulder bunched up in frustration. "You mean, you won't? You're here now."

He ran a hand through his impossible tangled hair. *It is not that easy.*

"Then explain it to me." Her eyes pleaded with him.

I am afraid of what it will do to you over time. I have never done this.

She regarded him with a blank stare. "You mean you think I can become addicted to you? That's absurd."

He raised a brow.

She grasped her loose hair at the scalp and tugged. "Yes, my lord. I'm addicted to you putting me to sleep with your boring nonsense." Her hands dropped back to her sides. "Are you sure it isn't the other way around? Maybe you will become addicted to me."

Without waiting for an answer, she hopped off the bed and made for the last of the tea. She considered offering him some, but a mere cup remained. He could find his own tea in town. The lukewarm contents of her cup was a welcome distraction from this whole bothersome conversation. She kept her back to him as she sipped.

He wanted her to spy, her, of all people. To make matters especially intolerable, he refused to help her get any rest because he thought she might become addicted to him. Of course, her attraction would be obvious to him, but addiction? She drowned the thought in tea.

In a burst of motion, she pivoted on her heel, meaning to be rid of the man before she lost her last nerve. Instead, she collided with a firm barrier, his chest, and sent her teacup spinning along the floorboards.

The air was forced from her lungs. He steadied her with a careful grip on her shoulders. At the flare in his eyes, the words asking him to leave were lost, and the teacup was forgotten.

Silence filled the air between them. Yet, the distance hummed with a vibration lost to sound. Her heart skipped in her chest. The sensation is like the space between words, intended but never spoken.

His gaze transfixed on hers, he discarded his gloves and reached up to touch her face.

Her eyes fluttered shut as the wave swept her away. The pain from his touch was now a welcome voice in her mind like the soreness after a pleasant walk or the sting of warmth over icy flesh.

She pressed her cheek into his hand.

Raw, unbound desire flowed through their link. She couldn't tell if it was his or her own, or both. Nothing mattered as his lips took hers.

His kiss sent the wave crashing into her, through her. Her heart collided with her chest, beating a charge to join the approaching crest.

His tongue tasted the surface of her lips. The hair along her neck rose as his attention grew heated, frantic. He pressed his body into hers as he nipped and licked, his hands wandered her body as though by their own accord.

She drank in his attentions. Her limbs were pliable as he swept her into his arms. Still, the waves crashed. Niko was the wave, carrying her into the sea.

She came up for air to find herself cradled under him on the bed. He trailed his lips along her jaw and down her neck, sucking and teasing the tender skin as he went. His breath came in pants as he pulled back to stare down at her.

"Oh, Dio."

A giggle burst from her lips, and she shook her head. "God has nothing to do with this."

His grin cast a wicked light to his eyes.

She gasped as his hand went to her breast. He moaned in return. His fingers found her nipple through her night rail, and he rubbed the sensitive peak. The wave raged, and their pleasure mirrored each other. The dampening between her thighs brought him equal arousal. His desire built on to hers.

He pushed up the thin fabric covering her and yanked it over her head. He propped up on his hands above her, and his whiskey eyes took their fill.

Taking advantage of his pause, she worked her way over the buttons of his waistcoat. For once, his impeccable clothes were not appreciated. She needed to touch his skin like she needed air.

He followed her progress as she disposed of his clothing. When she reached the buttons on his trousers, he lost patience and unfastened the flap in a heartbeat. A triumphant light sparked from his gaze.

Her frown at his still-clothed lower half made him roll his eyes, but he kicked off his boots and dropped his trousers in response. An empty moment passed where they lost contact. The urgency to reclaim his body prompted her into action.

She stretched her legs out to wrap around him, forcing him to lie on top of her. The resulting shock of their full-body contact stilled them. Their gaze held, and the world fell away. Nothing existed but the wave consuming her and the man above her. Warmth flooded where they touched, but the anticipation between bare spaces raised the hair on her skin. She couldn't get enough. She needed him now.

The pain as he entered her joined the pain in her ears. His lips took hers, and the discomfort washed away with her heightened pleasure. The manipulation should have bothered her, but she wanted him, every part of him, even the part that toyed with her senses.

Her acceptance must have traveled through their connection. His golden gaze blazed down at her. Every movement became a new forging between them until a rightness cocooned them. She tilted her hips up to meet him, welcoming him in every way.

He read her every need, moving to her unspoken directions. She met his rhythm, each motion of their hips sent her further into abandon. An unnamable pressure built at her core. Not the mounting expectation before the storm but the roar of thunder before the lightning strike.

Her body shattered, gripping him in bursts of movement.

The wave in her ears crashed as Niko lost control. The pain mixed with the pleasure of his release, and she shook around him once again.

His chest heaved as he collapsed on top of her. Even now, they fit together in harmony in a way she could never imagine. The moment would last forever in her mind but for only a short rest tonight.

He pecked a kiss on her forehead and rolled to the side of her. His breathing calmed, and a smile teased the corners of his lips. Still touching, exhaustion floated between them. He closed his eyes.

She yawned and put space between them, hoping to

regain a sense of her own emotions. The mistake smacked her straight in the face. Panic beat in her chest, a molten grip over her heart and neck. What had she done?

No explanation came to her. She gave herself freely to him, but she hadn't meant it to go so far. His touch made her drunk on him. She had welcomed the abandon of it, the sheer madness and desire. Never had she experienced such ecstasy.

She studied the sated form of Niko beside her. No, she didn't regret losing her virginity to him. Nothing else would have satisfied her desire for him. It was what came next that she regretted.

She couldn't afford another disappointment. Girls like Cassandra didn't marry lords. Her future was lost without such promises, but she would be damned before she begged a proposal out of him. In any case, he would tire of her as Mr. Barrett had, crushing her soul in a loveless marriage.

"I think you're right." She breathed out her admission in a near whisper.

He blinked toward her, and confusion marked his crinkled brow.

"I'm addicted. We shouldn't have done this."

He shouldn't have indulged her. Didn't he know what this would do to her? A man who could read emotions must see the cost of their actions. Cassandra knew the physical act of lovemaking could not rest at that for her. Her desire did not come without deep feeling, and when she loved, she loved with her whole being.

She swallowed, dismissing such thoughts and raised the familiar fortress encasing her heart. This would pass. Of course, it didn't mean anything. She wouldn't hold him to any promises. They could go back to the way life was before.

Her face paled. What if she was with child?

He reached out to her, his gaze creased with worry, but she couldn't be sure without contact. Still, she avoided his touch. It was how she had gotten into this mess in the first place. Craving gnawed in her belly. She ignored it the way she ignored his outstretched hand.

"Cara." He sighed and dropped his hand back onto the bed.

She fought against the sudden urge to join him. He raised his head from the pillows and focused his stare on her. He wanted her closer. The urge to nestle up to his skin was so intense she twitched toward him. She sent her focus on him and used his already exhausted state to suggest he sleep.

His eyes closed, but he tugged at her. It was the strangest game of tug of war she had ever faced, and the challenge sent a thrill to her breast. He wouldn't win this one.

The broad smile on his face presented an answer to her challenge though his eyes were still sealed tight.

"No, you don't." Just as the words left her mouth, she found herself in his embrace once more. She sensed no victorious celebration within him. A soft smile relaxed his face, and a snore escaped him.

She laughed to herself, ending on another yawn, and curled up enclosed in his arms.

Chapter 15

A light kiss on Cassandra's brow roused her from sleep. Niko sat up next to her, naked in the sunlight streaming from the window. His crooked smile delighted her half-conscious senses, and she reached out to him.

Before he could respond, a loud clatter startled them both. Alisa stood in the doorway, the breakfast tray she carried fallen in a chaotic mess about the floor. The maid's face turned crimson. She hurried to shut the door behind her.

Niko didn't bother to cover himself as he yawned and stretched from the bed. At any other time, Cassandra would have admired the view, but he needed to be gone. Still, her eyes lingered over the witch's firm backside. He craned his neck to meet her gaze. She looked away.

Not one to let Niko scare her away, Alisa stepped over the ruined meal and marched up to him, hands planted on her hips. She spoke in a rushed, angry voice that Cassandra could not follow. Alisa never dropped her gaze from his. His nudity cast a sharp contrast to her aggressive posture.

Cassandra watched with open-mouthed fascination. Her ears caught a few snips of words, but most of Alisa's sharp verbal beating was lost to her. The subject could have only been a few things, and she pulled the sheets closer as though she could regain her virtue or hideaway what they had done last night.

Niko stayed silent as Alisa lectured him. The smile on his face was plastered into place like the words did not affect him. When she finished, Niko swept his clothes off the floor and made a casual attempt to dress. Alisa scowled at him with crossed arms.

The two women watched as he transformed into his immaculate self, not that he didn't look appealing straight out of bed. He ran his fingers through his wild hair to complete the look. How she wished to touch his hair again, to pull at its length while wrapped in abandon.

With a short glance at Alisa, he leaned down to peck Cassandra on her cheek. The faint touch sounded a brief roar in her ears. He favored her with a wide grin before he lowered himself out the window.

Alisa frowned after his departing form.

A ghost of his kiss lingered on her cheek. She raised her hand to check if he left an imprint behind. How could she go about her day in any usual way after such intimacy? She ignored Alisa's gaze now directed at her and got to her feet to study her reflection.

Nothing had changed. A faint blush dusted her cheeks. Her eyes appeared a brighter blue, but other than that, she was the same Cassandra. Her golden-red hair crimped at her scalp, and she tugged at it with an amused grin. Her gaze fell on her belly. Would she know if she was pregnant already?

Alisa came up beside her and handed her the discarded night rail.

Cassandra spared a glance at the maid, then threw the garment over her head and pulled it into place. "I know you are cross with me. I assure you I'm angrier at myself than you could ever be."

Alisa gripped Cassandra's shoulders and turned her about to meet her eyes. "You misunderstand." The maid shook her head. She must have focused her attention on her every syllable for Cassandra to grasp her meaning. "Master Nikolas should know better, but I'm afraid I failed you."

Cassandra couldn't bring herself to regret it. Their bodies complemented each other while their abilities brought a rare heightened intimacy. She didn't know what it was yet and hadn't had time to process her own emotions. All she understood was the race of her pulse when Niko was near.

She shook her head. "Of course, you didn't fail me. I only have myself to blame for this. I have no doubt he would have stopped if I asked."

Alisa appeared to steady herself like she was about to deal with a troublesome child. "But his powers—"

"Can be used against him." Cassandra straightened her posture. "I'm just as dangerous. How do you know I didn't take advantage of him?" Her desire had consumed every thought. Perhaps she had transferred her urges to him.

An emptiness replaced where her stomach had been. Maybe he hadn't wanted her at all.

The maid huffed and busied herself cleaning up the mess in front of the door. So much for breakfast. Cassandra moved to help her, but Alisa waved her away and pointed toward the clothes Cassandra would wear. Another white dress.

At least she had renewed purpose. Niko and the witches of Spray Cove depended on her. Her first step involved accepting another white garment when she wanted black crepe. A small decision to an average person but a battle to Cassandra. Ever since Lord Lyme had provided her with ample white dresses, she carried herself as if she were the one who died, refusing to enjoy any of the events.

Now, she would wear her white as the costume it became. The high-waisted white muslin gown resembled nothing she had worn back in Coldon. It was too beautiful for a day around the house. The thought sparked a plan fresh in her mind.

"Alisa."

The maid looked up from her work.

"Do you think I could convince Lord Lyme to let me visit the church? My solitude has left me rather repentant. I think prayer would help me perform my duties with a new sense of the Lord's approval." Her wicked chuckle said otherwise.

Alisa's eyes shone, and she nodded. When the mess was cleared, Alisa poked her head out the door to speak to one of the footmen. She pulled her head back inside, her face awash with laughter as though she hid a private joke.

They finished dressing Cassandra and sat in companionable silence while they waited for Lord Lyme's answer. A visit to the church would be a welcome distraction, and the only plausible reason to leave her room. They could bring everything else to her. Since Lord Lyme had chosen to disregard her mourning, she would not expect him to accept her request.

When Mr. Barrett arrived at her door to accompany her to the church, she was more than a little surprised.

She had never been much of a churchgoer, but Mr. Barrett must have withheld that information from Lord Lyme.

He nodded in solemn greeting and glanced at her from time to time with a curious expression on his face she couldn't decipher. They didn't speak on the ride to the church even after Alisa handed her the chalkboard. Instead of his silence relieving her anxiety, the silence only heightened her restlessness.

Her hands twisted in her gloves, and she toyed with her bonnet ribbons. Perhaps a visit to the church was a poor idea. She had forgotten the vicar's presence and the underhanded blow she had dealt his wife. Mr. Powell would throw her out on sight.

Mr. Barrett interrupted her thoughts when he offered her his flask.

She wrinkled her nose. "No, thank you. What would people think of me if I drank before church?"

With a dramatic sigh, he opened the flask then sniffed the contents before tilting it to her. She accepted his unspoken request and braced herself for its sharp aroma. Instead, she inhaled the delicate scent of creamy tea. Her mouth watered. She blinked at Mr. Barrett.

She tested the smell again. It seemed harmless, but for some unknown reason, she wanted to refuse. The carriage hit a bump, and the contents of the flask slapped into her face. She licked the sides of her lips.

An unparalleled warmth settled her back against the cushioned seat.

She wiped the remaining tea off her face with her hand. Mr. Barrett grimaced. Since he had not offered her anything to wipe her face, she ignored him with a shrug and upended the flask to her lips.

The tea was almost gone before she recalled herself and offered some back to Mr. Barrett. He brushed her off with a scowl and turned to the window. No matter. Her unquenchable thirst craved every drop. Her morning tea had splashed across the floor, but she hadn't realized just how much she needed it.

The carriage stopped just below the hill where the church rose above the town. The haughty stone structure made no excuses for being the grandest building in Spray Cove, aside from Lyme House. The elegant steeple overlooked a graveyard and a path that ascended the hill. A pair of old oak trees greeted them at the bottom of the trail.

Mr. Barrett helped Cassandra down from the carriage, no need to injure the prized hunting dog. She peered up at the church, uncertain of her decision. The grounds appeared deserted as she had hoped.

She sensed her escort watching her, taking note of her failures. If she didn't show adequate piety, he would report it back to Lord Lyme. A slim hope had allowed her to believe her repentance would restore some of her employer's trust. Whoever heard of a devout witch? For that matter, would she burst into flames when she stepped over the threshold?

The thought checked her at the door for a short moment. She had been into churches before, and according to the witches in Spray Cove, she had been a witch her whole life. Why did the church make her uneasy now?

No burning hellfire consumed her. Hellhounds did not chase her from the hallowed ground. The windows of the church were free of misguided birds and locusts. The only life she saw was a common toad that occupied a headstone. It sat unaware or undisturbed by her presence.

Empty benches lined the inside of the church. "Where is Mr. Powell?"

A grim smile met her question, and he placed the chalkboard against the wall to write. *Dead. It's going around.*

"The illness took him too?" Disbelief wrinkled her brow. Who would be left of this town if the illness kept spreading?

Yes. Few escape the sickness. I know you are concerned, but there is nothing you can do about it. I am sure your crazy father works night and day for a cure. He has a better chance than you do.

Her crazy father? Mr. Barrett had always gotten along with her father. Perhaps she didn't know this man at all, or could someone change so much to make them unrecognizable? He had done her a favor leaving her.

She kept her opinions to herself and changed the subject. "Why is the door unlocked? I don't expect a new vicar has arrived yet."

His lips twisted up.

"You sent ahead?" She clenched her fists at her side. He seemed incapable of showing her kindness or respect.

His condescending smile only served to heighten the tension gathered at her shoulders. Enough of this. She had promised Lord Lyme prayer, and Mr. Barrett would not drive her away.

"If you'll excuse me, Mr. Barrett. I would like to be alone." Not waiting for another of his rude responses, she took a seat near the front of the church. She stole a glance back at Mr. Barrett who leaned up just outside the church door.

She wasn't foolish enough to believe she could escape. The church appeared to have no other exit, though she doubted that was the case. Even if she found another door, she couldn't outrun him. Her best chance would be the haberdashery, but Mr. Barrett would spot her long before she made the entrance.

Niko wouldn't thank her for bringing Mr. Barrett down on their sanctuary. Not to mention, her action would ruin any chance of success as a spy. Instead of indulging her impulse to escape, she stared forward but saw nothing.

The faint odor of cheroots met her nostrils. Mr. Barrett must be smoking outside. Her lips turned up in distaste. He could have at least waited until they returned to Lyme House, but he had always known she hated the smell. She blocked out his show of contempt and focused on crafting a plan.

Nothing came to her.

Her thoughts circled their familiar path, unable to come to any conclusions but the past. No longer did she have any purpose or any idea of how to move forward. Her only direction came from Niko, and she wasn't even sure she could spy. Healing her relationship with Lord Lyme seemed the best route, no matter her end goal.

A shadow fell over her, and she flinched forward. It wasn't Mr. Barrett who stood behind her but Morwenna, the tawny-haired witch from Morgan's Haberdasher. Cassandra almost didn't recognize her in her hooded green cloak embroidered with gold vines and leaves. The vibrant green brought out the color in Morwenna's eyes, a dark green reflection of the sea.

Her lips curved into a shy smile.

Morwenna wasn't beautiful in the same sense as the other witches. She was not mysterious like Selena, or shapely and elegant like Antoinette. She certainly wasn't alluring like Georgiana. Instead, she radiated the comforting warmth of a longtime friend or a sister. Someone you couldn't help but share your secrets. As a seer, an open mind must have only served to her advantage.

Morwenna slid down next to her.

Cassandra spoke in a whisper, and her gaze jumped from her new companion to the altar. "What are you doing here? How did you get past Mr. Barrett?"

Instead of responding, Morwenna stared ahead. Her eyes seemed to glaze over. A moment of silence followed, and Cassandra wondered if Morwenna had heard her.

Morwenna's bare hand clasped hers. The sound flooding her ears was like nothing else. If silence made a sound, it would be Morwenna's power. It was the air before a breath or the bell before the chime. An absence of sound or the calm before the storm.

Cassandra followed Morwenna's gaze. A rose window took up most of the wall above the altar. At first glance, she noticed the delicately crafted form of Mary in the center. She was surrounded by five circles, each containing another circle. On closer inspection, the circles revealed to be pentacles.

She squinted at the shapes, not sure of her own recognition. Morwenna had a faint smile resting on her face. The witch wanted Cassandra to see the significance of the window. It was hidden in plain sight.

Of course, Spray Cove—or rather, Scry Cove—

was a witch town. The building had every indication it was a regular place of worship for the Church of England. The pentagrams could be explained away as symbols of Christ. Yet, once she saw the pentacles, other oddities shouted out at her.

The rose window was surrounded by a thin border inscribed with what could only be ancient runes. Those same foreign markings were set into another circle in the tile on the floor, but instead of the image of Mary, they enclosed what appeared to be a series of tritons pointed outward and arranged in a circle. Other lines crossed the forks at their handles, and a circle joined them at the center. Runes seemed to pop out at her in the most obscure places as though they invited further investigation.

Morwenna squeezed her hand, bringing Cassandra's gaze back to her. The seer nodded toward the door where Mr. Barrett stood just outside. He still had her chalkboard, but nothing would convince her to ask it of him. Besides, he would want to investigate the newcomer, and it wouldn't take long before he realized she was a witch.

Cassandra lowered her head. "What is it?"

Morwenna's warm smile radiated her patience. Again, she nodded toward the door.

A thought struck her, and she never doubted the outside source.

Of course. Morwenna didn't indicate Mr. Barrett but the way Cassandra had come. Lyme House. The building was hundreds of years old, and it was as much a part of Scry Cove as the old church. If the church was built by and for witches, then Lyme House must have been the ancestral seat of witches. After all, Niko and

Selena had come from Lyme House though their curious accents told her they grew up elsewhere.

Cassandra shot to her feet then took a step for the door. On a whim, she turned back on her heel and hugged her new friend. Morwenna returned the embrace and released her with more of the same affection in her green gaze.

"Thank you." Cassandra's voice came out in an inaudible whisper.

Somehow, Morwenna had heard or sensed her gratitude. She gave Cassandra a slow nod as they parted.

At last, Cassandra knew what to do. She needed to get back to Lyme House.

Chapter 16

"Mr. Barrett, I believe my faith is renewed." She didn't elaborate on what her faith restored. "However, I think it would do me well to take my exercise. If it pleases you, I can be surrounded by footmen or put on a leash, but my health, and therefore, my powers would benefit from the movement. What do you say?"

They were in the carriage, returning to Lyme House. She hadn't spotted Morwenna leaving the church, and with any luck, Mr. Barrett hadn't noticed her. With Mr. Barrett close, she hadn't dared stay and question the seer further. Besides, the warm approval in Morwenna's eyes told Cassandra she had grasped the message.

Mr. Barrett's frown etched his displeasure at the idea of escorting her. He took up the chalkboard with reluctance.

I am not at all sure that is best for you, but your trip to the church pleased Lord Lyme. I will walk with you in the garden when we return, but any further adventures will have to be agreed on with our employer.

She gave him her brightest smile. He directed his gaze at the window, which was fine by her. Having any sort of conversation was ordeal enough, but when Mr. Barrett was her partner, it was like swimming against a current of anger and resentment. He wanted to find fault with her.

Being with Niko was the opposite, or it had been before they slept together. Her cheeks heated at the memory. She thanked her stars Mr. Barrett still looked away. The mere thought of Niko sent her heart into a frenzied gallop. Dread flavored her anticipation. How long would it be before he tired of her? Would he come to her again?

At least he hadn't given her any false expectations. They had never discussed any sort of relationship between them, and she had every reason to believe there wasn't one. She would be setting herself up for disappointment if she thought otherwise.

When they reached the house, an unknown carriage crowded the drive. Mr. Barrett let out a sigh when it came into view. Some of the guests for the house party had arrived. Mr. Barrett might see it as an inconvenience, but to Cassandra, the house party was the beginning of the end of her work for Lord Lyme. The man could only be acquainted with so many people.

Her stomach twisted as she realized Lord Lyme might want her assistance past his known associates. He would always meet new people, and new people meant new witches. What was to keep him from locking her away only to be released for periodic use like a child's toy or a riding habit?

They exited the carriage on the drive, not far from the house. She caught a glimpse of the owners of the other carriage before he led her toward the garden. She had to look again when she didn't believe her eyes the first time.

As if by design, a ray of sunlight broke through the

clouds and caught the golden strands of Georgiana Hart's pristine hair peeking out from her bonnet. A soft, secretive smile graced Georgiana's lips. All the footmen in attendance and Mr. Sutton came to her aid though it was clear she needed no assistance. If Mr. Barrett had been watching, she had no doubt he would have flocked to her as well.

He pulled Cassandra away from any possible conversation with Georgiana. The witch must have lost her mind to be here, but she doubted this was only her doing. Morwenna had guided her back to the church, and now Georgiana was here to enchant the guests. Perhaps Georgiana was sent to watch her or to spy in her place. She didn't know what to think of the risk. How did the witches expect her to ignore Georgiana's presence? Cassandra would have to test her like any other guest.

It was an impossible choice.

Cassandra struggled to hide her reaction at the touch of other witches. Niko had aided her in concealing his identity in the past, but he was an empath. She didn't even know if Georgiana's abilities would affect her. So far, she had only witnessed men succumb to her powers. How would she deal with women or other witches for that matter?

Cassandra's mind raced over the possibilities as she entered the maze with Mr. Barrett. Blinking in surprise at his choice, she wondered if he knew more about her and Niko than he let on. Being alone with him here in the maze sent an icy jolt down her spine.

The maze was more extensive than she remembered, and only a moment passed before she lost track of where they were. He seemed to take the passages at random, which was no reassurance. The last thing she needed was to be lost in the maze with him.

Her agitated gut almost made her miss the runes.

The markings on the stone path came and went at different turns with no obvious pattern. She had no idea what they might mean. The more she looked for them, the more prominent they became. How had she missed them before?

If Mr. Barrett noticed them, he gave no indication. Instead, he appeared consumed in his thoughts. He might as well have been walking a dog for all the attention he paid her. Perhaps her suggestion of a leash wasn't so far from the mark.

He ignored her attempts to slow him. Just as she prepared to plant her heels in the ground, he stopped.

Cassandra spun forward and would have collided with the awful man if she hadn't decided in a split second that the ground was preferable. Her knees struck the stone, sending a shock through her body. Fiery tracks of blood traced the wounds on her palms.

Mr. Barrett shook his head perhaps disappointed by her clumsiness.

She gritted her teeth and sucked in a breath.

She didn't bother to ask for assistance, but he didn't offer any. She rubbed her hands over her knees and crouched. Pain shot up her legs. She gulped down the discomfort, not wanting Mr. Barrett to see her helpless. She didn't need him now, and she didn't need him before. Her pride gave her every inch she needed to stand on her own.

They came to an alcove she hadn't seen before, a testament to the size of the maze. A bench nestled in the space, and Mr. Barrett dropped down. He rubbed at his leg. She moved to sit next to him. Glaring up at her, he shook his head and spread a hand out to indicate the walkway.

Cassandra sighed. He meant to watch her while she walked. Could she have chosen a worse walking companion? His company wasn't much improvement, but she would have greater freedom over the maze. If she went out of his line of sight, she could forget whatever trust she had gained.

She continued on, her eyes trained on the area for any out-of-place symbols. Aside from the occasional etched rune at crossroads, the maze appeared just as she would expect.

Mr. Barrett continued to watch her from his perch on the bench, his arms folded in a silent complaint. She didn't dare follow the runes, but they beckoned her. Her excuses to get out of her room were slim at best, and being alone again in the maze was a distant dream.

Niko must be aware of the rules, and yet, he hadn't mentioned them. It couldn't have hurt to let her know what to look for at Lyme House. The more she learned about Niko, the less she thought she knew him. The man was a riddle jumbled into a conundrum.

She resigned herself to return to Mr. Barrett. She couldn't hope to find any answers here today. Instead, she would watch for Georgiana back at the house. The witch was bound to be more forthcoming than Niko. As dangerous as it was, Cassandra warmed at the comfort of another supportive presence.

When she approached, Mr. Barrett slumped on the bench. He let out an exaggerated groan when he rose as though for her benefit. If the man thought she was about to apologize for her walk, he would be disappointed. She ignored him. Her gaze shifted to the area on the bench he had vacated.

A star was carved in the center of the bench, but nothing else in the area gave any indication of what it might mean. She frowned at the symbol until Mr. Barrett jerked her out of her trance to take the lead back to the house.

At the first major crossroads, she froze. Mr. Barrett was on her heels when her instincts took over. She made a swift decision to turn right. Her determination to not rely on Mr. Barrett and the position of the afternoon sun, helped her jolt her memory of the layout of the maze.

A few more turns and she only needed one not so gentle prompt from Mr. Barrett, which led to a dead end. After that, she relied on her own senses to find their way out. She allowed her mind to wander back to the star.

The decoration seemed almost random, but it must have something to do with the statue of Artemis at the center. The goddess appeared in many stories about the stars, and she didn't believe it was a coincidence. The creator of the maze seemed consistent there.

She had no doubt the runes would reveal their meaning. Right now, the maze appeared an exotic mess in her mind. A tangled thread that begged to be unraveled. Some excuse would have to present itself to her during this house party. A sense at the back of her mind told her she was running out of time.

At last, her efforts were rewarded when the house came into view, but before she had the chance to speed up, Mr. Barrett stopped her with a hand on her arm. His grip was light, but it seemed to burn through her sleeve.

She shook him off and met his eyes.

His smile was out of place, and the gleam in his eyes gave her pause. She scrunched up her brows at him, but he took little notice of her suspicion. He reached into his greatcoat and retrieved a small object covered in his grip.

Her eyes widened when he dangled the glass vial in front of her. It was the same vial Niko had thrown out her window. By some chance, the glass remained intact. How Mr. Barrett had located it in the yard was beyond her. Mr. Barrett wasn't the most observant man, and she suspected a servant must have retrieved it.

Without a second thought, she snatched the vial from his hand.

His smile widened, and he set off for the house. The spring in his step made his limp less noticeable. He peered back to her once for she followed him with slow steps.

The vial remained clutched in her hand. It seemed not a precious drop had been spilled. The glass against her palm set her mind at ease. At least, this was under her control. She could decide what was best for her. If only the rest of her decisions had been hers to make. Every person she encountered pushed her down another path of her own maze. She was tugged every which way, and all she saw were dead ends.

Lord Lyme offered her what she wanted. A way back to herself in Florence. Then she could go home, and her life would be restored like nothing had happened. She could forget she had ever heard of Scry Cove or witches.

Her thoughts put her doubts at ease as she entered her room at the direction of Mr. Barrett. She slipped off her shoes and bonnet. Her dress and corset were next to follow. When she was comfortable, she spread herself over the bed then unstopped the bottle. A couple of drops and Niko would never know.

Mist hopped up and stationed himself like a statue at the foot of the bed. His glare made her stomach lurch.

"What? I'm certainly not going to tell him. You don't need to either if you know what's good for your furry hide." She giggled at the cat's squinted expression. "Honestly, Mist, I won't make a habit of it." Why she bothered to lie to the cat was beyond her, but it meant lying to herself as well.

Mist gave her another irritated look and curled up where he sat, his eyes continued to watch her.

Cassandra let out a long breath as her limbs turned to jelly. Her thoughts drifted away from the pain, always at the forefront of her mind. Her body seemed to float as though Lyme House was far away, and with it, all of her concerns. Here, she didn't need fixing. Nobody would reject her or use her to hurt others. Only Cassandra remained and blissful nothingness.

She didn't sleep. The amount she took was no longer enough for sleep, but it would have been a blessing. No, she would have to ration the rest of the liquid. The loss of the drug had pained her when Niko so unceremoniously disposed of the bottle. She didn't think she could go without it again.

In her haze, she spied Alisa entering the room. The maid carried a tray and set it down on the table. She took a long look at Cassandra and exited the room. Another disappointed person, no doubt. Every choice she made seemed to displease someone.

Her chest lurched when she thought of home. If she had stayed in Coldon, none of this would have happened. Aunt Louise might be alive. She wouldn't need to worry about witches or crazy, old men, Mr. Barrett, or strange cats. She would be safe in her bed with no fear of a fiery-eyed man troubling her heart. Niko would be a distant stranger.

No time seemed to pass, and yet, the room darkened.

Cassandra sat up, blinking at the fading sunlight. She rolled her body off the bed then shuffled over to light a candle. The glow of the flame outlined the contents of the tray, a pot of tea, and some biscuits. An envelope rested against the pot.

Her unsteady hand spilled some of the precious tea over the side of her cup. It took every bit of concentration to finish filling it. The tea was cold, but she guzzled it as though for the first time. She bit off some biscuit and took up the envelope.

The bulge in the paper and weight of the contents hinted at more than a letter. She regarded it with a frown. The seal featured a lone feather that gave the illusion of being blown by a breeze. It was a clever imprint. She took pains not to break it to pieces as she got to the contents.

A pale blue stone rolled out into her palm. It was round though somewhat misshapen and thin but not quite flat with a perfect hole through it near one edge. A cord was tied through the hole. She set the stone back on the tray and pulled a letter out of the envelope. The script was written in a feminine, elegant flourish.

Darling Miss Poole,
I hope my letter finds you well, and your dear Alisa

delivers it safely. I arrived for this delightful house party at the invitation of Lord Lyme. Do not be alarmed. My family has been close to the Moores for generations, and it would be remiss for me not to attend. I am not concerned about what may trouble you. Trust me. Leastways, you could use an ally and not just the kind that peeps around corners and windows.

Cassandra's face burned as she read.

Since you have obtained a following, I will see you at dinner tomorrow. By then, many of the guests will be here, and our little problem will be much improved.

Was she insane? More guests would make her task more challenging.

I am not sure what our mutual friend at the church said, but I advise you to exercise caution. Things are never what they seem, as you may be well aware by now.

Your loving friend, Lady Georgiana Hart

P.S. I almost forgot. That dreadful Florentine passed the stone onto me to give to you. An adder stone for protection. Keep it well hidden. He would have you wear it, but I advise you to put it away in a pocket or any other useful areas on your person.

Cassandra reread the last line. The witch must have meant for Cassandra to hide it in her cleavage. Lady Georgiana was proving to be an unconventional woman, but Cassandra would welcome the help. How they would avoid Lord Lyme's suspicions were beyond her.

The Florentine must be Niko. Without her hearing, accents were a challenge at best. It was agony to identify them. He must know something more about the hospital there, but he had never mentioned it. In fact, he had made no indication he knew anything about Lord Lyme's plans for her.

He was hiding something. Whether on purpose or by omission, didn't matter to Cassandra. He could have saved her the trouble of working for Lord Lyme. The witches she had implicated would have nothing to fear, and she would be on the road to recovery.

Was he so convinced of the superiority of witches that he would prevent her from choosing her own fate?

The thought sent her stomach in knots.

Her hands tested the cord on the adder stone and toyed with what to do with it. Georgiana was correct. She couldn't keep this around her neck. It was too large, too rough for jewelry. Keeping a stone from Niko between her breasts disquieted her nerves.

Tonight, it would make little difference. She tied the cord to her bed's headboard. If the stone really helped with protection, then her bed was the best place for it. Much of her unguarded time was in sleep. Though it wasn't the knife she had brought, it shifted the weight on her shoulders a bit.

Chapter 17

Cassandra was summoned a short time after dawn the next day. To her surprise, Mr. Sutton came to escort her. Mr. Barrett was nowhere in sight. The bulky man waited expressionless outside of her door while Alisa dressed her with frenzied hands.

Something wasn't right, but Alisa refused to explain. Indeed, there was no time to write out her answers. Mr. Sutton emphasized the importance of a swift departure. The firm set of his jaw and his stern voice sent Cassandra and Alisa into a flurry of muslin and hairpins. She fetched the adder stone from her bed then stashed it in her skirts where it dangled against her skin.

In an impossible quarter-hour, Cassandra walked beside Mr. Sutton to meet Lord Lyme. The man remained silent with a frown etched into his brow. When she asked where Mr. Barrett went, his frown deepened, but he never replied. She kept her peace after that.

They entered the dining room, the long table lined with modest breakfast fare. Light filtered in through the windows, but gray morning shadows dominated the space. Lord Lyme sat alone at the end of the table. He gestured for her to join him. He hunched over his breakfast with thinned lips and ate with calm, deliberate movements. Something about his bearing urged her to run.

Instead, she busied her hands, choosing at random a boiled egg and well-buttered toast. She hadn't the stomach for jellies or sweets this morning. The drug still lingered over her body like a shroud.

Lord Lyme served her tea. She took it without hesitation. The brew was fresh, strong, and she delighted in its now-familiar texture. She had never brewed tea to such perfection. She made a mental note to find out the cook's methods.

Once he finished, he pushed his plate aside and hovered over the chalkboard Mr. Sutton had left behind. She hadn't noticed the man leave them alone. The empty space of the cavernous room sent a chill along her skin. The company of Mr. Sutton or even Mr. Barrett would be welcome now. Men more than twice her strength, who had no reason to favor her over the powerful man at her side.

It was Lord Lyme's eyes.

His brown gaze was milky, wandering the room without any aid from the rest of his body. He wrote, and yet, no thought seemed to enter his expression. It was as though he was lost. To Cassandra's relief, he tilted the board into her view. Her gaze cut to his words. His writing was scrunched and at sharp angles, just legible enough for Cassandra to make out the words. Whatever happened to his talking to her?

I cannot express enough the importance of this house party. You will be answerable to Mr. Sutton and me at all times. If you do not perform your duty to my satisfaction, I will revoke my side of the agreement.

With her nod, he erased the board and continued.

Furthermore, you will have greater freedom to

perform your task. Do not disappoint me. You will be watched closely. Niko has been spotted on the estate, and you must ignore his ramblings and report his behavior. He means trouble.

She peered up from the board to catch Lord Lyme, watching her over a cup of steaming coffee. "My lord, I don't understand why I must be watched. I am no danger to you, and surely you know I want my cure more than anything."

His expression was vacant as he spoke. Except his words were like gravel to her ears, they crumbled together into a grating mess of sound. It appeared that Lord Lyme had taken ill. He took pity on her, or rather, he lost patience with her and returned to the board.

Once we discovered your strength, we grew concerned that your power could be used against both you and us. It has been known to happen, with or without the witch's consent. Such phenomena are studied in Florence, and witches have been prevented from becoming deadly weapons.

The man held himself firm, but something was absent. "What of Niko? Have you offered him the cure?" She knew Niko would never consider such a thing. He was a proud witch who flaunted his abilities.

Lord Lyme tilted his head to study her a moment. His eyes cleared, and she saw Niko's own eyes without the golden tint. It was the first she had noticed a resemblance in them, and it twisted her stomach.

Yes, Niko has been offered the cure, but it would not serve for him to give up his abilities.

She pinched the bridge of her nose. "I don't understand. You want him to be a witch?" This made little sense in her understanding of Lord Lyme. He

170

expressed a desire to weed out all witches. Why would his son be an exception?

Lord Lyme let out a long sigh between his teeth. *He is willful and full of pride, but he has an advantage over other lords. It will serve him well.*

His words only scrambled her thoughts further. "Then why keep him out of Lyme House? Why not work with him?"

I do. Living away is the boy's choice.

Her mouth opened, but before she could speak, Mr. Sutton entered to remove Lord Lyme to the library. Cassandra was dismissed, left with conflicting answers, and a displaced mind. Not wanting to lose the trust she had gained, she went straight to her room.

Niko worked with Lord Lyme?

It contradicted everything she knew about Niko. She thought he hated his father and disagreed with everything the man stood for. How could he go against his own morals? That is unless Niko had lied to her.

Why did he sneak around if he was welcome there? Was it an act to draw her in?

Her heart pounded a sick thud against her chest wall.

Nothing made sense. Niko was his father's son, a con man set on revealing witches. No other explanation could account for his actions. If that was the case, none of the witches in Scry Cove were safe except perhaps his sister.

She couldn't grasp the betrayal or count the number of witches he already knew. Dear Antoinette with her gentle nature, and Dr. Scott with his kind wisdom. The shy and untested seer, Morwenna. The breathtaking Georgiana.

Georgiana.

Even now, the witch roamed the halls of Lyme House. Discovery waited at every turn. The thud of Cassandra's heart paused only to resume into a restless hammering in her throat. She had to warn Georgiana and force the witch to flee before Lord Lyme sent her to her mysterious fate.

Cassandra didn't hesitate. She pulled the bell to summon Alisa and made for the door. The footmen stood on either side of the entrance, but neither would answer her query about leaving the room. When she stepped forward, the one on her right raised his hand to stop her. So much for finding Georgiana.

She paced the floor of her room, and every moment added fire to her nerves.

Would Niko turn Georgiana over to his father? To be fair, he hadn't already, and none of the other witches seemed concerned. His objective must be deeper. Of course, why turn on a group of witches you already know when you can have all of England with Cassandra's help. She was a fool, a naive child with no sense of the world outside Coldon.

When she thought she could stand to wait no longer, Alisa entered and closed the door behind her. The maid's wide-eyed stare brought her back to herself.

"The woman who sent me the letter, Lady Georgiana Hart, do you know her? Can you take her a message for me?"

Alisa bobbed her head in agreement.

Cassandra held up a hand for her to wait and jotted off a note of warning to the witch, outlining her conversation with Lord Lyme and her further suspicions. Alisa took the letter then left to deliver her message.

The maid was not quick to return as Cassandra had hoped. She perched on the edge of the bed. When Alisa still had not returned, Cassandra laid back against her pillows and closed her eyes tight. Her stiff form was propped more than relaxed, and once the pinch of her clenched jaw took hold, she turned to Antoinette's remedy.

At this rate, she would run out before the house party was over. She settled for a drop to see how it would suffice. After an ineffective hour, she downed two more drops. Just as she dozed off, Alisa returned carrying a new dress.

Cassandra rose on her elbows. "Well? Did she get my message? Was there any reply?"

Alisa shook her head and set out the gown for use.

"No? To which question? Both?"

The responding nod grated along her dulled nerves. "I assume you had trouble locating her, and someone made you return to me to help me ready for dinner?"

Alisa scrunched up her nose in an uncharacteristic show of annoyance. She gave another nod and beckoned Cassandra to join her.

She wobbled on her feet. Either the ground or her feet had become uneven. Alisa watched her progress while shaking her head. Cassandra could almost hear Alisa's thoughts. This wouldn't do.

The greatest challenge involved keeping Cassandra on her feet while changing her into the new ivory silk dress. Alisa seemed hesitant to allow her to stand on her own. A rip in the fabric could prove catastrophic.

The adder stone tumbled from her. She blinked down at it without recognition. Alisa rescued it from the ground and offered it back to her. She flinched away, and an odd sense of revulsion crept up her throat.

Niko wanted her to wear it, but she didn't know what the man's motives were now. She would be safer without the thing. She instructed Alisa to hang it from the headboard as before and put it out of her mind. The stone could wait.

They finished her outfit off with a new set of gloves, altered again to suit her needs. The footmen outside her door escorted her to the drawing room, where the other guests were waiting. Two stiff-backed expressionless guards with no give in their duties. She almost wished for Mr. Barrett. Almost.

The walk sobered her, but her thoughts remained fuzzy like a fog had descended over her head. She pinched her arms whenever her mind wandered, and when that failed to keep her in the present, she bit her tongue.

She recognized much of the party as neighbors who attended the dinner party. Closer in proximity to Lord Lyme, they were some of the first to arrive. Mr. Carter, Mr. Tallmadge, and Mr. Jones were all in attendance. Their presence took her off guard. None of them must have been close to Mr. Harris, but it made sense if they were unaware he was a witch.

Georgiana stood to one side, giggling along with the long-absent Mr. Barrett. He stared at her with shining eyes and a half-open mouth, but he wasn't the only man taken by her. Most of the eyes in the room stared after the witch. It was a welcome change for Cassandra, who hated the attention of her position with Lord Lyme.

A group of ladies stood together, glaring at

Georgiana. A smile tugged at her lips as she made her way to the women. Mr. Sutton came along to introduce her. She hadn't much practice making contact with other women. Most of the women from the other events likely thought her clumsy or over-familiar. This group was no exception.

A woman's genuine smile set Cassandra at ease. It wasn't long before she ruled the group out. She continued to pretend to listen to the other ladies and found herself answering a few questions she heard. The conversation allowed her to stall for time in testing Georgiana and Mr. Sutton wandered off.

When they were called to dinner, the group of men came to gather up the women. Mr. Tallmadge's silver-gray eyes peered down at her from his self-absorbed height and offered her his escort. She accepted the gesture, knowing the alternatives were not much improvement. At least, she wouldn't have to tolerate Mr. Barrett.

Her mind drifted to Niko. She nearly slapped herself. She didn't need another traitor taking up her time. Better to forget she ever knew his name. Or his touch. His lips. What was the matter with her? Had she completely lost all sense of self-preservation?

Down the table from her, Mr. Barrett was making a fool of himself over Georgiana. The witch sipped her wine with a calm air that could pass as attentive or bored, depending on a person's preference. Mr. Barrett seemed to view her as besotted as himself.

It was a comical display. Even those guests furthest away from the witch attempted to speak to her over the distance. Both of her dinner partners were struck by Georgiana, freeing Cassandra to enjoy her meal.

With a sudden pang, she wondered if Niko was as affected by Georgiana. The witch was desirable even without her abilities. Cassandra washed the thought away with a gulp of her wine. The pang grew to a void, numbing her. It didn't matter anymore. He lied to her, and he could do as he pleased.

When the dessert course arrived, Cassandra had tired of the whole meal. She accepted the pudding with little enthusiasm but warmed to the mouth-watering texture. The brilliant cook had done it again. She looked forward to having tea after dinner, preferably in her room and away from these people.

For now, she needed to keep her head about her and off the thought of Niko. She would reserve those thoughts for when she could give him a proper verbal beating, followed by her hands around his throat. If he survived the encounter, she would never speak to the rat again.

A clatter down the table caught her attention between bites. Mr. Jones and Mr. Carter were on their feet, shouting down Mr. Barrett and each other. Next to Cassandra, Mr. Tallmadge rose, yelling across the table. Georgiana's expression hadn't changed. She took slow bites of her dessert as chaos erupted around her.

Mr. Carter smashed his fist into Mr. Barrett's gut, doubling him over. Cassandra dropped her spoon, and Georgiana frowned at the turn of events. Her expression was more annoyance than concern. Something told Cassandra that Georgiana was used to the violence over her.

Footmen streamed in to break up the fight. The men were taken from the room. Mr. Barrett toppled to the floor and was carried out. The remainder of the diners included the rest of the women and Lord Lyme who glared down the table at Georgiana.

A gripping fear seized Cassandra's throat as a footman bent down to whisper something to Georgiana. The witch's face paled, but she kept her composure. Another footman came to assist the first and made the mistake of taking Georgiana's arm. The footmen turned on each other. Blood sprayed across the white tablecloth. The remaining guests retreated from the table.

Mr. Sutton arrived with some of the returned footmen to break up the fight. He shot a look at Georgiana. She shrugged and smiled back at him. Mr. Sutton escorted her himself, his scowl chiseled into his face.

When the door shut behind them, the stillness of the room sent gooseflesh across Cassandra's skin. She rubbed at her arms to comfort herself. Her attention caught on Lord Lyme. His sharp gaze could not be mistaken for anything other than rage.

Chapter 18

While Lord Lyme hardened in tight lines of anger, and the women comforted each other in hushed whispers, Cassandra snuck out. Stealth wasn't necessary, she could have stomped out without any worry of being stopped, but it seemed appropriate given the atmosphere in the dining room.

Georgiana had gone undetected in Lord Lyme's company for years. The chaotic mess the witch created was deliberate. Whether it was to gain Cassandra's freedom or to some other purpose, she didn't know. Cassandra would thank the witch later, assuming she saw her again.

She needed answers.

Not for Niko. The man had used her for the last time. No, Lyme House had become her prison, but she needed to know why. What game was Lord Lyme playing? If she was going to win, she needed to know the rules and how to break them.

She made good time putting distance between her and the dining room, darting into rooms and hallways when she came across someone. So far, she had been lucky, but without any direction or any sign or runes, she would get nowhere fast. It was only a matter of time before someone spotted her. Georgiana couldn't distract them forever.

Another turn into an empty hallway and out of the

path of a maid. At least, the hall appeared empty. Mist sat at the center of a scarlet and cream-colored runner. He posed like a gatekeeper, waiting for her. The area was well-lit, but in her haste, she could have tripped once again on the feline.

"You're making a habit of this." She stared down the cat's gaze. "Are you going to help me, or do you plan to run off to play with toads?"

Mist's eyes slit, and he rose to his paws. He sashayed forward, his tail and backside mocking her as she followed.

"You better not be leading me to your last kill, either."

Mist's tail paused straight in the air a moment before he continued. She supposed it was the feline equivalent to a verbal lashing.

Without warning, the cat sped up, and Cassandra had to leap forward to try to keep pace. It was to no avail. She lost him almost at once and was left staring at the intersection of three hallways. Wherever he had gone, he was no longer in sight.

This was what she got for trusting a cat. As intelligent as he seemed, she must have imagined most of it. Maybe she had used too much of the drug. There was also the possibility that Mist led her into danger. He had known Niko first and was a long-time resident with Lord Lyme.

She picked the right hallway at random, but as she turned, a small imperfection in the floor made her pause. In the center hallway, the stone had a strange alteration in color. It was as though the stone had been replaced imperfectly.

She stepped into the center hallway. More odd-colored stone met her path. Someone must have removed the markings, and she guessed they were much like the ones in the maze. With her inexperience, the house was unnavigable, but to someone who had lived here their whole life like Lord Lyme, he didn't need the markings to find his way.

The discolored stones took her in what seemed like circles. The changing paintings on the walls were the only thing that convinced her she was not going over the same ground. Lyme House could not possibly be this big. She took so many turns she almost wished she was stuck in the maze or back in her room.

She was reminded of the stairs above the haberdashery. Something was off about Lyme House, and she couldn't begin to understand what it was. If she ever saw another witch again, she would make her explain it.

So intent was she on locating the next discolored stone, she almost missed the rune etched into the wall. The stones continued down the hall, but she stopped to investigate. The rune above the wooden paneling turned out to be several, but she had no understanding of their meaning. They appeared as carved nonsense.

On closer inspection, the wall was familiar to her. She hadn't noticed the runes before, but she hadn't seen the runes in the maze either. Morwenna had awakened her awareness either by pointing out the symbols in the church or by some seer trick.

Her fingers found the whorl in the wood again and pressed it. The wall moved forward. She stepped into the chill air of the atrium. The sun rested low on the horizon, giving her just enough light to see beyond the hall.

Mist perched at the edge of a still pond, watching the water. She hadn't seen him run past. Somehow the cat had gotten in without her and awaited her arrival. She came up beside the cat. He grinned up at her.

"Horrible beast, you could have saved me the trouble."

If Mist were human, he would laugh at her. She suspected he did.

"Is this some kind of punishment for being rude to you? Miserable creature." She turned away from him and absorbed her surroundings.

Vibrant green plants filled the space. Herbs and flowers, medicinal and edible alike, scattered among common garden plants, and a wooded area with a towering willow and aspens shaded the space beyond the pond. Beneath the water's surface, fish darted along the bottom.

The beauty of her surroundings enthralled her. Why go to such lengths to hide it?

She wandered along the edges of the scene, careful not to leave any marks of her passage. Her gaze caught movement among the trees, but it was gone before she could identify its source. More toads, she suspected.

Along the wall and out of view of the door, a wooden work table broke the vision of paradise. The table was well worn, possibly as old as she, but being exposed to the elements, it could be newer. A row of tools sat in neat order along the top of the table, from pruning shears to work gloves to knives. Baskets, bowls, and funnels were stacked along the side of the table, ready for the garden's collections. Above the table hung dried herbs.

By all accounts, it was an ordinary work table.

What caught Cassandra's attention was the group of vials set in a small open crate on the edge of the table. They were filled with a white liquid she had never seen. She lifted one of the vials and wiggled it in her fingers, but the liquid made little movement, more like pus than milk.

Curiosity got the best of her. She unstopped the vial and sniffed the contents. A wave of euphoria overcame her. It was like breathing fresh air after standing over a cooking fire for hours, or the smell of fresh bread after fasting for days. She dipped her little finger into the vial and brought it to her lips. Her eyes blurred as she slouched against the table. The effect was immediate but as potent as laudanum.

A lazy smile grew across her face. She took another taste. The world disappeared around her then she became lost in a bubble of comfort. Her limbs relaxed, and her legs nearly collapsed underneath her as she wandered to the door.

She didn't remember closing the vial or clasping it tightly in her hand. Mist led the way, but later she was not sure if she closed the door or not. Her only thought was for the toads and whether or not they would haunt her dreams again. Or would they follow her to her room and wreak havoc for disturbing their home?

In the end, she cared little for such things. Better to surround herself with the comfort of oblivion than deal with the poison of everyone around her. Nobody could hurt her where she had gone. Not Lord Lyme or Mr. Barrett. Not damn Nikolas bloody Moore or whatever he called himself.

She blinked, and she was back in her room. Alisa helped her ready for bed. Her feet kept stumbling.

Another blink, and she curled into the blankets of her bed. Mist nestled up beside her stomach.

Her eyes opened when light pierced through her window, slamming her in the face. Alisa stood outlined beside the drawn curtains. Cassandra pulled the blanket over her head, upsetting the cat beside her. Mist trotted off as she heard an exaggerated snort from Alisa.

"Leave me be." Cassandra groaned and pulled the covers tighter.

Alisa tore the blanket from her.

The light from the window crashed into Cassandra's head. A headache formed behind her eyes. "What is your problem?"

Alisa planted her fists on her hips and stared down at her. Accusation was etched into every line of her frown.

"It can't be that late in the day. The old fool can be patient for once. Better yet, he can find another witch to harass."

Mist plopped down next to Alisa. His expression mirrored hers, or so it seemed. Cassandra squeezed her eyes shut and open again. Mist stayed the same.

"Is everyone against me?" She huffed, dropping her legs off the bed.

Alisa yanked the night rail off of her and handed her a change of undergarments. She stood by with her arms crossed over her chest until Cassandra needed aid. They continued in this manner with Alisa finishing tugging her hair up into a simple style. Every pin in Cassandra's scalp screamed of Alisa's anger.

Cassandra met the maid's gaze as she rubbed at her scalp. "All right, I get it. You disapprove of my choices. What do I have to lose?"

Alisa closed her eyes and took a deep breath. She found the chalkboard which she must have retrieved from Lord Lyme.

What is this about?

"What is what about?"

Alisa narrowed her eyes at her.

Cassandra dropped her chin. There was no escaping the maid. Her door was once again guarded. "I don't know." She shook her head. "I just wanted to be out of pain. First, it was Antoinette's drug and the food. The tea especially. Then I found that white stuff. It made me forget."

Forget what?

A tear tickled at the corner of Cassandra's eye, but she bit her tongue to stop it. "This past year." She took a breath. "My world has been turned upside down. It's like I fell down a hole, and I claw, and I claw, but I keep falling. I thought coming here to Spray Cove and Lyme House would help me. It just gets worse."

A chaos of her own making. She didn't want the sad look on Alisa's face. It resembled pity, and the last thing she needed was someone feeling sorry for her. She had already done that for herself in abundance. Now, she no longer cared about what happened to her, but she would not be another sad story.

Is this about Master Niko?

"No, of course not." A blush betrayed her lie. "I shouldn't put too much hope into anything with him. After all, he's a future baron."

A smile tugged at Alisa's lips as she erased the board and wrote. *Master Niko is a good man. He would not hurt you on purpose. You should talk to him.*

"I don't know. He's working with Lord Lyme."

She frowned. "You could be working with Lord Lyme."

Alisa burst into a fit of laughter.

Cassandra's brows pinched. "What's so funny?"

Of course, I work with Lord Lyme. I am a maid. Before you get too excited, I am only a maid. I do not involve myself in his dealings. I listen, I watch, and I wait. If there is anything I can do, I will act. As for Master Niko, you will have to take this up with him.

"If I ever see him again, you mean."

Alisa wiped the board clean. *When you see him again, do not let that pretty face fool you. Show some teeth and bite it off. The man is a fool if he does not appreciate you, but all men are fools anyway.*

A stupid grin spread across Cassandra's face, and warmth flooded her chest. She had missed these conversations with friends. None of her friends back in Coldon had understood how to talk to her. Alisa saw something others didn't. Even better, she didn't tiptoe around her. Instead, she called her out for her misbehavior and made her listen. Not hear but listen.

Alisa grinned back at her and patted Cassandra's shoulders to signal she should rise. Cassandra did so, and they put on her slippers.

As she had first suspected, it wasn't late at all. Not as early as her breakfast with Lord Lyme, but also not an unreasonable hour to wake. Her sleep had left her groggy, and she suspected, so did the white liquid.

She examined the vial of the heady contents anew. Alisa joined her then scrunched her nose up when she sniffed it and gagged, turning her head to the side. Cassandra sniffed it herself, and then arched a brow.

A lazy sensation overcame her and the smell…oh, the smell. It was like iced cinnamon bread. Her mouth watered from the short inhale.

"How can you not like the smell? It makes me want to swallow it all and lick every drop from the vial."

Alisa squeezed her mouth shut and shook her head.

"Maybe if you tasted it?" Cassandra shrugged. "It's divine." She nearly dropped the bottle at her own words.

Her friend widened her eyes in question.

Cassandra set a hand on Alisa's shoulder. "It's divine. The tea. The food." She stared forward in astonishment. "My god. Do you know what this means?"

Alisa picked up the board and scribbled a swift message. *They have been putting it in your food and drink. Why?*

She shook her head back and forth, unable to stop. "I don't know. It doesn't make sense." Her gaze shot back to Alisa's. "What about you? Do you drink the creamy tea?"

It smells vile. I never touch it. Lord Lyme insists you have it. I never understood why.

"I've done everything he has asked of me. Why would he drug me? Don't I already have guards? They never give me enough to put me asleep. I've been tired since I got here."

Alisa shrugged in reply.

If Lord Lyme's goal was to keep her calm, he was doing a poor job. Cassandra had been attempting that herself. Whatever his purpose, it couldn't have been good.

Do you want me to prepare your meals myself? Pour out the tea?

Cassandra tapped her lip. "No. We need to behave as before. Bring everything here, but if you could include food from somewhere else."

Alisa nodded.

"They mustn't know. We need to find out more."

She had the sudden urge to talk to Niko and shake the answers out of him. He must know about the atrium and the white liquid. Even if he didn't, she would shake him anyway. Maybe she would push him out the window for good.

The man owed her answers. Their conversation was sparse. She had allowed it because of her hearing. He held back his words but filled the void with touch. She had encouraged his attentions and thrilled in the sound of crashing waves at their contact. Not this time.

Someone must have knocked at the door, but she hadn't heard it. Alisa peeked out the opening and spoke with someone in the hall. She shifted from foot to foot, wanting to finish with the man at the door. Then, her back stiffened, and Alisa went silent. The man in the hall left then she closed the door again.

When she faced Cassandra, Alisa had gone pale, and she blinked a few times as though to regain her senses. Her hands clasped together, her knuckles white. The maid seemed as if she would faint or scream.

"What is it?" Cassandra's voice sharpened.

Alisa took a deep breath and picked up the board. She wiped away the last message, taking her time. At last, she set her hand to the chalk.

Your presence is requested. Master Niko has returned.

Chapter 19

Cassandra's jaw dropped. She stared at the words, reading them over and over as if she could decipher some hidden meaning behind them. If the chalk held more answers, she didn't find them.

Her eyes jumped to meet Alisa's gaze. "What do you mean he's returned?"

Instead of answering, the maid pushed her toward the door.

Cassandra protested, but it made little difference once she was forced out the door. Mr. Sutton stood waiting, his posture as rigid as always. She spared a brief thought for Mr. Barrett but banished it from her mind.

When they reached the drawing room, she realized this was no ordinary meeting. Lord Lyme spent little time in the room. Her stomach growled in protest, and she swallowed back her hunger upon entering. It wouldn't do to have them see her discomfort.

She straightened her back and lifted her chin as she traversed the room. Lord Lyme sat composed in his wheeled chair, a wool blanket covered his lap. A cup and saucer rested in his hands. Across from him, Niko sat with a leg crossed over the other. He held a teacup identical to Lord Lyme's, his saucer rested with the other tea things on the small round table between them.

It was Niko who sat there. His well-tailored dark

brown coat and checked fawn waistcoat were all Niko, but the wild curls she loved were pulled back neatly. His eyes were dark pools of brown without much of the usual golden spark.

He regarded her with a raised brow and sipped his tea without further acknowledgment. He smiled at his father, who watched the exchange with little interest. She clasped her restless hands in front of her and waited for someone to speak.

Mr. Sutton appeared beside her with the chalkboard. A pair of footmen brought in additional chairs. At his insistence, she took the chair between him and Lord Lyme. Niko sat across from her in their little circle. Father and son continued to sip tea, ignoring her.

Mr. Sutton dutifully scrawled on the board. Why had she been called here when it was clear they would rather she wasn't?

I believe you are acquainted with Master Nikolas. He has agreed to assist us where Mr. Barrett has failed.

Cassandra concealed her flinch. After the disapproving stares and lectures, Niko would join his father and become the thing he preached against. By now, she was convinced his actions were all for show to keep her in line. Since that tactic hadn't worked, he would try the more direct route.

What had happened to Mr. Barrett? Her throat caught before she could ask the question. The possibilities made her uneasy, and few of them were good. As horrible as he was, she wished him well. At least, she had known where she stood with him. It was under his boot, but at least she knew where he aimed.

Niko continued to deny her presence. He radiated

arrogance the way the upper-class did, taking small sips of tea and sporting a false smile. She recognized the self-assured confidence in him, but his haughty manner was something else entirely.

Her gaze shot back to Mr. Sutton, and her hands clenched into fists. "You mean he has come here to control me."

All eyes flew to her. Lord Lyme's deep frown was the worst of the lot, but the lack of recognition in Niko's foreign gaze formed a sour taste at the back of her throat. He showed no signs of sensing her discomfort, but she knew he must have.

I assure you that is not our intention. We want only to help you perform your duties to the best of your ability. Your time is limited, and we mean to make the most of it.

Without Mr. Sutton's tone, she could not be sure if the last line was meant as a threat. She sensed the message was multi-tiered, but she had often made too much out of a man's words when everything was on the surface.

"Was there anything else? I haven't yet broken my fast."

"Indeed?" It was Lord Lyme who spoke in his rare, clear voice.

He said something else, and she assumed when Mr. Sutton left that he had sent for her meal. Before he left, he handed off the chalkboard to Niko, who passed it onto Lord Lyme with a shake of his head. So, the coward refused to talk to her.

Lord Lyme placed his cup and saucer on the table and took up the board. *I am told you went on an adventure.*

Her pulse hammered as she looked between the two men. "I'm not sure what you mean, my lord." In truth, he could have meant several occasions.

Lord Lyme's gaze sparked in the depths of his brown eyes, looking every bit Niko's father. *My workstation. Do you think it fit for an apothecary? I do like to dabble.*

The atrium.

Her mouth went dry. Then she must have left the door open, but how did they know it was her? She met Niko's eyes, and it was like an alarm sounding in her head. Niko knew somehow, but the only way he could have found out was through Alisa, who had found her with the strange white liquid.

"It's a worthy pastime, my lord." Her tone was wary, the words narrowly slipped from her lips. She cleared her throat in an attempt to regain herself. "Perhaps you will unlock the mystery of this disease." Once the words were out, she wanted them back.

Lord Lyme smiled, a sick, toothy widening of his lips and the sight forced her to lower her gaze. *That is my objective.*

She had spoken to both men about the mysterious illness, and both had blamed the other in some way. By their expressions, it was unclear if they had come to terms or if they still harbored blame. The depth of their working relationship and trust was yet to be determined.

She was saved from further conversation on the topic when Mr. Sutton returned, followed by two footmen. A table was arranged beside her laden with the usual tea and small meat pies. She should not have mentioned her hunger. Now, she would be forced to consume more of the strange drug.

Under the watch of all, she took a hesitant bite of the meat pie. Before she knew it, she pressed leftover crumbs onto her fork. She didn't care if she appeared a glutton. The drug possessed her actions. The creamy tea went the way of the pie, and she looked around for more when she was through.

A different, darker brew occupied Niko and Lord Lyme's teacups. She bit her lip and tried to get control of her craving, but Mr. Sutton ordered her more tea. As bad as she wanted to protest, she couldn't bring herself to speak. The taste of tea lingered on her tongue.

She was halfway through her second pot of tea before the drug reared its head. Her muscles relaxed into the chair, and she sipped in contentment. She sensed Niko's eyes on her, but her vision was unfocused. It was early yet, but surely a nap wasn't out of the question. She yawned into her hand and struggled to keep her lids open.

Mr. Sutton handed her the chalkboard. His words wavered in and out of focus as she read. *You had better rest before the concert tonight. Your services will be required. Of course, Master Nikolas will escort you. Go now before I have to carry you out.*

When she rose to her feet, Mr. Sutton and Niko stood with her. Both moved to assist her, but she waved them away. Had she imagined the concern spark in Niko's eyes? It was probably a dream or a drug-induced memory. When she looked again, she only saw contempt in his tight-lipped expression.

Tears pushed at the corners of her eyes, but she hadn't the energy to cry. The weight in her chest was ready to burst. She wished she had made some excuse not to consume the drug. If only she could clear her mind, she was sure she would make sense of everything. All she could see was the disapproving gaze of the man who had taken her innocence. The witch she had thought her friend and perhaps something more.

The drug was in full force when she reached the drawing room doors, and she remembered little of her trip back to her room or getting into bed. The adder stone swung over her head as she collapsed onto the blankets.

She clenched her teeth tight when she opened her eyes. It was a dramatic shift from the drug-relaxed state she was accustomed to. Her head and jaw throbbed. She suspected she had ground her teeth in her sleep. She stretched her mouth, but it only opened the floodgate of anger.

She berated herself for drinking so much of the tea. Not only had she lost time, but she had also shown Niko and Lord Lyme her dependency. She remembered her cravings for the tea all too well. Much like the laudanum, the white drug left her wanting more, and when she couldn't have it, she suffered worse.

Already, the gnawing urge to soften the edge haunted her. She didn't know how she would resist, but without restraint, she would be under Lord Lyme's control forever. The white substance was foreign to her. Nothing her father used looked even the slightest bit like it, nor did any drug she knew act the way it did.

In small doses, the liquid produced a relaxed state. In that respect, it was much like the laudanum. What made something smell delicious to one person while being odoriferous to another? It was one of those rare occasions where the smell was almost as overwhelming as the taste of a fine cheese.

The door clicked open and shut. Alisa busied into the room. Without any prompting, Cassandra threw herself out of bed. She tugged off her clothes then helped the maid dress her for the concert. The soft silk ivory gown with embroidered lilies and seed pearls went unappreciated. By the time Alisa finished her hair in an array of curls, she could no longer sit still, shifting and fidgeting at every opportunity.

When a firm knock sounded on the door, she hurried into her slippers and allowed Alisa a brief adjustment to her appearance before opening the door herself. The breath caught in her chest as her gaze found Niko.

She couldn't find her words. The anger blinded her in silence, but she had no doubt he sensed it. The air between them buzzed as she took in his formal black coat and waistcoat next to his bright white cravat. Not a hair on his head was out of place. Some of the golden spark had returned to his eyes, but the man before her was a stranger.

He glanced toward the footmen beside her door and caught sight of Alisa behind her. Then he gave Cassandra a graceful bow. Nothing of the old playful Niko inhabited his manner. Who was this civilized nobleman? She had misjudged him. He had made her into a fool.

She ignored his formal gesture and stepped around him into the hall. A wave of surprise stopped her. She aimed a glare at him. How dare he push his emotions on her. How could he possibly be surprised by her response?

Pivoting on her heel, she stalked off down the hall.

His bare hand clasped her arm above her glove. The rush slammed into her head and chest, pushing her against the wall. She gasped, twisting his wrist to release her. He flinched away and rubbed at the area.

Her action opened a heavy pit in her stomach. She took off down the hall before he could respond. It wasn't until she paused at the top of the stairs to catch her breath that Niko caught up to her. He avoided contact and stayed silent as he passed her.

He peered back at her with a sharp gaze, but she followed with reluctance. This new arrangement was worse than she could have imagined. She had been right about him all along. Alisa had warned her, but by then, she had been too far gone to listen. Too seduced by his touch and too consumed by drugs as she chased the path to oblivion.

They walked in silence. Waves of emotion floated back to her, making her stomach turn, but she ignored his manipulations. He wanted her to feel hurt as well and to experience his annoyance with her. She had her own emotions and didn't need the contrast of his.

Her nails bit into her palms through her gloves, keeping her anger steady. She wouldn't apologize for hurting him. What he had done was far worse than any injury she could inflict. The pit grew as she tried to push it away. It consumed her every thought by the time they arrived on the terrace.

She avoided Niko as she took a seat near the back. Other guests were already arriving, but she saw no sign of Georgiana or Mr. Bennett. Lord Lyme and Mr. Sutton sat near the front. Everyone else was scattered around on the gathered chairs. No musicians were present, but a piano was brought out for the occasion.

They waited for more of the seats to fill up, and most of the guests were unfamiliar to her. She predicted a long night and hoped Lord Lyme would at least allow her time throughout the house party to meet everyone. Lyme House was large, but she hadn't realized just how many people could visit comfortably.

Footmen escorted a woman who Cassandra didn't at first recognize. When they reached the area set aside for the performance, the woman came into view. The golden blonde hair of Katrina Powell was unmistakable. Gone was her bright smile and captivating presence. She wore a pale yellow dress that brought out the color in her hair, but it did nothing to help her pale skin. Her eyes were downcast, and she slouched forward. Otherwise, she seemed unharmed.

Cassandra's mouth stayed agape until Niko nudged her with his foot. Her gaze shot to his polished shoes, and she considered slamming her foot down on his. Raising her chin high, she bared her teeth at him in a grim smile. He held up his hands as if in surrender and gave her a wide smile. A smile belonging to the Niko she thought she had known. It raised the hair on her neck.

The footmen sat near the front of the audience and confirmed Cassandra's suspicion that they were more guard than an escort. Katrina settled herself down at the piano. The instant her fingers touched the keys, the world flew away.

Cassandra floated among the clouds, transported to a paradise of musical notes. Her hearing had no bearing on the sweet hum and soothing vibrations. She could not distinguish Katrina's voice from that of the instrument; they were one and the same. The notes carried through her like the pulsing of her blood. She spun and dove with the song.

When the song came to a close, Cassandra's breath escaped all at once. Her head was light, and her mind dazed. Her hand clasped tight to Niko's. The firm press of her glove made an imprint on her skin. She jerked her hand back and flexed her fingers while her mind caught up to her emotions. What she had experienced could only be described as witchcraft.

Her cheeks heated as she trained her gaze ahead, but the amusement that hovered from Niko was unavoidable. Moments passed as Katrina selected another song. By the time the music resumed, Cassandra's cheeks were crimson, and Niko was a second from bursting into laughter.

On the fourth song, Cassandra no longer cared that her hand rested in his. Her body seemed no longer hers. Niko and the rest of the audience were in similar rapture. Even Katrina nodded at the piano. Her abilities must have drained her as much as Cassandra's did her.

The concert only ended when Katrina slumped unconscious onto the keys. The resulting bang failed to awaken everyone as it might have before the performance. The guests exited the room as if drunk or sleepwalking.

Cassandra had no chance for introductions, but she was able to touch a few guests on the pretense of helping them. She revealed no new witches. Even if she had found one, she doubted anyone would be able to take action with the footmen, all swaying on their feet.

Niko accompanied her. When she could stand no more, he helped her back to her room. He avoided skin contact with her. She didn't know if she should be grateful or disappointed.

Her heart flipped against her chest as they neared her unguarded door, and she shook herself. This was foolish. Niko had betrayed her, why did having him at her door put her stomach into knots?

She stopped outside her room, and their gaze met.

He tugged at his pulled-back hair. She wanted to run her fingers through his wild hair, to pull on the strands as he kissed her. His proximity would drive her out of her mind.

She didn't have to act to show him her emotions, but she could speak to drive him back. "How could you work with Lord Lyme? Why did you use me, manipulate me?" Tears threatened to take over, and she hardened her anger. "I would have cooperated. All I ever wanted was to restore my hearing and go home."

He studied her face, tracing over every corner of her skin. The confusion set around his eyes echoed the mood of the air between them.

Her body trembled like her fury possessed her limbs. She faced away from him. "You're no better than them."

When she glanced back, he was gone.

Chapter 20

Cassandra pushed herself away from the door and pivoted on her heel. Nobody would lock her away in her room again. Not Niko and not Lord Lyme. Doubtless, they expected her to be dutiful now. Their little puppet ready to give up any witch.

They thought wrong.

Seeing Katrina alive had lifted a weight. Cassandra had banished the thought of dead witches out of her head, but it had always been a possibility. Lord Lyme's hatred had known no bounds.

Of course, the witches were more useful alive. Katrina, Niko, and Cassandra had proven that. It would be dangerous to leave them roaming free, but a dead witch was wasteful.

She had been a fool. Lord Lyme would never let her free, never let her seek healing in Florence. If her suspicions were correct, she would lose her abilities when she regained her hearing. The thought would be unthinkable to Lord Lyme, and Niko, well, he had advised against her seeking healing, hadn't he?

She had to escape.

It was no use taking her things. It would only make her escape more obvious. None of her possessions were necessary anyway. Her mind lingered over the adder stone, but she gave it up as another tool Niko had used to control her. How did she know it wasn't for something other than protection? Antoinette did specialize in curses.

She swore under her breath as she raced down the hall. The servants' staircase was nearby, she had seen them go this way often, and if her guess was correct, she was near the edge of the house. The servant exit couldn't be too far from there.

A maid exited one of the rooms and strode past her, not sparing her a second glance. Cassandra's breath caught in her throat, but she rushed on in the opposite direction and hoped the maid wasn't one to talk.

A light glowed over a narrow set of stairs, and she knew she had reached her objective. When she gained the first step, a silhouette from below came up to meet her.

The light sent sparks from his golden eyes.

Her face paled, and she took a step back. Niko held the chalkboard as though he had come back to torment her. He stared at her for a long moment. His gaze seemed to peer into her mind as was his way. His sudden step to the side made her flinch.

Niko sighed and gestured for her to pass with a wave of the chalkboard.

Cassandra hesitated. He wouldn't let her leave; he worked for Lord Lyme. As soon as she moved close, he would stop her.

An unintelligible shout sounded behind her.

Niko closed his eyes tight and took the last step between them. The chalkboard clattered to the floor. He grasped her around the waist with his arm and spun her around.

This time the crash of ocean waves was unwelcome, unbidden. Bile rose in her throat, and she fought against his embrace.

Mr. Sutton strode toward them with a faint smile. He nodded to Niko and shouted to the footmen behind him.

Her body shook against Niko. Her chest tightened as she fought for the chance to breathe. He squeezed her with his hand, but she couldn't tell if it was to keep her in place or comfort her. She craned her neck back to look at him; her face a whisper away from his.

The waves refused to reveal what he thought, or more accurately, what he felt. She saw her reflection in his golden eyes. She stared back at herself. The witch in gold had wide startled eyes and parted lips, a frightened animal on the brink of frantic escape.

Gentle hands stole her away from Niko.

He blinked once, twice.

The footmen pulled her away. The bubbling panic inside her erupted. She kicked at them with all her strength. The man on her right took a slippered foot to his shin and dropped his grip as he stumbled back.

The other footman tightened his hold and secured his other arm around her neck.

A mistake.

She clamped her teeth onto his arm like a mad beast. Blood pooled into her mouth, and he howled. The sound echoed even in her ears.

Another pair of hands grabbed her and then another. Struggling was no longer sensible, but she continued until her body could no longer sustain it. Her muscles went limp, and they carried her with her weight between them.

She fought inwardly with her anxious mind, and her thoughts were left unformed.

The two footmen and Mr. Sutton held her as though she were a child to be put to bed. Indeed, she must appear as a child throwing a tantrum to them. Niko, the man who had stopped her escape, was no longer in sight. No doubt unable to face the result of his actions.

They passed her room. She tried to crane back to look at it to confirm. It was already too far away. She closed her eyes and hoped they would vanish with her sight. "Where are you taking me?"

One of them grunted, but no other response came.

Her mind raced across the possibilities. Nothing made sense. Would they take her to where they kept the other witches? Or worse, would she be interrogated? Of course, the places were likely the same.

She opened her eyes. The last thing she should do was lose herself. She had become accustomed to letting go, to floating through the present to escape. This time, it wouldn't work. She had to know where she was headed and leave mental breadcrumbs along the way so she could break free for good.

They passed through the hallway with little ceremony. They paused in front of a door, and Mr. Sutton released his hold on her to grab a key. Her chest tightened again in anticipation of whatever horror lay behind the door.

Instead of a room of torture, they descended a flight of stairs and then another. They came out into a hallway. This one lacked any connecting passages or doors, and continued straight for as far as she could see by the light of the candles set into the walls.

No windows or artwork accompanied them, only the bare stone walls. They must have gone underground, but the hall traveled beyond the bounds of the house. She had seen nothing to indicate the presence of an expansive basement.

Or a dungeon.

A dungeon was the best way to describe it. The hall met a set of doors on either side, but they walked on until they came to a fork. Mr. Sutton took the right path without hesitation. The scent of fresh straw and stale piss met her nostrils. Dozens of cages like the ones that housed wild animals lined the walls, but the only animals were the witches behind iron bars. She saw only women and guessed the men were down the other passage.

Mr. Sutton stopped at one of the cages where a form huddled against the back. He unlocked the door. It swung open to allow the footmen to drop her inside. She jerked around and slammed into the closing door. Mr. Sutton waggled a finger at her while he secured the lock.

Silence fell as their footsteps faded away. All that remained was the low light offered by the few remaining candles and the company of witches she had helped condemn to cages. She supposed she deserved to join them. She had put herself here as she had put some of them.

She startled when the form in the cage with her stirred and a low murmur came from a dry throat. She studied the witch wrapped in a wool blanket sitting on a bed of straw. When the woman returned her gaze, she recognized the large blue eyes of Georgiana. She appeared as beautiful and unwavering as ever despite her circumstances. Her disheveled hair gave a wild look to her that only heightened her appeal.

A spark brightened behind Georgiana's glowing smile. She patted the place next to her.

Cassandra studied the straw, and then, the witch. Did she have anything else to lose? She steadied herself down on the straw. The pieces poked into the fine silk of her gown.

Georgiana inched over to Cassandra and wrapped an arm around her shoulders without touching her skin. She seemed to instinctively know Cassandra had no desire to experience her abilities. Yet, the witch knew how to bring the most comfort. Even though Cassandra did not aid in Georgiana's capture, she was still the cause of it and needed every ounce of forgiveness.

Neither of them spoke as they sat for a time and stared forward beyond the bars. The room was silent other than the occasional cough or snore. If anyone could escape, they were kept elsewhere.

The other witch squeezed her shoulders once more then forced Cassandra to face her. Georgiana's gaze sized her up. Her smile never left her face. She was a bright light in the dim reality around them.

Georgiana opened her mouth and paused to consider her words. She cleared her throat. "How are you?" She mouthed the words as much as she spoke.

Cassandra's eyes widened. "How am I? I'm fine. You're the one who's been down here." She shook her head. "How are you?"

Georgiana tilted her head and gave a short nod. "Good." She stretched out her legs as if she had awoken from a deep sleep atop a bed of down feathers.

"I wanted to talk to you. Did you know Niko works for his father?"

A giggle echoed from Georgiana's lips. The sound

was almost barbaric in the cage. She nodded to Cassandra, the gesture easier to decipher than any words.

"You knew? Why didn't anyone tell me? He used me, convinced me to stay in Lyme House. He spoke out about his father when all along, he was working with him. The cad handed me over to Mr. Sutton without another thought."

Georgiana frowned and somehow looked pretty doing it. "Hmm." She shook her head.

"No, what?"

"Not right. Niko…no…"

Cassandra scrunched up her nose. "What?"

"No choice," Georgiana repeated.

She made a strangled sound in her throat. "We all have a choice. I made a stupid one by coming here. I see now that it was selfish and cruel. I didn't stop to think about what would happen." She exhaled, releasing her frustration. "But, Niko was aware. He had to know about this place." She gestured with her hands to indicate the large room. "He works with Lord Lyme knowing what the man is."

The side of Georgiana's lip twitched up.

"How can you be amused? You think I'm wrong?"

Georgiana's eyes creased as she smiled. "Yes and no."

"Niko doesn't know about this place?"

The witch shook her golden hair in response.

Cassandra's eyes widened. "But he knows what a horrible man his father is?"

Georgiana didn't answer. Instead, she favored her with her glowing smile. Cassandra wanted to smack the cheerfulness out of her. Nobody had told the woman they were in a cage sitting in straw.

If Georgiana were telling the truth, Niko would search for the witches after Georgiana disappeared. It was the only thing that made sense. Why hadn't he told her? He had let her believe he was his father's faithful servant, the wayward son returned and forgiven. Her heart had broken under his cold behavior, having known nothing but rejection in the past. Surely, he would know that she of all people would understand.

She swallowed hard. Unless, perhaps, he also doubted her loyalties. She had stayed behind even after betraying other witches, and even after Lord Lyme's promise seemed a distant dream. He had stepped aside.

She hadn't trusted him.

Georgiana watched her with a thoughtful cast to her eyes. Gone was the happy smile from before.

"Maybe I've made a mistake." She wanted to bury herself under the straw. "Now, I'm a prisoner." Her hearing was the least of her problems. She didn't know what to think anymore. If she were wrong, she would lose her last chance to apologize. How could he ever forgive her? How could any of them?

"I'm sorry. I've been a horrible witch."

Georgiana rested her head on Cassandra's shoulder as if she was the one needing comfort, but it passed for the witch accepting her apology. Underneath Georgiana's gorgeous exterior, an iron will of strength resided. Even so, Cassandra allowed her to maintain the illusion.

Cassandra spoke into Georgiana's hair. "He came back for you, didn't he? Does he love you?" Her skin turned cold at the possible answers.

Georgiana raised her head and caught Cassandra's

gaze. Her soft brows creased together. "How ridiculous." She spoke as though trying out the words on her tongue for Cassandra's benefit. Her bare hand clasped the skin above Cassandra's gloves.

A sharp cry pierced Cassandra's ears, and she flinched. Georgiana maintained her grip, and the sound settled into the sharp melody of the nightingale's song. She could hear the specific notes of Georgiana with more exposure. Perhaps the same instance had brought her closer to Niko.

She understood why Georgiana had touched her. A better understanding was formed despite her hearing, or rather, the ability offered her an advantage over normal hearing. Georgiana's touch caused her to square her shoulders and toss back her head. She wished she had a mirror to see if the effects were outward as well. Being this alluring would have its advantages.

Georgiana's giggle transformed into full-throated laughter. The emotion was so much more understandable now. It was no wonder Georgiana radiated happiness. The power she wielded was not what one would expect.

The witches sobered, and Georgiana cocked her head. "No. There is no love between us. I can't have love." The bond between them rang with her voice though Cassandra wasn't sure the witch had even spoken.

"You can't have love?" Cassandra wanted to spit out the words like they were poison.

Georgiana nodded.

"The pound of flesh?"

The witch looked wistful.

"Then, why? Why did he come back for you?

Unless I'm mistaken, you can get out of this cage without much effort."

An enthusiastic nod answered her. "It is insignificant."

Cassandra gaped at her. "Then, why stay?"

Their eyes roamed the room together. Some of the witches were there for months, long before Cassandra had even heard of the existence of witches. It made sense that Georgiana wanted to help them, but she couldn't have done it alone. The state of some of the women was questionable, and their numbers were too many. Now that she had discovered their location, she could find a way to help them.

"You're the new inside man?"

Georgiana made a face at her phrasing. "The Florentine did not want to involve you anymore."

"What?"

The witch started to repeat herself, but Cassandra waved her off.

"Why didn't he?"

A short shrug answered her.

She had been right. Niko didn't trust her. She had given him no reason to, but the realization was like a shard of glass opening up her chest. "How did he get Lord Lyme to forgive him? Wasn't Niko responsible for Lord Lyme's legs and his wife's death?" She had to ask while she was getting actual answers. Having a real conversation was refreshing. She wanted more, wanted Georgiana to talk to her until they both slept from exhaustion. The loneliness of her hearing loss hit her full force.

Georgiana bit her lip in thought, doubtless an endearing expression to men. "If you were fighting a war, would you throw away a valuable weapon because you hurt yourself with it? A well-trained dog may bite back, but the years of training and end result are worth the pain."

The concentration and fragmented sentences exhausted Cassandra. The last bit had been the worst. True, she had grasped the meaning behind the sounds, but the work was far worse than she remembered as a hearing woman.

Niko and Lord Lyme were using each other. Like father like son. One wanted all of the witches under his control, while the other wanted witches free and proud in their abilities. When they were tired of each other, it would be catastrophic. Cassandra was stuck in a cage where she could do nothing about it.

"I don't suppose you could get me out of here?"

Georgiana used her free hand to pat Cassandra's. "If you leave now, you'll miss the ball."

Cassandra snorted. "I'll miss the ball locked up in this cage." Was her pretty little head full of air? Who cared about the ball? They should get out of there and find help. The other witches of Scry Cove would know what to do. Then, she would locate Niko and make him tell her about Florence and the cure, even if she had to throttle him to do it.

"The guest of honor won't miss the ball, and neither will I," Georgiana said in a firm voice, like putting her foot down. Cassandra had no doubt Lady Georgiana was accustomed to being obeyed.

"How do you purpose that?"

"My dear, we are part of the entertainment." Like Katrina.

Lord Lyme would parade his witches around the

ball like prized hunting dogs or horseflesh. She didn't want to stick around to be flaunted. It wasn't like she had a demonstrable ability like Katrina or the obvious beauty of Georgiana. She couldn't imagine what Lord Lyme had in mind, but it didn't sound pleasant.

If she stayed, she would be able to help Georgiana free the witches, and she would have the opportunity to confront Niko. She still wasn't sure if she understood him or who was lying at this point. All she knew was that she would have answers.

Chapter 21

Her ball gown rivaled all her other clothes. Not because it was finer or more elaborate, it wasn't. It was a shimmery white like the glimmer off of fresh snow, but it was trimmed in blush ribbons. The hint of color thrilled her more than her escort from the cage.

Some, but not all of the women were taken to rooms in Lyme House to prepare for the ball like they were dishes served with dinner. Cassandra was allowed back in her old room, where Alisa waited for her.

When they realized Lord Lyme reclaimed all of her gloves, it became clear that her dress was more costume than evening attire. This time, her bare skin would allow the guests to touch her, and her contact with other witches would display her abilities like a spectacle at the theatre.

She met up with Georgiana on the way to the ball. They clasped hands as they walked and became a united front in their powers. If it was a spectacle they wanted, it was a spectacle they would give them. The footmen guarding them didn't bother to hide their stares. She wouldn't be surprised if one of them ran into a wall.

The two witches shared a smile.

Niko came around a corner and tripped over his feet when he spotted them. His eyes were wide as he froze in place. The footmen trailed away when they saw him, presumably to take up their duties in the ballroom. They must think Master Niko was a force to be avoided. She quite agreed.

Georgiana let out one of her endearing giggles, and it echoed from Cassandra's lips. Georgiana patted their clasped hands with her free one and led her past Niko. He opened his mouth, ready to speak, but no sound came from him. Cassandra could get used to this.

As much as she wanted Niko to explain himself, she had more pressing worries right now. She would keep her distance from the information and reexamine it later. She wanted to believe Georgiana, but experience told her to remain wary.

The first face she saw when they entered the ballroom was Morwenna. She leaned into Dr. Scott. Her kind face appeared lost in concentration, and although her eyes were closed, she nodded in their direction. The ballroom was full, and nobody seemed to notice the exchange.

Georgiana and Niko moved toward them, forcing Cassandra to do likewise. So much for caution.

Morwenna and Georgiana exchanged whispers with Niko. His eyebrows shot up. The witches argued in frantic gestures. Georgiana must have won out because Niko frowned and nodded.

Dr. Scott, Georgiana, and Morwenna strode away with Morwenna between them for guidance. Cassandra watched after them. Of course, they had left Niko behind to fill her in.

Cassandra tried to look at anything but him. The room was decorated lavishly in wide elaborate fabrics streaming down from the ceiling. Bright Indian silks created an illusion of an otherworldly forest. The result was enchanting, but it made seeing the rest of the room difficult. Even the countless candles, set well away from the flammable decorations, did little to help with visibility.

If it weren't for the numerous footmen, she would expect all the witches to escape. The doors she had seen were double guarded. If the three witches headed out, she couldn't guess where, but she had no doubt Georgiana could handle the men. If only she had taken Cassandra with her.

Niko grasped her arm with a gloved hand, preventing her from following the trio. It had crossed her mind.

She raised her brows in question but accepted his escort. He led her through the fabric jungle, passing witches and guests alike. Katrina's unmistakable voice carried toward her; the entertainment had begun.

Niko gestured to one of the footmen who handed him the chalkboard. Not only was she going to have to perform, but she would also have to converse. Maybe she should have stayed in the cage.

They headed away from Katrina's song, and Cassandra studied him with a frown. His eyes remained forward as they neared the edge of the room. It was an echo of the previous ball, but that was an easier time when so much hadn't come between them, and he was a fellow witch stealing a dance.

A wistfulness overcame her, and she didn't bother to protest when he urged her behind a curtain-like area along the wall. She opened her mouth to speak, but his lips met hers, forcing all thought from her mind.

A roar overcame her senses like a plea for acknowledgment. He released her arm and used his hand to cup her cheek. He pulled his lips away and settled his forehead against hers, whispering something in what sounded like Italian. He sipped a brief taste of her lips again and stepped back, releasing their contact.

The air rushed out of her with the wave.

He kept her gaze, an uncertain smile tugged at his lips.

"Niko, we can't do this." She drew back, hoping she could dislodge the desire coursing through her. "I don't even know who you are anymore. Why would you want me after everything?"

He searched her eyes a moment and held up a hand for her to wait. He brought up the chalkboard and placed it against the wall to write. At least the chalkboard made their privacy complete with no chance they would be overheard.

There has been no time. What I know is this. He gestured between them.

She took the chalkboard from him and rubbed his words out with a fury only skin deep. *I need more. What side are you on?* She handed him back the chalk.

His gaze flew up to the ceiling. He shook his head. He rolled his eyes at her before writing. *Ours. Witches. Especially yours.* He waggled his eyebrows at her.

She jerked back the chalk, breaking it in half, and struggled to write with her small stub. He gripped the larger piece. *How can you work against everyone?*

How can you?

Of course, he had a point, but she wasn't going to allow it.

That's different.

Is it?

She rubbed out the short phrases and wished this

conversation over. The longer they were away, the more likely Lord Lyme would grow suspicious. She still had hopes of helping save the witches, and she couldn't do that locked up.

We need to go. What if someone finds us?

His grin put her on edge. Was this some sort of witch trait she hadn't picked up on? *It won't matter. He already knows I slept with you.*

She dropped her chalk, and it rolled away past the curtain. "You told him?"

He shook his head, his grin never faltering.

If Lord Lyme knew, then the whole household probably knew. A blush burned up her chest and heated her cheeks. Hopefully, she could escape the shame when she went back home. That is if she ever saw home.

"I don't understand. Why were you so cold?"

Before he could answer, a scream erupted somewhere in the room. Niko glanced beyond the curtain and took off. She did her best to follow him, weaving in and out of the fabric, but she lost him. She clutched the chalkboard in her hand then searched the floor for her lost chalk.

The man continued to speak in riddles. She knew he only teased her, but she had had enough of half-truths and hidden passages. Lyme House could burn to the ground for all she cared. As the thought struck her, she spotted the cause of the commotion. One of the witches had set fire to the fabric. The witch shouted at the crowd, eyes blazing as she was led away. The footmen doused the fire in no time. Someone had already foreseen such possibilities.

She fetched up the chalk that had lingered over one

of the trailing streams of silk. When she rose, Georgiana stood beside her.

Cassandra huffed out a breath. "Care to tell me what happened?"

Georgiana cast her gaze around and took the nub of chalk and chalkboard. *I thought Niko would tell you.*

She shrugged.

Georgiana puckered her lips. *Very well. I told them where the witches were held. They went to meet up with Selena and Antoinette.*

Cassandra took the chalk back. *Should we join them?* She handed back the chalk.

No! We are needed here, and we still need to discover this illness. If we leave now, all will be lost. When the time is right, we will join them and release the others.

Cassandra wiped off the board with her palm. *Why not escape before they put us in cages again?*

An exasperated sigh came from Georgiana's lips. *Why give my capabilities away?*

She supposed it made sense, but the thought of returning to the cages made her wish to abandon everything. Lyme House was terrible enough without beds of straw and cramped quarters. At least the cages were mostly clean.

Georgiana tugged on her sleeve to get her attention, showing her the writing on the board. *We are wasting time. You still have a job to do.*

Her friend wove her arm into Cassandra's. The high-pitched squeal in her ears took less time to subside, but the residual ache made her want to rub her head. This time, it was necessary. If they were going to put on a show, they might as well do it right.

Heads turned as they traversed the ballroom, and the fabrics billowed as they passed. It was like walking in a dream. Almost floating, their footsteps made no sound on the marble floor. They must have been a sight, displaying a grace Cassandra knew she didn't possess. It made her wonder if Georgiana held such sway from her abilities or if she possessed skills to compliment her power.

Georgiana led her to Lord Lyme, who sat between Niko and Mr. Sutton. The three men studied the pair of witches. Lord Lyme and Mr. Sutton held their mouths slack. Niko smirked and leaned over to his father, whispering something in his ear.

Lord Lyme's eyes widened. He gave a short nod in reply. He beckoned Mr. Sutton to lean closer to him, and they exchanged a few words. Mr. Sutton glanced at Niko and rose to his feet to do his employer's bidding.

The haughty version of Niko had returned. She wanted nothing better than to flee back to the cage. No sign of the playful, loving Niko was in evidence. Perhaps he had dropped his facade, and this was his real nature.

"Nikolas."

She was brought back with the sound of Lord Lyme's voice. Her erratic deafness unnerved her. His pronunciation differed from the nickname, and it matched the English sounds, throwing Cassandra off guard.

Niko gazed toward his father with a small smile and rose to his feet. He bowed to Georgiana. His bow to Cassandra was flashy, a graceful bending of his well-formed limbs. It reminded her of his naked body strutting about her room. He saw her blush. His wry grin appeared mocking. Her stomach dropped. He offered her his hand, his gloves discarded. Cassandra refused the offering, and Georgiana glared at Niko.

Instead of showing disappointment, he gestured for them to follow. Guests were gathering along the dance floor. The open area was sporadically interrupted by a stream of near-translucent silk. In any other circumstance, she would be mesmerized.

When Niko ushered her to the floor, her heart all but stopped in anticipation. Instead of taking her hand, he introduced her to a dance partner. The pale, red-headed gentleman bowed, and Niko shook his head at her over him. If he already knew the man wasn't a witch, why was she troubling herself? This ball was more theatre than party.

Still, she accepted the man with a kind smile, and they moved off with the other couples. Katrina's voice rang out over the room, and the dancing began. She glided along the silk, wishing for the power of Georgiana's touch.

Then the witch appeared, dancing with another gentleman though her brilliance overshadowed his appearance. She was a distraction, if nothing else. It was no wonder she was placed inside the house. Nobody could do it better.

The song ended, and Niko introduced her to another partner. The greasy man repelled her. She scowled at Niko over the man's bent head. He grinned back and moved off to watch her from the side. Her partner was no witch. She began to doubt there were any hidden among the guests. Otherwise, why not get it over with?

She knew her next two partners, but she was

unable to refuse their requests since she could not plead them off if she would keep dancing. Her feet grew tired, and she was about to ask Niko for a break when she saw her next partner.

She shook her head at Dr. Scott as soon as he offered. Why had he returned? She couldn't pretend he wasn't a witch. She doubted he had the same empath ability as Niko, and he certainly was no Georgiana.

"I must plead exhaustion, sir."

Niko's brows pinched together.

"Truly, maybe Lady Georgiana is free." She hoped both the men would take the hint. She couldn't be a part of Dr. Scott's capture, not after the kindness he had shown her aunt. Her gaze swept toward Lord Lyme, who watched her.

Dr. Scott continued to insist though he didn't speak. He offered her a warm smile that reached his kind, hazel eyes. His gaze told her he knew his decision. All she could do was accept his hand.

He leaned into her unexpectedly, and her hand went to his unclad wrist. The ripple of pain spread through her. She clenched at her stomach to keep herself from upending her last meal. Although she had released him, the pain lanced behind her eyes and echoed in her bones. Whatever his power was, it was nothing like she had experienced before.

As she righted herself, a footman came to escort Dr. Scott away. Niko joined her and brushed a hand along her cheek. The pain dulled enough for her to witness Dr. Scott leave. His steady smile told her he held no anger toward her. He seemed more pleased than concerned with the turn of events. Witches were contrary people.

Her eyes stung and not from the use of her powers. "Care to tell me if you're going to throw any more witches at me?" Why must she bear the weight if Niko was already aware? He could have just told his father himself, but then he would also be revealing his knowledge. Perhaps, Niko was on her side, whatever side that happened to be.

He offered her his hand, and she took it without hesitation. The wariness ached through her bones, and she hadn't the patience to protest. The usual crashing wave came in as a sedate ripple. She didn't know if it was from her exhaustion or his manipulations, but it was a refreshing change from the mental assault.

He beamed at her, not the haughty smile of before, but the wide grin that crinkled his eyes. She glanced toward Lord Lyme, but Niko captured her chin in his hand, moving her gaze to his. The gold in his eyes flashed as he led her to the dance floor.

The musicians took up a waltz, and Katrina accompanied them. The music resonated through her, entwining her movements with his. No doubt a scandalous performance, but Cassandra was consumed. They danced as if by familiarity though she had no formal dance lessons. His powers flowed and ebbed over her in tune with the steps.

It was the way she pictured Georgiana on the floor. A dreamlike state of swirling silk. His eyes captured her gaze like a spell. The other dancers fell away and turned to faceless background noise, leaving them alone to the steady pulse between them.

He moved closer, and his lips brushed her ear as he spoke. The words were like a brush of wind she could not translate, but his tone sent heat between her thighs.

He inched back to meet her gaze. A tide of pleasure radiated from him, making his intentions clear. The man was direct, she'd give him that, but the more she wanted him, the more she doubted her own desire.

She was kindling to him, ready to burst at his touch.

The music tampered off, and she remembered where she was. Men and women gawked at the future Baron and the nobody witch standing far too close. Had they been deaf to the music? Had they not experienced the call of Katrina's voice to abandon all reason? Surely, they had not become enthralled by Niko's magnetism.

Niko stepped away and released his hold on her. It was like dropping out into another world, and witchcraft was nothing more than an illusion.

Then, a sudden round of applause broke out, echoing off the walls to drown out all sound. The guests clapped for them, but she couldn't imagine why. Had they been the only ones listening?

She turned to face Niko to ask him what he thought, but he had disappeared.

Chapter 22

Cassandra spun in place in an attempt to catch a glimpse of the fiery-eyed man who had set her aflame. Men began to surround her and flood her with invitations. She accepted each of them in turn, but her mind had left with her heart moments before.

Her body went through the paces, each step a chore as she scanned the ballroom. Niko was nowhere in sight. Nor did she encounter any other witches that night. Perhaps Lord Lyme had captured everyone not entertaining the guests.

A pang nestled into her chest. If Lord Lyme had tired of his son, Niko could be trapped with the rest of the witches. As powerful as he was, he was fallible. Maybe he had pushed his father too far too soon. If Lord Lyme had learned of their plan to free the witches, she doubted he would excuse Niko's behavior. It wouldn't matter if Niko were his only heir. A man could only handle so much betrayal.

Her mind raced frantically with her dancing feet. Lord Lyme gave her a knowing smile as if they shared a secret. What if his forgiveness were an act? Another ploy to get his son close where he could strike the hardest. His hatred of witches ran deep, how could he ever forgive the one witch who took his wife and his ability to walk?

She spotted Georgiana sipping lemonade on the

edge of the dance floor. One of the guests appeared to plead with her for a dance. Several of the female guests stared at her with open hostility. Georgiana gave her a calm look, which clouded Cassandra with doubt. The witches of Scry Cove had a plan, and it didn't include her. Niko had made sure of that.

She pushed her thoughts aside and set to the task given her. After all, Lord Lyme watched, and she needed to get out of there alive. If they wanted her help, she would gladly give it, but in the meantime, she had to keep her head above the water.

Several bone-aching hours later, Cassandra dragged herself after the pair of footmen assigned to her. To her surprise, they brought her back to her room. She said nothing as they allowed her entry, in case they had made a mistake. Who was she to correct them?

She closed the door behind her and rested against the surface. The sigh that rushed from her lips spoke of her mental and physical exhaustion. The room was crowded in darkness. She widened her arms, searching out the mantle for a light. She managed to light a candle, only burning herself twice.

The room came to life in shadowed colors, and she nearly dropped the candle when she noticed a form resting on her bed.

She shook her head at the golden-eyed witch lounging on her bed. "By all means, make yourself comfortable." He had discarded his coat and waistcoat. His bare feet rested against the blankets. She had worried he was shivering over a bed of straw.

He patted the bedside next to him as if it was his bed and not hers. He tapped his stub of chalk against the board she had thought lost in the ballroom. If she had the energy, she would throw something at him, something heavy and sharp like Mist. The cat lay curled up on the windowsill and seemed oblivious to his surroundings. She would never make that mistake. Mist and Niko shared an innate knowledge of their environment.

She did as he requested if only to rest her aching feet, or so she told herself. "If you're planning to speak in riddles, I suggest you do it elsewhere. My mind is already dead tired with worry. I'd rather not torture myself further."

His lips quirked up, and he tapped the board again. She bent toward it with her candle, and he wrote across the surface by the light. *I am sorry. We were not trying to be deceptive, but we needed someone in the men's area. I could not do it, or I would have taken his place. There was no time to tell you. You have shown you are a brave woman standing up to Lyme, and I won't shut you out again.*

She set the candle down on the bedside table. "Then why did you leave? Surely, Lord Lyme wanted you to look for other witches."

He wiped the board clean. *He knew the rest of the party was safe. I had other matters to attend to.*

"You're being vague. Give me straight answers or jump out the window." She rubbed at her temples, hoping to dispel some of her exhaustion.

He slipped the board in front of her. *The host refuses to walk the rounds, so I have to do it for him.*

She squinted at him. "What do you mean? That isn't funny."

He waved the chalkboard like he would hit her with it. *The old bastard can walk. He has convinced himself otherwise. Thinks I did something to him. The doctors can find nothing wrong with him.*

"He's mad at you for something that didn't even happen?"

He wiped away the board in an uncharacteristic urgency to reply. *No. He is right to be angry. It is because of me that Mama is dead.*

Cassandra searched his face for more answers. "That can't be right. I haven't known you very long, but I don't think you are the type to kill your mother. Your father is a scoundrel, and yet, he still lives."

I appreciate your faith in me, but I can assure you I am responsible.

As much as she wanted answers, she wouldn't argue the point. She couldn't bring herself to ask what he meant.

He seemed to perceive her curiosity and, for once, obliged her. *When I came into my abilities, my mother was closest to me. The emotions were too much for her.*

Without thought, she rested her hand on his leg to comfort him. He gave no indication he noticed the action. "What happened?" Her voice dropped to a whisper.

She drowned away her thoughts with opium.

Cassandra's gaze jumped to the two bottles resting on her bedside. Two distinct liquids with similar effects, to help her forget. Her gaze shifted to Niko, but his focus was on the bottles. A deep frown wrinkled his brow as he took up the brown liquid. He let out a weary sigh and set it back down without comment.

He clasped the bottle from the atrium. He studied the contents. He held it up before Cassandra and shook it lightly in question.

"I don't know what it is. I found it in the atrium where Lord Lyme does his research."

He raised a brow in encouragement. She filled him in about what she and Alisa had discovered. She told him about her suspicions of being drugged, and her attempts to stay away from the substance. He listened without interrupting, his face expressionless.

"One thing we don't understand is why I find it so intoxicating, but Alisa can't stand a whiff of it."

He opened the bottle and sniffed. His eyes snapped wide, and it seemed he couldn't close the bottle fast enough. The drug was back on the table the next moment like it had burned him.

"Then, you don't like it either?" She squinted her eyes. "Maybe there's something wrong with me."

He scribbled over the chalkboard, his offense still plain on his thinned lips. *No, the aroma is like nothing else. Amazing. Delicious.*

"Then, what's wrong?"

Nothing should have such an effect. From what you are telling me, this is powerful stuff. I do not take such chances.

The fearless witch didn't take chances. It was like a bad joke. He had warned her before, but she thought he had been overcautious then. Now, knowing what she did about his mother, his choices seemed reasonable.

"Niko, listen. I'm sorry about the drugs. I can't seem to help myself. It's like the way men flock to Georgiana. It's a need like breathing air. I can't seem to shake myself of it. It isn't working the same as it was, I already need more." Her eyes went to the bottle, only a quarter of it remained. "I don't know what I will do when I run out."

She sensed his eyes on her, weighing her words. At first, she didn't realize he had spoken. His voice was quiet, and the sound could have been the rustle of fabric or the wind outside. He spoke again, and she was sure this time.

She met his gaze, the gold illuminated by the candlelight, or was it simply him?

He spoke louder. "Throw it out." This time she caught the fragments and pieced them together with the previous sentence.

"Why don't you?" Her hands trembled in her lap.

He shook his head and gestured toward the bottle, not bothering to hand it to her.

"What if I don't want to?"

His hand went to the chalk, but she caught his wrist. The rush slammed her eyes shut, but she pushed on. "Please, talk to me. I want to hear you."

He stilled under her grasp, and his pulse pounded under her fingers. She blinked open her eyes, and he gripped her hand. Warmth crept up her arm with calm patience behind it.

He cleared his throat, maybe he meant to prepare her, but it got her attention all the same. Still, she couldn't puzzle out his words, and he repeated himself.

Her cheeks burned with embarrassment. She had asked this impossible task of him, and still, his tireless persistence drifted through their clasped hands. He squeezed her hand and spoke again. His intonations changed as he switched up his words. Finally, she grasped them.

"It's the only way."

A bubble of laughter burst from her throat. She was so relieved to understand that she almost forgot what they were discussing. "Yes, yes." She laughed again and let out a breath. She grew calm, her face sobering.

"I don't know if I can." She ran her free hand over her skirts. "You see, it calms me. I'm afraid of what will happen. I can't control my mind."

He captured her chin in his palm. "I will be here." He seemed to take care with his words, working through his accent. He repeated himself to be sure she understood him.

"Don't be silly. You can't possibly be with me all the time. We have to save the witches and find out what's killing everyone. No empty promises."

He gave a short nod and tried again. This time, her nerves sent her mind wandering. She didn't catch everything.

"I'm sorry. Something about now?"

His mouth twitched up. "Now." He leaned into her, taking her lips with his.

The kiss sent a tingling sensation straight from her lips to her core. He cradled her head in his hand, his tongue tasting her as he held her firm. She melted into him, opening up to the gateway of his emotions. A teasing arousal fluttered through her.

He pulled back, his lips parted.

Her eyes focused on his soft mouth and the ache for more.

"Now."

She blinked as those tantalizing lips formed the word. "Now?" A whoosh of air burst from her chest.

His lips widened into an open-mouthed grin. "Now."

She made a strangled sound and dropped to her feet. Pushing off the momentum of their kiss, she plucked up the offending bottle from the table and strode to the window. She glanced back at Niko. He nodded. Without another thought, she upended the bottle, draining the liquid onto the ground below. She tossed the empty container after it.

The weight she expected to lift had crashed down on her shoulders, and she dropped down next to Niko again. She rested her head in her hands and hoped the world would disappear around her.

The bed jostled under her, and Niko's hands settled on her shoulders.

She shrugged him off. "No. How do I know the difference between you and your abilities?" Niko was a drug, and she wanted to curl up inside of him.

The bed moved again, and Niko knelt in front of her. She gave him a faint smile, but he didn't return it.

"Cara."

"I'm sorry, what?"

He reached for her chin, and she dodged away. "There is no difference."

She shook her head. Either she wasn't hearing him or his English was worse than she thought. "What do you mean?"

"The same. My powers and me. Same."

"But when we don't touch, it isn't the same." She knew her defense was weak before she even uttered a word. She had experienced him using his powers without touch. He could be using a more subtle effect on her now.

He gave her a level look, and she fought to still her gaze. A shiver ran up her spine, and her voice worked on its own. "I don't know anymore."

Accepting Niko as a witch meant accepting her

own abilities. She wasn't prepared to do that. What she wouldn't give to hear in complete sentences, to understand his pretty words, and learn his language. She needed to be as she was and not as she had become.

He said something while she was lost in thought. He had to repeat himself.

"Please?"

She squinted her eyes in confusion. "Please, what? You know, maybe we should just get the chalkboard. I'm being ridiculous."

Without warning, his hand took hers. The torrent rushed inside her, and the comfort of his warm skin was a second thought. She could not hear him through the waves. He mouthed the word again. "Please."

She nodded in understanding, and he nodded back.

He spoke again. "…you."

Her eyes filled with tears, but she waited for him to continue.

He searched her face and settled his other hand on her cheek as if he meant to catch any falling tears.

She blinked away the cloudiness and gasped as a blanket cocooned her like bathing in warm honey. He grinned as her limbs seemed to melt beneath her. He held her steady to prevent her from tipping forward.

"This is nice."

A slow smile and nod answered her.

She leaned back and propped herself on her hands. "What were you saying?" The tension had exited her muscles, and she wanted to rest, but Niko knelt before her, and she couldn't think of a better time to get answers.

"Let me show you. I am my abilities."

She wondered if maybe she had imagined his words or if her relaxed state had helped her understand. Even so, she was curious about what he might mean. "All right, show me."

He gave no signs of relief at finally being heard. Instead, he leaned forward and nuzzled her skirts. She giggled at the strange gesture, and he beamed up at her with a wide grin.

His hands moved to her slippers, and he gently tugged them off. His fingers slid over her stockings until he reached the top.

Her breath caught in her throat, where her heart beat in frantic hiccups.

He paused, cocking his head, and his grin reached his golden eyes. He rolled her stocking down with exaggerated slowness. He did the same to the other side.

"Niko."

He raised his brows.

"If you're going to spend all night undressing me, we'll have no time for the important part."

He threw his head back and laughed. The sound became muffled as he tossed her skirts over his head. The heat of his breath tickled her thigh, and his hand nudged her legs apart. She fell back onto the bed.

His fingertips brushed between her legs, and she gasped, attempting to regain her seat. He pushed her back and patted her thigh, telling her to leave well enough alone.

"Niko, I hardly think…"

He stroked the sensitive skin, and her eyes went back. The rolling waves pooled through her, consuming her. All at once, his circling fingers became all she knew as he teased and glided along her center.

His lips closed on her peak. She arched to meet him. The heat of his arousal from her reaction rippled over her, bringing her higher. A low moan rewarded his efforts, and they ignited together in blazing heat.

Her pleasure mounted until she no longer knew her name, nor cared. Her head thrashed to the side as she grasped his head, begging for her release from the torment wielded by his tongue.

When she thought she would burst, he pulled away, leaving her frantic and gasping for more. He lifted her skirts and favored her with his wicked grin. She reached out to him, but he only shook his head and gained his feet.

She whimpered and fell back to stare at the ceiling. If he meant to hold out on her, she wished he'd leave so she could finish on her own. Before she could complete the thought, a naked Niko crawled beside her.

He brandished a knife. She flinched back, but too late as he dipped the blade along the fabric covering her chest. Without explanation, he ripped the garment in clean tears, the meticulous tailor through and through.

"Sir, there are less harmful ways of removing a woman's clothes. At least, you could have given me some warning."

The glint in his eyes told her his method was more enjoyable. He tore away the layers of the now useless garments, unpeeling her remaining defenses. He threw them over his head to land unceremoniously on the floor. The blade clattered along with them.

"Aren't you concerned you might hit Mist?"

He snorted. The cat either had nine lives, or he dodged harm like a trained fighter. Probably both.

He hesitated above her, his eyes devouring her skin.

"What are you waiting for?" She rocked her leg back and forth, widening and closing her legs.

A growl rumbled from his throat, loud enough to send shivers along her skin. He nestled between her legs and propped himself on his arms as his lips possessed hers. His kiss was hungry, augmented with the roar of his emotions.

She answered his call, deepening their kiss in desperation. He pushed his way inside her. She nearly burst from pleasure. She hugged her legs around his hips. They rocked together. They were twined in body and mind, joined in the throes and chaos of passion.

He sank his teeth into her neck, sending her over the edge.

She convulsed around him as he thrust. He refused to release his hold on her neck. He claimed her, possessed her, and with a final thrust, he marked her as he spent himself deep inside her, bringing her back to ecstasy once again.

Chapter 23

Niko collapsed beside her, his eyes closed, and his breathing heavy. Cassandra panted next to him, her body melted into the mattress. Her hair tangled beneath her head. The adder stone swung over their heads like an aftershock.

The pendulum swing of the stone captivated her. Niko opened his eyes and followed her gaze. A strangled sound came from his throat. He rolled off the bed. He paced when his feet hit the floor.

"Whatever is the matter?" She rose on her elbows to watch his quick steps.

He gestured to the stone and started rambling, whether it was in English or Italian, she couldn't say.

"Please, Niko. You aren't making sense."

He stilled and took a measured breath as if to calm himself, but when he glanced back at Cassandra, he renewed his pacing. His face paled, and his rambling continued in a steady stream.

"Have you lost your mind?" As much as she enjoyed his nude form on display, he needed to put something on and leave before someone saw him.

He raised a hand to silence her. She dropped back on the pillows. If he insisted on this insanity, she would at least get some rest. If he would just stop talking for five minutes, she would be dead asleep in no time.

She started to doze anyway. The sound of his voice

became a lullaby for her rest. She shook awake when he scooted next to her. She squinted open her eyes, hating the light of the candle in her face. The adder stone swung anew with his abrupt movements.

"Do get the light out of my face. What's this about?" She shielded her eyes, and he brandished the chalkboard at her in question.

"Fine. I'm too tired to argue the point, and I'd imagine something has you too worked up to manage basic speech." She smirked and rolled to face him.

He set the candle back down and wrote, stopping now and then to peer at the adder stone. *I apologize for the board. It will help me think before I speak. Why is the stone there? Haven't you been carrying it?*

He wrote the message with careful attention to his letters, but the strokes were dark from pressing hard on the chalk. She read the note a second time, unable to understand what he wanted.

"I did carry the stone, but I stopped. I was too angry with you to keep it around. Besides, I thought it would be more useful in my room while I slept. Isn't it for protection? I doubt anyone would harm me openly at Lyme House." She bit her lip to keep the words from coming.

He gritted his teeth. *Why there?* He pointed at the headboard.

She shrugged. "It was convenient."

His hand rubbed out the chalk. His mouth opened and closed as if he might speak. Instead, he wrote. *Was it there when you were locked away with the other witches?*

"Of course, I didn't have it on me."

He covered his face with his hand, and chalk

powder streaked over his skin. She touched him lightly on the shoulder but jerked her hand back. His raw anger burned through her and tugged at her heart. What had she done now?

His hand fell away. He wrote with pinched brows. His firm hold on his anger was fading fast. *Mr. Sutton personally cleaned out your room. I did not see the stone for lack of light, but he certainly did.*

"What does it matter? It's just a rock." She doubted it worked at all anyway, but to be fair, she hadn't been harmed while it was present.

He glared at her over the board. *It is not just a rock, and it is not just for protection. It is used for fertility as well. I had no idea you would put it over your bed. If Mr. Sutton knows, then my father knows.*

All she could do was stare while Niko detailed her stupidity. Fertility stone? Why hadn't anyone warned her? Of course, she had known there was a chance of her conceiving, and she didn't need to make it any easier.

I don't think you quite understand. I asked that you have your room. They knew what I wanted. Still, they left the stone. They must have known I would see it.

"But why?" Her voice sputtered like his rambling from before. "Does everyone know about these rocks?"

He wiped the board with care, but his jaw was clenched. *Around Scry Cove, they do. I don't know why. I mean to find out what my father intends.*

Setting the board to the side, he rushed to dress and nearly tripped on his pants. She watched his quick movements, her eyes growing in alarm.

"This is silly. It's just a rock with an interesting hole. I'm sure nothing will come of it. Never you mind."

He shook his head while he buttoned his shirt in a crooked manner. She would have laughed if she wasn't so concerned.

Her voice quivered as she spoke. "I'm sorry. I didn't know. You know I would never do such a thing. You couldn't possibly want to be pinned down by a girl like me."

His hands froze. He turned on her with wide eyes. He strode over to the bed and bent down, his lips caressing hers.

Her skin buzzed with the thrill of him. His soul-shattering power thrashed through her veins. The anger remained, but it seemed blurred with confusion and concern. The emotions were so tangled she couldn't be sure. Anger wasn't a simple emotion to decipher.

He licked the bottom of her lip as the kiss ended. His eyes flared as he watched her face transform with the emotions she knew he already read. A slow smile played on his lips. He dipped down again and pecked her on the tip of her nose.

He yanked the adder stone off the bed—the cord holding it snapped without any effort. Disheveled and wild, he dashed out the door to find whatever answers the dark hours held. She doubted anyone was awake.

Cassandra stared after him in hopes of his swift return. Her careless behavior may have ruined her life though she knew her parents would accept her decision but dreaded facing her neighbors. It wasn't too late for her to take something to prevent a baby, but she couldn't bring herself to consider the possibility.

Her father once treated a young woman pregnant out of marriage. Some quack doctor had given her a remedy from his personal recipe. The baby died prematurely. If it hadn't been for Cassandra's father, the woman would have passed with it. Her father had said the quack had given the woman poison. The woman's parents believed she would be out of her misery. After all, a dead woman could have her disgrace covered up.

Cassandra swore to herself she would never take that path. Perhaps her family could put her away where nobody would know her. When she came back home, she could fabricate a story about a dead husband who fought against Napoleon.

The time inched by, and still, Niko did not return. Sleep was impossible when the sun began to work its brutal light through the heavy curtains. She might as well find her answers. Alisa would see to her waking anyway.

Cassandra rubbed at her heavy eyelids. Was it too late to try more of that delicious drug? It was all she had left now that the bottle from Antoinette was gone. She sighed and threw herself to her feet. It wouldn't do for her to be muddled right now. No good could come of it. With that thought, she poured out the container onto the ground below her room. Niko had the way of it, better not to flirt with temptation.

A quarter-hour passed before Alisa came to help her dress. Lord Lyme summoned her once again. This time, a footman escorted her to the library, where he worked at his desk. She was offered tea but declined, choosing a clear head over the drug.

She read his understanding in his wry smile and wondered how much the man hid from her. How many of her secrets were not actually secret. "You wished to see me, my lord?" She attempted to break his silence.

He held up a hand and continued writing, sipping his coffee in a leisurely fashion. She suppressed the urge to tap her foot. Her gaze wandered over his desk. The adder stone rested on the surface. So, Niko had been to his father.

Her stomach lurched in distress, and she clasped her hands together to prevent them from shaking. If he had already confronted his father, why hadn't he returned to her? Her past fear of his capture resurfaced, but the possibility seemed remote. He was more use to everyone out of a cage, and she doubted he would allow himself to be locked up.

Had he at last abandoned her? She remembered the sweet kiss he gave her when he left, was he saying a final goodbye? She swallowed back her fears. Her thoughts were becoming their own, better to stop this madness now. Niko always came back.

At last, Lord Lyme set aside his quill and waited a moment for the ink to settle. The smeared ink had never bothered him in the past. Must he draw out her torture? He sipped his coffee and gave her a wide grin, not unlike Niko's playful smile, but his was full of bared teeth.

He said something. She didn't catch a word of the quick phrase. His smirk told her he knew she hadn't understood him, but she refused to ask and give him pleasure in her suffering. His face fell, and he handed her the page he had written on. *Miss Poole, It has come to my attention that you have lured my son to your bed on more than one occasion. I had not taken you for a fortune hunter, but alas, I was wrong.*

Fortune hunter? The thought had never crossed her

mind. She knew the Moore family was well off, but it had never mattered to her.

Niko has agreed to cease all connections with you after you have conspired to trap him into bearing his child.

She reread the sentence until the meaning became clear. Niko believed she would use the adder stone against him? He seemed to accept her explanation before. She wished she had a way to contact him and learn the truth. She forced herself to read on.

If you perform well for the rest of the house party, you will travel to Florence, where you can give birth in secret. You will be cured after the child is born, and I will take custody of the child.

Her heart slammed into her throat. She stared down at the angular slope of his letters, not wanting to meet his eyes. "What if I refuse to participate in the house party?"

He remained silent, and she raised her gaze to his face. His grin had returned. He drew a line along his neck with his thumb. He would accept nothing but complete cooperation. Any deviation from his plans would endanger her and her possible child. He would take her child.

No child of hers would be raised by this madman and used for his or her power.

"No." Her voice came out sure, but her insides tangled. She tried again. "You will never have my child." Her child. A shiver ran up her spine. She had no idea if the adder stone worked, but she wouldn't let this man think he controlled her body.

He cocked his head and made a gesture to Mr. Sutton, who had entered the room without her hearing.

Mr. Sutton brought in her chalkboard. He had been in her things while she was here. She itched as if she were dirty. Another violation. To be fair, she preferred the chalkboard to the smeared ink. Everyone had lost patience with her hearing.

Lord Lyme passed the board to her. *You have no choice.*

"There's always a choice." She folded her arms across her chest.

If you want your cure and value your life, you will do as I say. He wrote under his last message.

"Damn my cure and damn you."

Lord Lyme stared at her a moment and took back the board. *You cannot refuse if you cannot leave.*

She knew he would say something to that effect. Her freedom had always been in question. "How do you know I won't spread the illness to you? From what I understand, people I come in contact with keep catching the disease." She grasped at bare threads, but what choice did she have?

He laughed, the sound resounding across the library walls. *Because Miss Poole, you cannot get the disease.*

"What do you mean?"

He set his lips into a twisted sneer. *You are stupider than I thought. You are barely fit to hold my grandchild. It will not kill a witch. Nor will it kill anyone I do not wish to die.*

The color drained from her face. "I don't understand. What did you do?"

My dear wife found solace in common toad venom. It worked like a charm, but she needed more and more over time. She would harvest and drink it in astonishing quantities. One day, a group of footmen became drunk and dared one of them to drink the venom. It wasn't long before he died.

Her jaw slackened, still not understanding. She had heard of people licking toads but never anyone dying.

When my wife passed, I caught my two children drinking the venom with no ill effects besides exhaustion and a belly ache. It seems the stuff is rather addictive and irresistible to witches. Common toad venom requires too much to be an effective weapon. It doesn't kill witches. Months ago, I found a way to concentrate it and used it to test suspected witches. You can see the flaw. I found witches, but most of the people died. Then you came around.

A flare of anger lanced her breast. "Aunt Louise was no witch. When I came here, you had me to rule people out. Why would you kill people needlessly?"

Lord Lyme sighed and wiped the board with little enthusiasm. *By then, it was already considered a contagious illness going around. Nobody knew what was going on. The venom was a perfect weapon.*

Her voice dropped to a whisper. "Why Louise?"

Do you think your aunt would let you come here and be in my employ? Your parents would never allow it.

It was as though the floor had fallen out from under her. She grasped onto a chair to prevent herself from falling. "My parents. Did you even write to them? Did they receive my letters?"

He shook his head.

Her parents would be searching for her. What had they thought when the body of her aunt had arrived? Or had it arrived at all? She wasn't sure she wanted to know. She couldn't do anything about it now.

"You can't watch me every minute. Sooner or later, I will escape or slit my wrists."

Both men's mouths hung open. Lord Lyme finally blinked and wrote on the board with hesitant motions. *You would end your own life to prevent me from giving your child a better life?*

Of course, he believed life with him would be better than living with a meager apothecary's family. The idea had occurred to her, but she doubted he cared one bit for the wellbeing of her child. This was about power. Any child parented by her, and Niko would be a powerful witch, and she would die before seeing Lord Lyme mold a witch to his purposes.

She raised her chin. "Hell would be a pleasure garden compared to living in a world with you in it." She had sealed her fate.

Chapter 24

Cassandra was escorted out of the library without further explanation. Lord Lyme returned to his work as if she was of no consequence, but the hard set of his jaw said otherwise. Mr. Sutton clamped down on her arm and jerked her from the room.

He brought her to the door leading down to the underground cages and directed a glare at her, an unspoken command to stay put so he may unlock the door. This could be her only chance to escape. Yet, she couldn't bring herself to care. If she somehow made the door and found her way into town, she would still have to get home. Once there, they would find her, but she would be endangering her family. She had nowhere to run.

He nudged her to descend the stairs, and her balance teetered as she caught the railing. She knew then she didn't want to die. If a child grew inside her, she wanted it to thrive. Each step underground hardened her resolve. She would not let Lord Lyme destroy her. Already she had been foolish enough to allow him to prey on her when she was weakest. Now, she had someone else to consider.

Her inner strength faltered when they reached the cages, and he set her in a separate cage all to herself. She hadn't realized she had counted on seeing Georgiana until the witch was nowhere in sight. The cages were cast in shadow. She couldn't see anyone she recognized.

Mr. Sutton grunted as he walked away, taking the brightest light with him. The scant light from the wall sconces made a faint outline of her chamber pot and straw bed bunched against the bars. She pushed around the straw and hoped it was still fresh enough not to contain vermin. She wasn't sure she could handle the possibility.

Best not to think about it.

Instead, she plagued herself with thoughts of Niko. She pictured him now sipping brandy on the terrace, a contented smile on his face. Nobody would find fault in the baron's golden child, and if they did, he could manipulate them to change their ways.

She no longer knew what was true with him. Her chest ached when she thought of the night they spent together. Had any of it been real?

Her raw confusion overwhelmed her senses, and time had no meaning underground. She sat in blurred stillness, nothing moved, but her mind played games with her. There was no sense to make out of the darkness.

After a time, she attempted to sleep, but the straw poked into her skin, and her neck cramped on the hard surface. For once, she didn't wish for the comfort of laudanum. Her stomach churned in disgust at the memory of her cravings for toad venom.

All the times she had sipped tea or feasted on sweets, she ingested the very poison that killed her aunt. Doctors and apothecaries studied and searched the countryside for a cure. The answer had been at their feet the entire time. A mad baron out to find witches had taken innocent lives instead.

The witches floated as everyone else drowned.

A loud sob ripped her from her doze, followed by a mind-numbing screech. Silhouettes gathered around one of the cages. Quick, jerking movements interrupted the otherwise still room. A thud slammed into the floor. The blow startled Cassandra to her feet.

Other witches had risen, and they stared between the cages hoping someone held the answers. A startled cry issued from the other side of the room and all turned toward the sound. Someone forced the witches from their cages. By the sound of it, this was no heroic rescue.

Lord Lyme had reached some juncture. After months of gathering witches, he moved his plans forward. Perhaps he had tired of them, or her actions had forced him to rid himself of them. Whatever his reasons, they were being moved one by one.

The cages steadily emptied. Some struggled while others walked out, their postures forlorn. The feeble were carried between men, raising protests among some of the witches. She couldn't understand their shouting calls, but their tone was hair-raising fury.

Two men stopped outside of her cell, and she recognized them as footmen who had taken turns guarding her door. One of them carried a lantern while the other a strange garment. Their wary eyes took her in as they unlocked the door.

To her knowledge, none of the witches had succeeded in escaping. She opted to reserve her strength. She lifted her arms, palms up, and waited for whatever they planned for her.

The man with the lantern nodded, and the man with

the garment advanced on her. The garment proved to be a strange backward shirt that fastened in the back, pinning her arms in place. It would prevent her from touching anyone. An interesting idea but not a sound one. Even she was unsure of her range.

They shackled her ankles and connected the garment to iron chains. She couldn't help but shake her head. Iron had never repelled or restricted her before. The constrictive jacket was more than enough to keep her from escaping.

Naturally, she tripped all over her bindings, and their advancement from the cage came in slow, measured steps. This time, they brought her around to the other side of the room. On her way out, she spotted Katrina, who avoided her eyes.

The man with the lantern unlocked a door set into the far wall, and the light illuminated steps beyond the door. She took a step and raised her leg as high as she could, but the chain proved too short. She toppled backward into the man behind her.

The man bent before her and slammed his shoulder into her side as he tossed her headfirst across his back. The startled cry she made ended in a jolt as the breath was knocked from her.

The footman reeked of old sweat and tobacco. She wrinkled her nose as she thumped against his back with each step.

He shifted her as they reached a landing and swatted her backside. If she could move, she would kick him. For now, she settled for slamming her chains into his front. What she hoped was his groin.

He bent forward with a jolt, his hands like claws in her sides. He raised a hand to hit her again, but his companion shouted something back to them. Her footman muttered under his breath as he renewed their ascent.

They exited a door at the top of the stairs, and sunlight blasted Cassandra in the face. After the time spent underground in the weak light, the faint sun on the eastern horizon overwhelmed her. She blinked in rapid squeezes and allowed her vision to adjust to her surroundings.

The blurry forms of hedges met her gaze. She continued to bob against the footman as the statue of Artemis rose above her. The cages were under the maze. She wanted to slap herself for not figuring it out sooner.

It all came down to the runes. She doubted even when Lyme House was built that runes were familiar among the common people or any written language for that matter. What better way to mark passages than by using a secret language.

The footmen exited the maze without hesitation as if they had walked the trails dozens of times and no doubt carrying witches. Lord Lyme's loyal followers. How many did they number? Her stomach rose in a panic. It seemed she was about to find out.

Rows of people lined up across the green. Every guest in the house and probably some of the villagers. At least fifty people stood facing a cluster of witches kneeling on the ground.

She spotted Georgiana and Katrina among the women. Dr. Scott knelt with the men, along with the other witches she had identified. Each of the witches was restrained according to their abilities. Both Georgiana and Katrina were gagged and bound. Some of them were blindfolded while one unlucky witch had a thick chain around his neck.

The footmen brought her forward and tossed her in front of Lord Lyme. The baron lounged in a cushioned chair underneath an open tent. Beside him sat a long table of refreshments as though the guests were having a picnic.

Cassandra squinted up at him, the rising sun blocking much of her vision. Unfortunately, it did nothing to hide the man standing beside Lord Lyme. Niko avoided her gaze, and his expression was blank. The rest of the party flanked the tent, looking on in curiosity.

A shout went up from behind her, but she couldn't turn to see the commotion. Mr. Barrett was thrown down beside her. He struggled to regain his feet and failed when Mr. Sutton shattered Mr. Barrett's bad knee with a calculated kick.

A scream ripped from Mr. Barrett's throat. The sound pounded through Cassandra's head. He whimpered, and tears glistened in his eyes. She struggled to find the words to comfort him. Her throat clenched shut as her tears were forced to the surface. She beat them back. It wouldn't do for them to see her pain.

Lord Lyme raised his voice above the din of the crowd. Although it was the loudest sound in the area, she could not separate his words from the rustle of clothes, the distant call of birds, or the occasional cough among the bystanders.

Mr. Sutton raised a full glass above his head, and a ray of light hit the surface to show it to the assembled parties. He leaned down in front of her and pushed the glass between her lips. The unmistakable scent of toad venom made her mouth water. She thrashed her head from side to side.

The footman who had carried her braced her head in place. Mr. Sutton forced her lips apart. As the first drop hit her tongue, she relaxed her mouth and drank in eager gulps. He took away the glass when she had downed half of its contents, and she slumped forward, moaning at the loss.

Her gaze trailed the glass as her vision grew hazy. Mr. Sutton stood before Mr. Barrett. The fight all but gone from her former fiancé, he gave a hopeless whimper of protest.

"Please." Cassandra's voice came out unsteady. She swallowed, summoning her strength. "Please, I need more." It was all she could think of to spare Mr. Barrett from the venom. They wanted an addicted witch. She would give them one.

Laughter erupted across the lawn. Lord Lyme grinned down at her. She caught Niko's gaze and saw the spark ignite there. His fists clenched at his sides, where only she could see.

Mr. Sutton moved back to her. She made a show of struggling toward him. The footman pulled her back against him, her head snapping back and forth. Her vision refocused in time to see Niko take a step forward, but he restrained himself.

The glass hovered over her head. This time, the cry from her lips was real. Tears streamed down her face at the pain in her head. The world was no longer stable, the ground tilted to and fro. She would have fallen if it weren't for the grip on her shoulders.

Lord Lyme spoke again. She heard the amusement

in his voice. She closed her eyes against the sound, and the growing oblivion enveloping her. When she opened her eyes again, Mr. Barrett was curled on his side, his eyes wide and lazy. A stream of mucus escaped the side of his mouth. He stopped moving not long after. The once full glass of venom was now empty in Mr. Sutton's hand.

Cassandra's gaze fixed on Mr. Barrett's glassy eyes as Lord Lyme gave another speech. Something about this sick demonstration. Mr. Sutton towered over her, holding a new glass of venom. She shook her head at the man, but he ignored her refusal.

She clamped her lips shut. Her compliance would only entertain the guests further now. Drinking more of the venom wouldn't save Mr. Barrett or any of the witches. She needed to focus. Her mind was foggy enough as it was.

Her mouth was forced open, and the footman held her jaw tight as they pried open her lips. She screamed as loud as she was able. Her eyes stung with tears. She had never had so much of the venom. What if it killed her like Mr. Barrett? Or worse, what if her mind never recovered?

Her gaze darted to Niko, a silent plea for assistance. His face was pale, and when their eyes met, he was tense like a coiled spring ready to jump into action at any moment. He leaned down to whisper to his father. His movements were frantic. His lips worked in rapid speech.

Lord Lyme narrowed his eyes at Niko, his displeasure at his son shone in every crease of his frown. He shook his head and waved for Mr. Sutton to continue.

Mr. Sutton complied with a thin smile and tipped the glass to her lips. She jerked an inch, but only a taste landed on her tongue before the glass was knocked from her lips. The footman released his grip on her. Mr. Sutton was thrust to the ground.

Niko's wide defensive stance shielded her from the men. He tremored with equal parts rage and fear that clouded the space between them. The same fear had overcome her in the hallway when Mr. Sutton came to take her away. Niko was afraid, and she experienced every drop of his panic without any contact. It was a wonder he hadn't bolted.

Lord Lyme spoke in an angry snarl. She caught the word whore. Maybe she heard it because she expected it from him, or perhaps because the sound shocked her. It was plain Lord Lyme denounced her, but if what he had told her was true, he wouldn't have to.

A trickle of hope grew in her chest. Niko cared enough to defend her life, but did he care enough to defend her character?

If Cassandra's arms were free, Niko was close enough to touch. His voice fell, and she barely recognized that he spoke. It took her a moment to realize he was using Italian, and she wouldn't have understood him if she could hear clearly.

Lord Lyme seemed to understand, and his face went from bright pink to purple while Niko spoke.

When he was finished, Niko spat to the side as though to emphasize his words. He stepped back and pulled Cassandra toward him, his hand cupped the skin of her neck.

The wave struck her like an oncoming hurricane. Her drop of hope blossomed into firm confidence. He spoke to her through the contact, not in words but in emotions. It was like a gentle caress that said he was with her no matter what unfolded.

Mr. Sutton roared something, and a half dozen footmen surrounded them. Instead of the swelling fear Cassandra would expect, Niko hardened his resolve. He rose to his full height and caressed a hand over her cheek before releasing her.

He raised both hands to his sides as if to prevent the men from advancing. The men froze in place. Cassandra couldn't tell what repelled them. Distracted, she nearly missed the man racing toward them out of the corner of her eye.

She cried out to warn Niko, but her efforts only distracted him, and his defenses fell. The men rushed him and slammed a fist into the back of Niko's head. Niko crumpled to the ground.

Cassandra sniffled in the silence.

The man stood over him, parading over his catch. She recognized him then as the man from the maze who had met with Mr. Sutton.

"Niko." Please let him be alive. The witches needed him more than her. He was a powerful witch who worked from a base of rightness and selflessness. He was everything she wasn't.

He didn't move or make any sound audible to her.

She dropped herself to the ground, meaning to squirm her way over to his side. The man in the shabby clothes pinned her with a booted foot to her back.

A footman brought the man a pistol.

The shabby man kicked her side, forcing her onto her back. What she saw stole the breath from her and ended the scream in her throat before it started.

All of the members of the house party were armed. Pistols and rifles seemed the preferred choice. Some of them were more creative. Mr. Tallmadge hoisted a crossbow and an excited smile full of teeth. Even the butler, Mr. Snoot, had turned out, a hammer rested on his shoulder.

A handful of witches were brought to their feet, including Cassandra, Dr. Scott, and Katrina. The shabby man cut their bindings and removed Cassandra's chain. A footman held them at a distance with a pike and another held a pistol ready.

Their actions would have been laughable if it weren't for the crowd drawing near. The small group of witches backed away until they were at the edge of the lawn, where the woods began.

Katrina opened her mouth around her gag.

A gunshot cracked, and all other sounds fell away. Katrina collapsed to the lawn, and blood pooled over her pale gown.

An icy stone lodged in her stomach.

The shabby man stepped forward and aimed a pistol into the air. A malevolent gleam shone in his eyes as he met Cassandra's gaze.

"Run." He mouthed the word to her.

The crack of his pistol echoed off the hillside.

All at once, they bolted into the trees.

Chapter 25

Without the use of Cassandra's arms, she soon fell behind the others. Her feet stumbled over the uneven ground, catching on undergrowth and fallen branches. She lost sight of the other witches and knew she didn't stand a chance against the hunters. At least she didn't have to attempt to outrun them with the chain binding her ankles.

The hunters didn't bother to hide their approach. Their progress could have rattled the windows in London. She was running out of time, and every short minute tightened the breath out of her chest. The worst part was she couldn't tell how far away they were, but only that they pursued her.

Her foot caught on a crooked root emerging from the ground. Her body skidded forward, scraping her cheek. An angry burn slapped her face. She whimpered into the dirt. The drug purged itself from her stomach, and a long moment ticked by before she rolled onto her back.

A swarm of birds fled overhead, and the unmistakable yelp of a dog sounded in the distance. Perhaps they believed hunting dogs would give them an equal chance against the witches. They were cowards to send the animals to do their work.

Cassandra struggled to rise, but without the aid of her hands, her efforts were futile. Her gaze jumped over her surroundings, looking for anything that would give her an advantage.

She wiggled over to the side of a fallen tree and nestled close to the trunk. It was her last bit of hope. Her chances were slim at best.

She had left a clear trail behind, and if the hunters didn't see it, the dogs would smell her. She closed her eyes and steeled herself against the terror clawing along her skin.

The head-rattling bark feet away from her wasted all her efforts.

A chill sped over her nerves. Running was impossible in her state; she couldn't even manage to get to her feet or a decent crawl. She pressed her body tight against the ground and held her breath, willing the hunters away from her. In her mind, the dog's teeth were already a soggy breath away. Her body stiffened as she waited for impact.

It wasn't a dog who disturbed her. A booted foot kicked her in the ribs. She curled in on herself and pushed herself into the ground.

A man's laughter rewarded her efforts.

Her body froze. She came eye to eye with Mr. Tallmadge, and his cold gaze left no question as to his intentions. He raised a pistol toward her as a sleek hunting dog watched at his side.

In the moment before the pistol went off, her mind flew over the witches of the past. How many had faced similar slaughter? How many times had these woods seen the death of innocents simply because they were different?

If she died now, she would not be the last. No, far from it. "Please, Mr. Tallmadge." She did her best to dignify herself in her current state, straightening her back and keeping his gaze. "Perhaps we can come to some kind of agreement."

He didn't respond, but he didn't fire either.

She decided to take a chance, throwing all her self-respect away for the sake of life. "I know you must hate Master Niko." His scowl deepened as she spoke. "He has taken a liking to me if you take my meaning." She lowered her eyes, feigning embarrassment.

She cleared her throat. "Don't you agree, killing me would be the least you could do in Niko's eyes? A mercy really." She didn't know where she was going with this, but she needed more time. She hoped she wouldn't live to regret her words.

He lowered his pistol a fraction. She spotted the overdressed form of Selena behind his shoulder. Her unbound curls settled along her shoulders as though she had just emerged from the fairy world, and perhaps she had. Gliding along among her skirts was Mist, all pride and pomp.

Selena nodded at her, and Cassandra took the hint.

Cassandra dropped her voice and looked at her enemy through her lashes. "I never got to show you how much I appreciated meeting your acquaintance. It has been a shame we didn't get to know each other better. Wouldn't you agree?"

He grunted and took a step closer. The man was as arrogant as she had expected.

"Your confidence drew me from the start. How can a woman subject herself to a slug like Niko when you're around? It has been a trying time." She let out a long, exaggerated sigh.

Selena crept up a few feet behind Mr. Tallmadge,

and Cassandra rushed on in her speech. "You wouldn't deny a woman one last chance at pleasure before she took her last breath? Lord knows I haven't found it elsewhere."

Mr. Tallmadge lowered his pistol and snickered.

Selena struck then, slamming her fist into the back of his head. He dropped like a useless toy, lifeless and unmissed.

While Selena dealt with the man, Mist circled the dog. He swished his tail across the dog's muzzle, who bared his teeth at the cat, ignoring the attack on his master. Mist swatted at the dog's nose, and all at once, the chase began. The pair darted off into the trees.

Selena bent down to Cassandra and flipped her over. She tugged at the contraption confining Cassandra but soon gave up. Instead, she hoisted Cassandra over her shoulder. The garments between them were too numerous for them to make contact, or Cassandra would consider using Selena's strength and ripped through her confines. She couldn't summon the focus to try without touch.

They rushed and bounded through the trees. Selena made no sign she was tiring. Her breaths were even, and her pace never slowed. It wasn't long before they joined another group of witches. Still, Selena held her firm.

When she swung around, Cassandra spotted most of her group who were chosen along with Antoinette. She wiggled in Selena's grip, but the witch only patted her backside and directed the others to move forward.

Cassandra caught glimpses of their progress as she bumped along. From the undergrowth below, she guessed they advanced through the forest. No one spoke, but she doubted she would hear anyone without seeing their face. Still, it would have been nice to be included.

They continued until she spotted a dirt road below. Her back screamed in protest when Selena finally eased her to her feet. She stretched her lower back while Selena gave her a wide grin that reminded her of her brother.

Cassandra's face froze. "We have to go back."

The smile dropped from Selena's face, and she shook her head.

"They have Niko. We can't just leave him."

A line of carriages waited for them. Selena tugged her arm toward the front one.

"Please. I think… no, I know he saved my life. He's your brother." Her head spun and pulsed with each step. The venom made her thoughts a sluggish mess. It was a wonder she had gotten this far.

Selena ignored her protests as she hoisted her into the carriage like a small child. The rest of her group was crammed in next to her.

"Damnit, Selena—"

Dr. Scott cut off her words with a gloved hand over her mouth. He raised his brows at her, and she nodded in understanding. They were not out of danger.

The carriage jerked forward. She tried to get a glimpse of Selena and Antoinette as they left but to no avail. She hoped they would save the others. More than anything, she wanted to see Niko again.

She didn't realize she was crying until a faint tickle trailed along her cheek. Dr. Scott took pity on her and wrapped an arm around her shoulders. The tears streamed in pools over Dr. Scott's coat, which was still clean but for a few wrinkles from his stay underground.

"I'm sorry," she said in a choked voice. "I'm sorry." She spoke to Dr. Scott, but all she saw was Niko.

He removed a glove and stroked her hair. The pain jolted anew in her head but only to be replaced by exhaustion. Niko's face winked at her in her mind, and she drifted as though she sailed along a river. "I'm so sorry." Her voice was a whisper as she floated off.

Her whimper woke her. She had lost time. It was impossible to tell how much time, but when she gazed up, the sun shone through the window above her. She had seen a similar window before though not this one. She glanced around at her surroundings with no recognition.

The bed beneath her was filled with soft down, and she melted into the deep green blankets. For once, her head was clear. The venom had worn off, and the realization made her panic. How long had she been asleep?

She stumbled out of bed and steadied herself on the writing desk against the wall. A picture frame toppled off the surface, and she bent to retrieve it. Her breath caught when she glimpsed the portrait. A raven-haired woman with golden-brown eyes stared back at her.

The woman resembled Selena, but she saw more of Niko in her. The familiar gray cat perched on her lap told Cassandra another story. This must be Niko's mother with Mist. She would recognize Mist's stance anywhere. Niko hadn't been joking when he said Mist had been around a while.

She set the portrait down and surveyed the rest of the room. The small dressing area was strewn with a man's breeches and waistcoats. Niko's immaculate attire or not so much anymore. The man was a slob. She smiled to herself but then a moment later, her smile fell.

What was she doing in his room? The room was cold and hollow without the man himself.

Someone had changed her into a night rail. Her hair was loose about her shoulders. A crimson banyon hung over a chair, and she wrapped it around herself before trying the door.

To her relief, the door was unlocked. She headed out into the hall. When she shut the door behind her, she had to blink to adjust to the low light of the hall. A few candles were scattered about, and she almost took one up when a voice startled her.

Morwenna stood outside one of the doors, and she gestured for Cassandra to join her. The candle forgotten, she followed the other witch inside the room. Two beds took up most of the small space.

Morwenna aimed a small smile at her and took a measured step toward a round table. She brushed her fingers over a chair and settled herself down. Cassandra took the other chair without invitation.

"Where is everyone? Did they go back to get the others? To get Niko?"

The witch held up a hand and cocked her head as though she were listening. Her dark turquoise gaze seemed intent on something far away. After a long moment, she gave a short nod and held out her palm to Cassandra.

On contact, the strange silence filled her and raised the hairs on her arms and neck.

Cassandra met Morwenna's eyes, but the witch didn't appear to notice. The color shifted in her eyes like the swirl of green agate. The sight stole her breath, and all at once, she found herself in the forest again.

Georgiana raced behind Antoinette, whose limber legs bounded over the ground. Antoinette stopped to assist Georgiana. They rushed forward hand in hand.

Cassandra's vision shifted. Selena carried an older woman over her shoulder, much as she had done with Cassandra.

The picture shifted again, and she was back in the cages. All of them were empty, that is, all of them but the one she occupied. Niko sat on the straw, his head rested in his hand, and the adder stone was clenched in his white-knuckled grip.

"Niko." Her voice came out a gasp. She swallowed and raised her voice. "Niko, can you hear me?"

His head stayed in his hand, oblivious to everything but his misery.

Niko vanished, and Morwenna sat before her. She released Cassandra's hand, a worried frown on her face.

"We have to get him out."

Morwenna looked thoughtful. Her gaze still not quite taking Cassandra in. She grabbed Cassandra's hand once more, and the world fell away.

The vision appeared in flashes. Cassandra was alone curled up in the straw of a cage. Her sobs would break the hearts of the hardest of men. Then she appeared, a mere skeleton of her former self, kneeling before Lord Lyme, his walking restored. He grabbed a fistful of her stringy hair and threw her across the floor where she stayed, not moving but not dead, only hopeless.

The last part emptied her to the bone. Her hands were fastened behind her back, and jeers went up around her. She was tied to a pole in the ground with kindling piled at her feet. Mr. Sutton raised a torch over his head and threw the flames into the wood. Her raggedy clothes caught first. The smoke choked her until her lungs burned. The air showed her no mercy as a wind took hold of it, and the flames licked at her legs. The crackling of the fire accompanied her screams.

As she struggled against her bonds, a hooded figure appeared in the crowd. His head was bent, but Cassandra knew it was him, and she knew he had promised not to reveal himself but to protect their child. The little girl that stood beside him with the light red curls. Their child who came to say goodbye against Cassandra's wishes.

When Morwenna pulled away, the tears had already taken hold of Cassandra. All she saw was her daughter and her confused frown as she clutched Niko.

"Why?" Cassandra wiped her tears with the back of her hand. "Why did you show me this? So I wouldn't help him?" She got to her feet and paced the room. "You know, I must. It's better me than him. You must know that."

Morwenna's brows pinched together, and she shook her head.

"I don't care. I can't leave him to rot in some cage. If it's not me, then it's him. I can't see him burned. Don't you understand?"

Morwenna raised a palm in a shrug.

"Are you even sure your vision will happen if I save him? What if we take extra precautions? Or what if I threw myself out a window?" Of course, she knew she wouldn't do that, but the possibility would change the future.

The other witch puckered her lips and shook her head once more.

Cassandra's posture straightened. "If there is any chance at all of saving him, we must take it." Her thoughts refused to form a plan. They trudged in circles the way her feet did.

The safest bet would be to send someone else in her place, but she couldn't bring herself to stay behind. If she surrendered herself in exchange, Morwenna's vision would likely come to pass. Her helplessness was agony, a caged monster waiting to be set free.

Morwenna seemed content to sit quietly by as Cassandra mumbled and cursed to herself. The seer gave no sign of what she thought, but Cassandra suspected she already knew what path she would choose. The die had been cast when Morwenna showed her the visions. Already, change would be in motion.

Cassandra stopped mid-stride and pivoted on her heel to face the seer. Morwenna gave her a warm smile though her pink-framed eyes were closed.

The framework of a plan formed in her mind. She would need help if she were going to avoid capture. She needed the witches of Scry Cove. Her powers alone were useless, but with the presence of other witches, she would be part of a united force to tear down Lord Lyme.

Her duty to herself and her future child was to stay free. At least, she knew her child would be with Niko if she were captured. Yet, the thought of dying and deserting her daughter to live without a mother was cruel. Her parents would probably never see her again.

She started pacing again. It wasn't for another half hour before the other witches returned. Selena pushed the door open wide and looked Cassandra up and down. She snickered then took the chair next to Morwenna. Her ridiculous navy ball gown sported a few tears at the hem but was otherwise intact. She must share her care of appearance with her twin.

Georgiana floated in after her. Her golden hair was disheveled, but it only added to her appeal. Other witches waited in the hall, but Georgiana waved them down the hall to another room. She embraced Cassandra, and then, she dropped down on one of the beds.

"Is Niko with you?" Cassandra already knew the answer from Morwenna's vision, and the last bit of her heart was shredded when Georgiana dropped her head.

"We need to free him. Morwenna saw him locked in a cage."

Selena favored her with a scowl and crossed her arms.

Cassandra stopped in front of her, hands on hips. "I know you blame me for this, and I agree with you. I'm not ready to abandon him."

When Georgiana pulled a paper from her bedside, she knew the other witches were exhausted. Nobody wanted to expend the energy in contact with her abilities.

He will not like it.

Cassandra snorted. "Since when do I follow his directions?"

A taut grin split Selena's face. Georgiana and Morwenna looked thoughtful but unmoved.

"He's of more use to you than I am." She took a breath. "Look, I'll do everything I can to avoid capture. If anything, it will prevent more witches from being detected." She deliberately omitted mention of her child, and Morwenna didn't say anything.

"Were you able to rescue everyone else?"

Georgiana shook her head and scribbled on the paper. *Most.*

"What happened to the others?"

Nobody answered, but the pain lining Morwenna's eyes was enough. They had been hunted down like animals for a few minutes of entertainment. She could have been part of the slaughter. Gratitude warmed her chest, and her gaze focused on Selena.

Before she could thank her, Selena ripped the paper from Georgiana. *It was not my idea. I would have left you to the dog.*

Cassandra had forgotten Selena's minor empath abilities. At first, she thought Selena was joking, but the set of the woman's jaw told her otherwise.

"Then you'll help me? If you don't care if I'm captured, then you have everything to gain by freeing your brother." She would take this as a win if she could get one.

Selena's wicked smile made Cassandra want to run from the room. *When do we start?*

Chapter 26

The other witches refused to get started until after dark. By then, Cassandra had nearly run a trail through the floor. Georgiana attempted to calm her with little effect. When Antoinette joined them with Dr. Scott, Cassandra refused to take anything offered to her. She suspected they would have her sleep through the rescue.

Georgiana found her a more sensible outfit, a dark brown walking costume and sturdy boots. She found a set of daggers in Niko's room and armed herself with them. Her knowledge of weaponry was fragmented at best, and so she declined the pistol Georgiana offered her. The rest of the witches accompanying them armed themselves. Two carriages were readied to transport them.

Selena chose only volunteers and had to refuse some of them, bringing only those who would be of the most use. As with the ride there, they would split into two small groups. Anything larger than a few people would only take up space.

Cassandra would go with Georgiana and Antoinette. Mr. Manchester Harris would join them. He had forgiven her with the wave of a hand when she apologized for identifying him at the dinner party. After all, he said, if it wasn't her, then it would be someone else. The four of them would release Niko from below the maze while Selena and Mr. Shaw would create a distraction. Dr. Scott would stay with the carriages until they returned.

Mr. Shaw insisted on going, he was bent on bringing down Lord Lyme and would not be refused. He was one of them, after all. Cassandra secretly wished they had left the man back in the cages where he couldn't do them any harm. Not to mention, Mr. Shaw was already injured from his interrogation. His arm and hand were bandaged. She loosened up when she learned he wouldn't be in her group. She didn't know how Selena could trust him after demonstrating his controlling nature.

Selena refused to tell Cassandra her plan but made sure Cassandra knew not to confront Lord Lyme and to flee if anything went wrong. They would work with what Morwenna could tell them.

Cassandra caught a glimpse of herself in the mirror just as they were about to leave. Her long reddish blonde hair was tied up into a sloppy updo. She stared at it for a moment and tugged it down. She took out one of her daggers and hacked away at her hair. In all the visions Morwenna showed her, she had long hair. If she could change one thing, she reasoned she could change more.

Her hair came away and cascaded to the floor. She stopped just below her ears and tried out a smile at her reflection. It would do. Now, they would avoid these visions and rescue Niko.

Cassandra strode out the door without another glance. The other witches had mixed reactions to her appearance. Georgiana giggled. Morwenna was the only one who seemed to understand and favored her with a short nod.

The night was overcast with no moon in sight. She didn't know how they would see where they were going without being detected until Mr. Harris raised his hands, and the clouds in front of the moon seemed to evaporate into the sky. He winked at Cassandra. She gave him an uncertain smile.

The ride back to Lyme House was nothing short of torture. Cassandra tapped her foot against the inside of the carriage. Her hands twisted in her skirts until Georgiana grabbed them and gave her a level stare. She stilled her foot and took a deep breath.

What seemed like thirty hours or thirty minutes passed. They pulled over to the side of the road. Mr. Harris helped them out of the carriage. Selena and Mr. Shaw had arrived before them and were gone when Cassandra's group pulled up.

Only Antoinette knew the way, and she led them into the trees. Mr. Harris followed her, sending the occasional spark in front of them. Controlling the weather had its advantages, and Cassandra itched to try it out. She followed behind Mr. Harris, and Georgiana took up the rear.

Cassandra concentrated on keeping her feet in the low light. The chill air kept them at a steady pace. They had no reason to believe anyone lurked in the woods, but their progress was slow going. Nobody wanted to be left behind because of a turned ankle.

Her foot caught on fallen debris. She held up a hand to stop Georgiana. She bent down to free her boot and came up with an arm. She dropped it at once.

Horror mirrored hers in Georgiana's wide eyes.

The arm must have been from the hunt, but who it belonged to was a mystery. No other body parts were present, and animals had gnawed away at the flesh. The smell was sour but not yet rotten. Lord Lyme had left the bodies in the woods. She wondered if he was even aware who survived.

Georgiana nudged her and nodded toward Mr. Harris and Antoinette, who waited up ahead. Cassandra caught up to them, trying to shake away the sight of the limb. Unfortunately, that was not the last body part they encountered.

Mr. Harris illuminated a slipper with the foot still dangling from its soft kid leather. Once they noticed the parts, other remains revealed themselves. Some of the bones were old, having been worn away from weather and scavengers.

She covered her mouth, her gaze forced aside. Her attention was drawn to a bright red stringy plant, until she realized the plant was hair attached to a skull. The gaping mouth appeared to laugh at her as she urged everyone to hurry on. She didn't want to be in this graveyard any longer than necessary.

Her hand settled on Mr. Harris's greatcoat. She matched him step for step. No use in everyone seeing these things. Georgiana followed her lead and did likewise. They continued this way for a time and reached the edge of the woods without any trouble.

Antoinette slowed when they made the lawn. Mr. Harris brought a thin fog cover to obscure their passage. Georgiana took up the lead, and she hurried them to the side of the maze. Her feet skipped over the lawn, fae-like. Mr. Harris stayed near Cassandra as Georgiana found the entrance to the maze.

Cassandra studied every path they took, skeptical of their direction. She remembered little of her exit from the maze, and when they came across the statue of Artemis, her steps became lighter. Georgiana opened the hidden door in the ground without hesitation and hopped in first.

Her heart hammered through her limbs and against her bones. She paused beside the door then stepped off after Georgiana. Darkness swallowed them whole.

After Antoinette skidded into Cassandra and nearly toppled them both down the stairs, Mr. Harris chanced a spark. Their progress was at a crawl again.

Every step set Cassandra further on edge. Her skin caught an itch of impatience that could not be rubbed away. The ache in the pit of her stomach told her something was wrong. The feeling grew as they came closer to the bottom.

The stairway ended all at once, and again, no light greeted them. Nobody moved.

They exchanged glances, but silence seemed to seep from the passages and into their blood. Together, they waited. The dungeon was dead as the stone beneath their feet.

The witches moved as if they shared a mind. Georgiana and Cassandra hurried after Mr. Harris and Antoinette. Turns came and went, but their steps raced on until they crossed the threshold of the men's dungeon.

Antoinette's gasp startled Cassandra. When they halted, the silence became so consuming she had thought her hearing had left for good.

The cages were empty.

Either Niko was taken out, or he had never been there. Georgiana dragged Mr. Harris into the women's section, and the other two witches trailed after them.

Again, the cages were empty. Where then, were they keeping Niko?

Cassandra wasn't satisfied until they searched every cranny of the tomb-like structure. Their feet slapped from wall to wall until the last glimmer of her hope seemed at an end. A weight settled across her chest.

Their goal thwarted, they followed Mr. Harris back into the maze. None of them spoke, but each of them carried their failure like a sentence of death. Perhaps it was. Their assumptions might cost them more than Niko's life but their own as well.

Cassandra's only thought was to return to the carriages. Maybe Selena had returned with news, or even better, perhaps she had found Niko. She turned toward the woods when the earth trembled out from under her. The other witches dropped beside her.

Wary of detection, Antoinette checked for injuries. When Cassandra regained her shaky legs, all eyes found Lyme House. The house party had concluded on the evening of the hunt, and few lights illuminated the windows. The library was one of them.

A ripple of motion blew into them, and Cassandra gripped Georgiana to steady herself.

"Selena," Cassandra said the name, an accusation more than a statement. As far as she knew, Mr. Shaw and Niko could not unsettle the earth in such a way.

Antoinette nodded beside her and strode toward the house.

The three of them hurried to catch up with Antoinette's long strides.

She noticed nothing of their progress except the lawn streaming out beneath her. Her desperate thoughts occupied all corners of her awareness. What had caused Selena to lash out? Was this her idea of a diversion? Cassandra had to give the woman credit. It was an effective distraction. To Lord Lyme and the rest of Yorkshire.

Antoinette collided with Mr. Snoot inside the door. While they were both dazed, Georgiana slammed a fist into the man's stomach. Mr. Harris sent a spark through the man's limbs, toppling him to the ground.

Mr. Snoot thrashed along the ground as they rushed past.

Georgiana was first through the library door, and she was thrown against the wall before the rest of them gained the threshold.

Mr. Harris paused inside the door, which was his mistake. He was sent flying into Georgiana, where they both lay still.

Antoinette grabbed ahold of Cassandra's hand, and they raced inside side by side. A bigger target, they took the blow together and managed to land behind a fallen bookcase. The spine of an oversized volume of Shakespeare caught Cassandra in the shoulder, and Antoinette landed at an odd angle against the bookcase.

Breathing through her teeth, Cassandra pushed the book out from under her and rubbed the angry area up and down. She silenced a groan when Antoinette held up a hand to her lips.

A chair crashed into the wall behind them. Cassandra flinched.

From their vantage point, the room was a chaotic mess of broken furniture and strewn papers. She couldn't get a glimpse of the occupants of the room. She crawled forward to peer around the bookcase.

Antoinette grabbed her ankle, but Cassandra only shook her off.

Her gaze fell first on Lord Lyme, who sat still behind his desk. His tight-lipped expression was the only indication he was aware of his surroundings. Mr. Sutton lay in a pool of blood in the middle of the room. Off to one side stood Mr. Shaw, arms raised at his sides.

One of Mr. Shaw's hands aimed toward Selena, who stood holding a bust of Julius Caesar shaking over her head. She struggled to maintain her hold of the bust while Mr. Shaw bared his teeth in concentration.

Niko was at his other hand, his eyes wide and wild as he scanned the room. He knelt near Lord Lyme's desk. The adder stone lay broken and useless in front of him. He caught Cassandra's gaze. His shoulders moved a fraction as though he struggled against a rope.

Mr. Shaw must have caught the movement when he closed his fist. Niko flinched back. His focus left Selena for a brief moment. The bust dropped from her hands and rolled across the floor in chunks. Her arms drooped at her sides.

Mr. Shaw threw his head back and cackled. His laughter resounded through the library. He babbled something through his laughter, and for once, she was glad she couldn't understand.

Then, she heard Niko's voice. It was clear like he stood next to her, a caress like the first time they spoke in her family's shop. "Cassandra, it is quite safe. Do come out."

She rose to her feet and took a step.

The sound mesmerized her as much as a favorite memory etched in her mind. It was too late before she remembered she hadn't heard Niko's voice so well since she had lost her hearing.

Her knees struck the hard floor in front of Lord Lyme's desk with no recollection of how she had gotten there. Mr. Shaw placed her well away from the other witches and himself. Niko kneeled a half dozen paces away.

Selena took her chance then and rolled forward, elegant dress and all, feet first into Mr. Shaw.

The blow landed on Mr. Shaw's stomach. He folded inward as he tumbled backward.

Selena continued her roll onto her feet and rushed him.

Free from his binding, Niko crawled the distance to Cassandra and pulled her behind him. The crash in her ears reassured and distracted her. She pulled away, pushing herself beside him.

In their chaos, no one had paid attention to Lord Lyme, docile and helpless behind his desk. A shadow fell over Cassandra's view of the fight unfolding, and she gazed upwards.

Lord Lyme sat in quiet leisure. His weight rested on his desk as he leaned forward. A pistol was aimed toward her head. The barrel was so close she thought she could see the ball waiting for her death.

Niko uttered a cry, and a thud followed somewhere in the room. In the corner of her eye, Mr. Shaw limped toward them.

Niko's frantic voice was unlike anything she had heard from him. The fear and desperation from his power was a physical force. The beautiful Italian language slid off his tongue the way English never could.

She raised a hand to soothe Niko but froze when Lord Lyme shook his head.

Mr. Shaw's smile belonged among vermin as he approached.

Niko rambled on until Lord Lyme gave a short nod toward him. Mr. Shaw flashed his hand up, his palm toward himself. Niko's voice cut off.

"Mr. Shaw, how can you take his orders? The bloody devil locked you in a cage." Cassandra dared not move as she tried to meet Mr. Shaw's gaze.

He opened his mouth to speak but must have thought better of it when he answered with a grunt. Instead, he steered his sharp gaze toward Lord Lyme, whose eyes widened.

The older man must have sensed danger when he leaned away, but Mr. Shaw had already taken control. With quivering limbs, Lord Lyme rose to his feet, one painful degree at a time.

"You're mine," Mr. Shaw said in clear syllables.

A gurgle that was half-gasp and half-choke broke from Cassandra's throat.

Lord Lyme stared down at his body, his face twisted in horror. His hands grasped in desperation for the support of the desk. His movement was checked with a flick of Mr. Shaw's wrist, and Lord Lyme aimed his pistol at Niko, who was frozen in place and unable to speak. His father's eyes nearly bulged out of his head.

The madman controlling Lord Lyme seemed to enjoy every torturous movement he inflicted on them. After a long moment of shock, Cassandra found herself unwatched. He directed his intent at Niko, now the most dangerous adversary in the room with Cassandra untested and unsure of her own powers.

Before she could think better of it, Cassandra slid her hand back toward Niko and caught ahold of his thigh. Encouraged by Mr. Shaw's lack of awareness, she grasped Niko's hand.

The wave crashed through her fingers and crowded her veins. No more. She was a witch, and witches made up the distance.

Mr. Shaw caught her movement. His head snapped toward her, but she was prepared. She brought up every memory of pain. Her little dog, Otto, slaughtered by a carriage when she was five. Her dearest friend moving away to the continent when she was fifteen. The loss of Ashley Barrett's love and friendship with his abandonment from their wedding. The sudden rupture of her life when her hearing left her. Lord Lyme poisoning her aunt.

Niko.

Her heart quaked in her chest.

She locked eyes with Mr. Shaw, and she sent every last drop of pain his way. She gave him her longing, her loneliness, and her lost hope. The anger she harbored at the unfairness in the world traveled along for the ride.

He staggered back. Lord Lyme slumped into his chair.

Niko squeezed her hand, and together they directed their focus on the man meant to murder them all.

Mr. Shaw curled onto his side, tears streamed down his face, but not a sound came from him. All at once, he began to babble.

Cassandra's throat tightened at the sight. Her hand squeezed Niko tight to ask him to stop. His acceptance trickled over the bond, and she nodded, her gaze still fixed on Mr. Shaw. The waves brought Niko's comfort, and she sent the sensation along to Mr. Shaw.

A heavy sigh rocked the man to stretch out over the floor.

She smiled at the strange sight and turned her gaze to Niko. Just as she met his golden eyes, his face blanched.

In Niko's line of sight, Lord Lyme aimed the pistol at Cassandra's head and fired.

Chapter 27

A fractured moment passed in infinite thoughts. The crack of the pistol shook Cassandra into a frozen state. No past swirled through her mind, nor did she see the regretted lost future. Her life up to this moment ceased to exist, and all that mattered was the man beside her and the time in between seconds.

Her heart took a beat, and the cloud of smoke stung her nostrils.

A half-beat and Niko cried out.

The world sped forward. Lord Lyme slammed to the ground. Cassandra gazed into nothingness, unblinking and unmoving.

Her attention jumped to Niko, whose mouth remained open. She leaned toward him, her eyes and hands searching his body for injury. He stilled her hands and got to his feet, pulling her with him.

Selena crouched next to her father. Her dress ripped and disheveled, a thin trail of blood ran down her face. Instead of the contorted anger Cassandra expected to see marring her haughty beauty, a listless sadness furrowed her brow and slackened her mouth.

Lord Lyme lay sprawled in an awkward position like a cat in a misshaped box. His chest was crushed in.

Niko released his grip on her hand, silencing the waves that had become part of the moment, a natural background to their circumstance. He moved beside his sister, placing his hand on her shoulder. She knocked his hand away and pulled herself to her feet with the help of the desk.

Mr. Shaw had wounded her, and yet, Selena kept a firm grasp of herself as she stormed out of the library. Antoinette called after her next to the bookcase, but Selena ignored her.

Niko sighed. "Lay still…"

Cassandra only caught the first of his shouted reassurance. He said something about Dr. Scott, and that seemed to satisfy Antoinette.

He hurried through the room and stopped. Looking back, his golden eyes sparked as he regarded her with a small smile. It was a mercy the bullet had gone awry.

She burst into a wide grin. His lips stretched up to crinkle his eyes. His rare dimple appeared, and she wanted to kiss it.

Then, she did.

She didn't know who moved first, but a moment later, she found herself in his embrace, the crash sounding between them. His lips played across every surface of her face as if she would disappear at any moment. A cry issued from her throat, and she couldn't help the tears that dampened his shoulder and neck.

He pulled back to look at her and wiped at her cheeks with his thumb. "Shh."

She didn't need their connection to see the unchecked joy that shone in his eyes. They were alive. Anything else could be managed. Her heart beat as if to remind her of life's fragility. She cherished and drank in each breath like a drug, or like a lover.

He took her lips with his, his kiss soft and undemanding. His hand cradled her head, and he rested his forehead on hers, his eyes closed. They stayed like this for a while, simply being. Without words or reservations.

Cassandra was called back to their surroundings with the crash of Antoinette tossing a book toward them. Niko grinned at her and set off to help the witch and check on the others.

****

The clean-up was no small feat.

Dr. Scott saw to injuries with Cassandra's assistance. Niko busied himself with concocting an excuse for the carnage and settled on the rampage of Mr. Shaw, who was secured with a chain and gagged. Mr. Shaw showed little resistance. His mind seemed reduced to that of a child's, but Niko took no chances.

Antoinette suffered the worst injuries. Her leg and at least three of her ribs were broken. Although Selena had taken a great deal of beating, her wounds proved to be minor scrapes and sprains. It seemed her strength did not just rest in her brute force.

Georgiana and Mr. Harris were unconscious when Dr. Scott examined them, but were roused after some ministration. Georgiana had suffered a head injury and a bruised back. Cassandra stayed with her until she sat up and agreed to stay awake. They watched as Mr. Harris woke, a stupid grin on his face. His only injury was his pride.

When the magistrate was brought in and the maids set upon the library, the house descended into chaos. Cassandra busied herself with alternating between keeping Antoinette company and joking with Georgiana. The chalkboard was well-worn by the end of the week.

She saw little of Niko during this time. He had taken up the mantle of being a baron and seemed worn to the ground when she happened to pass him in the hall, his gaze ever fixed ahead on his tasks.

As happy as she was to assist her new friends, her heart ached for home. When Georgiana and Antoinette were well enough to care for themselves, Cassandra set about returning home to Cauldron, the witch name now stuck as though it had never been otherwise.

Her parents greeted her with enthusiastic hugs, having heard no word from her since her time at the inn. They had thought her kidnapped or dead, which was not far from the truth. All of their neighbors and friends descended on the house as if she had never pushed them away when she had been so low.

Aunt Louise's body had never arrived, and her parents were distraught to hear of her death. Nobody seemed to know what had become of her. Cassandra wrote to Lyme House for answers.

She waited on a reply by post for over a week when she was working at the counter in her family's shop, her chalkboard ready for business. She was engrossed in a novel when a shadow fell over her light. Having not heard the bell over the door as she rarely did, she jumped at the interruption during a particularly engaging passage.

Even more startling was the presence of Niko at the counter during his hectic clean-up of Lyme House. His wild hair was tamed back from his face. He was dressed in a neat black greatcoat and a striking royal blue patterned waistcoat. He was every bit the baron, the part of him she loathed. The man couldn't be any more out of place in the apothecary shop.

Mischief played about in his golden-brown eyes. For once, he seemed to keep his abilities in check, and she was unable to read his expression to any effect.

Her mother chose such a time to enter the shop from the door connecting the living quarters from the shop. She froze at the sight of Niko, but recovered quickly and favored him with her businesslike smile. No doubt, the presence of such an overdressed man had caught her off guard.

Mrs. Poole gave Niko her usual speech, which Cassandra had long ago memorized. "Good day, sir. How may I assist you? May I suggest my husband's celebrated poultice? It is indispensable among many a customer in no less than four counties."

Cassandra had always doubted the sincerity of these lines but had never dared to say so. As always, she played along, giving Niko her widest smile. His eyes crinkled, and he turned his attention to her mother. Her mother continued to explain the benefits of her father's poultice.

Cassandra rolled her eyes, but Niko seemed occupied by the topic. With a nod, he agreed to purchase some of the concoction and spoke to Mrs. Poole in a low voice that Cassandra was at a loss to hear.

Her mother's brows shot up, and her mouth formed an oh as if the sound had frozen on her lips. She gave a glance to Cassandra, and then ushered him through the door to the house.

When Cassandra moved to follow, Mrs. Poole shot her a look, a warning not to leave the shop unattended. She sighed and leaned onto the counter, eyeing the passage in her book with no real interest. What could

Niko possibly want with her father? Had Antoinette taken a bad turn? Maybe he had decided a response to her letter would fare better with an answer in person.

She didn't dare hope beyond those possibilities. Once she was allowed to dream, she was forced to accept disappointment. For now, she only allowed the events of the moment to occupy her thoughts.

The unmistakable roar of her father shook the glass beneath her hands. Her book clattered to the floor as Niko backed into the room, the color drained from his face. Her father's ruddy face stormed after him. His hand raised to strike him.

Cassandra rushed between them and faced her father. "What is the meaning of this?"

Her father shook with a rage she couldn't grasp. She had never seen him so agitated. Mrs. Poole appeared behind him, worry tightened her lips, but her mother had the good sense to snatch the chalkboard from the counter. She beckoned Cassandra toward her, but her daughter was reluctant to leave her father alone with Niko. Her mother repeated the request, and the set of her jaw told Cassandra not to argue.

Mrs. Poole took her aside and set her graceful hand to the chalk. *Lord Lyme has requested your hand.*

Cassandra blinked at the message a moment before she gathered what it meant. Of course, Niko was now Lord Lyme, what a disturbing notion.

"And Papa doesn't approve?" By all accounts, her father should want to have her settled, and a match with Niko couldn't likely be improved upon.

Quite the contrary.

Cassandra narrowed her eyes at her mother. "What then?"

The man insists on taking you back with him, and you just returned to us.

She folded her arms across her chest and frowned. "And I wasn't consulted in the matter? I have given no consent to this."

Her mother rubbed away the writing and gave her a quizzical look.

"Let me speak to him. He can't possibly know what he is asking. Indeed, I am certain he must have taken a blow to the head."

Mrs. Poole gave a great shrug and waved her away, but she called out to her husband and Niko who stared each other down in the center of the room.

Niko stepped back toward them and assured himself Mr. Poole would not attack before turning his back on him. He joined Cassandra, and Mrs. Poole forced her husband from the room.

Her parents gone, he didn't hesitate before taking her into his arms. She pushed him away and glowered at him when he laughed.

"How dare you consult my father without speaking to me. Have you no sense of decency? What is it to him where my heart lies?"

The side of his lips twitched up, but she would have nothing of his pranks.

"Lord Lyme, this is no joke. Are you drunk or blind? You can't possibly want a common wife. What would people think?" She emphasized his new name to make her point.

His hand rose to touch her, but he lowered it when he saw the alarm in her face. Niko's voice was soft at first as he gained confidence. He repeated his words and spoke with an understanding of her needs she had rarely seen. Still, it was a battle to understand his accent, but he did his best to take care of his pronunciation.

"Cara mia."

The phrase came to her over a wash of memories and his caressing voice as they lay in bed. Her cheeks reddened, but she kept her composure and waited for him to continue.

"What of our child?"

His assumption and reasoning disarmed her, and she nearly fled. Was a child what he had come for? Of course, he would need an heir. She wanted to kick herself for her foolish romantic notions.

"What child?" In truth, she had missed her courses and had kept the fact a secret from everyone. The adder stone had proved her false. She wasn't about to tell Niko that.

His eyes cast down a moment, and then, he looked up with a shyness she would never have identified with him. "Is there?"

Instead of answering, she busied herself with the excuse of retrieving her book from the ground. When she thought she could delay no longer, she pivoted to face him. The uncertain set of his shoulders and the small box in his hand nearly undid her.

Her breath caught. She took the offered box with a shaky hand. She didn't dare meet his eyes as she opened the polished wood. On a bed of red silk, a brilliant gold and rose cluster ring of citrines and diamonds sparkled back at her. The citrines nearly matched the shade of Niko's eyes, and she realized at once the arrogant man knew it.

She would have thrown it in his face if she wasn't

so enchanted by it.

"Cara." He repeated himself until she looked up. His hand took hers, and she allowed him to place the ring on her finger. The light in his eyes put the ring to shame. The rush in her ears was not just from their touch, but the drum of her heart through her veins.

"English, Niko."

His features brightened with humor. "My dear."

"One condition."

His face perked up at her near acceptance.

"I want to go to Florence and seek the help of the hospital your father spoke of." She watched his rapid change of expression when his lips fell into a tight line. He must have preferred a witch for a wife.

He cleared his throat and ran a hand along his neck. "What you ask…" he repeated himself twice before she grasped these words. "There is no cure."

"He assured me this hospital existed."

Niko nodded. "In a sense, it does."

"Then you are refusing? You don't want me to be cured, do you?" She puffed a breath from her nose and cast her gaze away.

His frown upset the beautiful planes of his face. "Cara." He forced her attention back to him. "It is no cure." He paused to make sure she understood his words. "The hospital experiments on witches."

"What?"

Mistaking her meaning, he repeated his words.

"No, I heard you for once. Of course, they must experiment on witches if they are to see the benefits of a cure for everyone."

His eyes dimmed, and she knew from his touch that what he said weighed on his mind, a time in his past he didn't wish to relive. "The witches never come out."

Her stomach twisted and a sour taste filled her mouth. She sensed a deeper meaning to his revelation, but he had drawn away from the conversation. She wouldn't force him to talk about it.

"I am sorry."

She had so much trouble with the three little words that she feared they would have to resort to the chalkboard. The sound of his voice soothed her, and she didn't want him to become silent. "Why are you sorry?"

He picked up the chalkboard. She protested, but he held up a hand to still her objections. He scribbled out his words and turned the board to her, but instead of allowing her to read the message, he spoke. "I know how much your hearing means to you."

His method of communication sent a thrill along her spine, and she wondered why she hadn't thought of it before. "It isn't just that. It's as though I'm half a person. The chalkboard is all well and good, but what of the sounds I miss? Just now, I didn't hear the bell on the door. What of when our child is born? How will I hear his cries?"

Niko scrawled his next message in record time and blurted out his words. "So there is a child? You are sure?"

She slapped his shoulder playfully, and his face lit up. "Are you not listening? Yes, I'm fairly sure. What does that matter if I can't care for him?"

"Pish." In his excitement, he nearly forgot to write on the board. "You will be an excellent mother, and besides, you have a whole house of witches to help you."

"You mean a coven?"

He waved her comment away as he wrote. "You're just as whole as anyone else. Don't you dare think otherwise."

Her sigh echoed the empty longing she sent him. "What will society think? Even if they accept my poorly state, they will surely object to my class."

Without warning, Niko brushed his lips against hers. His gaze pierced the depths of her own, and she had the odd thought of him reading her mind. He set about the board to make his meaning clear. "Cara, it does not matter to me what they think. I want you. Your family, your background, and your hearing are all outshined by my love for you."

"But how can you—"

He silenced her with his lips, his mouth demanded her attention. She forgot what she was about to say. His tongue teased her until she opened to him and surrendered to his whims. Their touch became heated as they fed off of each other's reactions. Niko drew back from their kiss before it got out of hand.

The whimper from her lips was foreign to her ears. His knowing grin only heightened her frustration.

"You love me?" Her voice was quiet, and if she hadn't been the one speaking, she would not have heard it. She repeated herself, giving him the same courtesy he gave her.

His grin spoke volumes, but he seemed to enjoy writing on the board, no doubt basking in his words written down as he seemed to enjoy the sound of his own voice. "Yes, you fool. I love you. Have I not told you in a thousand ways? I want you. All of you. Be my wife."

It was everything she wanted. His love, his acceptance. She could not imagine any answer that would rival what he had given her. "Niko, I…" He waited with calm patience, already reading her reaction. "I love you, too."

He held her against him and stroked her back. It was no kiss, but the touch was more intimate than any chaste embrace she had experienced. Their reactions to each other collided much as it was when they were last in bed together.

When her parents entered the room, she didn't bother to move and pretended not to hear as her father addressed Niko. "Then it is decided?"

Niko nodded into her.

Her mother cried out and raced to the couple, pulling Cassandra out of his grasp for a hug.

Niko looked on with an amused half-smile and shook Mr. Poole's hand. Her father must have forgotten his reservations at her departure with the happy news. More likely, Mrs. Poole had convinced him how foolish he behaved. After all, Lyme House was not so far away as to render frequent visits beyond their means.

At last, her mother released her, and Cassandra hugged her father. A bear of a man, his arms swallowed her up. Her parents beamed at the couple until her mother remembered herself and rushed back to the kitchen to prepare their evening meal. Mr. Poole went to find champagne to celebrate the occasion. It was up to Cassandra to close up the shop, but her head was not about her, and the shop remained open.

Instead, she lost herself in Niko. Loved, wanted, addicted.

A word about the author...

Mae Thorn enjoys being romanced and terrified—a combination not normally found in books so she writes them. Her favorite stories include kickass women and the men they fall for. She writes historical romance, fantasy, and horror. She has published three historical romance books: Notorious, Dangerous, and Rebellious.

Mae holds a Bachelor's degree in English from the University of Utah and a Master's degree in Library and Information Science from San Jose State University.

She is the co-president of the League of Utah Writers Romance Chapter, and she lives near Salt Lake City, Utah with her cats; Church, Shadow Moon, and Sabrina, and a puppy, Whiskey.

https://maethorn.com/